Acclaim for
THE RED CORVETTE

"A great gang of characters and some rip-roaring adventures. Wish we could go along for the ride."
—*The New York Times Book Review*

"A satisfying whodunit with a melancholy tone set to the high, lonesome whine of the prairie winds." —ALA *Booklist*

"A marvelous piece of Americana."
—ROBIN W. WINKS,
The Washington Post Book World

"The ending crackles with energy and humor." —*The Herald*

"Reid skillfully introduces memorable characters, creates an impenetrable mystery, and writes some hilarious scenes."
—*St. Louis Post-Dispatch*

THE RED CORVETTE

ROBERT SIMS REID

Carroll & Graf Publishers, Inc.
New York

First Carroll & Graf cloth edition 1992
First Carroll & Graf paperback edition 1993

Carroll & Graf Publishers, Inc.
260 Fifth Avenue
New York, NY 10001

ISBN: 0-88184-990-1

Manufactured in the United States of America

This is for my parents and grandparents,
who have held fast with me for a long time.

Thanks, also, to Ken Lawson for some technical
assistance . . . and for not arresting me
twenty-five years ago, when every now and
then I gave him the chance.

I forget the names of towns without rivers.
A town needs a river to forgive the town.
Whatever river, whatever town—
it is much the same.
The cruel things I did I took to the river.
I begged the current: Make me better.

—Richard Hugo,
from The Towns We Know and Leave
Behind, the Rivers We Carry
with Us

1

S ome people call it creation science, for others
it's creation mythology. When I was a kid, I
always thought of mythology as something
that had to do with ancient Greeks or Romans. Tem-
ples and togas and all that bullshit. It never occurred
to me that people once took Venus as seriously as I
might take the Madonna, or even the Los Angeles
Raiders. For that matter, the whole notion of "ancient civilization" had an abstract quality, something
far removed from human beings who once prepared
food and raised children, worked and loved, and are
now dead. I knew about American civilization, of
course, because we studied that in school. But nobody
ever taught me that history and mythology—to say
nothing of science—might be the same subject. It
took an amateur's interest in fossils, and too many
years of police work, to do that.

During that first summer after I retired from the
Rozette, Montana, police department, I spent an
alarming amount of time trying to get over the sense
that my own life was ready for the boneyard of an-

cient civilization. Many people have melodramatic preconceptions about retired policemen. For the most part, we tend to be just guys who earned a pension, had enough, and moved on. I tried letting my beard grow, hoping to cover the fine scar just below my jaw, where my throat had been cut years before. After two weeks, though, the beard turned out to be mostly gray, and I gave it up.

Living alone, I managed to make ends meet without the necd for another job. That's not the same as saying I didn't need something to do. For several months, I kidded myself into believing I could spend the rest of my life dabbling in yet-to-be-invented hobbies. But it happened that even paleontology, once I had unlimited time to pursue it, could not hold my interest. Roscoe Beckett persuaded me to try bartending at Angel's, the joint he owns downtown. Within moments, I realized that I didn't know much more about mixology than drawing beer and pouring shooters. Worse, I wasn't inclined to learn. After all the hours I'd spent listening to shitheads in interview rooms, why set up shop again behind a bar? You hear one guy confess, you've heard them all.

In the middle of June, I loaded up my old pickup and spent a long weekend east of the mountains, rooting around for dinosaur bones. I always enjoy spending time on the east slope of the Rockies. The mountains erupt in a long, black spine from the margins of the northern plains. The plains seem to extend forever, an impossible expanse of grass, jammed up in the west against those mountains, which are the birthplace of wind. The plains, though, are the graveyard of dinosaurs. Fossilized skeletons are frequently found and, by law, become the property of the State of Montana. Many end up in the Museum of the Rockies in Bozeman. Who knew, maybe I'd get lucky, stumble across a previously undiscovered model. Call it the Leo Banksosaurus. Or the Tyrannosaurus Banks.

The weather turned cold and stormy, typical of Montana in June, so I headed back west at White Sulfur Springs, crossed the mountains over White's Pass, and came out along the east shore of Canyon Ferry, a large reservoir on the Missouri River near Helena. After spending several hours digging through sediments along the shoreline, I came across a mastodon tooth. The tooth was half again as big as my fist, and looked at first like just another chunk of rock. God only knows what had happened to the rest of the mastodon. I considered the legal admonition against collecting prehistoric relics, and decided that there are all kinds of laws, and the mastodon was a long time past caring.

I got back to Rozette on Sunday night. While I was still unloading my gear, Pastor Roscoe Beckett came downstairs with a message. The Pastor and I share the carved-up remains of a big old house that was built in the last century by Ronald Hollingshead, one of Montana's original timber and cattle barons. The house sits on the bank of the Holt River, across from downtown Rozette, and the surrounding residential area was once part of Hollingshead's ranch, which once extended clear into the mountains over twenty miles to the south. When I first moved in, the house was owned by Hollingshead's daughter, Leona, herself a relic, who lived in a converted apartment on the ground floor. The second floor was rented out to a young married couple, and I rented the studio on the third. A few years ago, Leona crossed the divide. Became, you might say, ancient civilization. Between us, the Pastor and I scraped up enough money to buy the place for back taxes. Now, the Pastor lives on the second floor, I live on the first, and we rent the top.

"Was some folks here," the Pastor said. From inside the huge folds of his dark blue overcoat he drew a small white envelope and handed it to me. "Man and woman and their two kids. Looked like Mr. and Ms. America. See the USA in their Chevrolet. That kind of shit. You hear what I'm sayin', Jim?" The Pastor calls everybody Jim. With his three hundred pounds, his long, black beard and hair, his black beret and the tiny gold cross dangling from his left ear, no one would ever confuse Pastor Roscoe Beckett with Mr. America. Chevrolet probably wouldn't even sell him a car.

The scribbled handwriting on the envelope said, "For Leo Banks." While Beckett hoisted a duffel bag from the back of my truck and lugged it inside, I stood under the porch light and read.

Dear Leo—

Some surprise, huh? We were out this way on vacation and decided to look you up. Sorry we missed you. The man at your house, Roscoe, said you'd be back this Sunday. We're off for a few days in Glacier Park, but plan to be back through here on Tues. or Weds. Hope we can catch you then. Been a long time—too long.

Gerry Heyman & Sarah

Gerry Heyman. Gerry Heyman and Sarah. Well, that was just dandy. I folded the note and shoved it into the hip pocket of my jeans.

"What in the hell is in that bag, Jim?" The Pastor, breathless from carrying in the duffel bag, walked back to the truck, where he fished around inside my cooler and came up with a can of Rainier beer. "Jim? You there, Jim?" He popped the tab on the Rainier. Drops of spray on my face brought me around.

"Rocks," I said. "Just a bunch of goddamn rocks."

"Good, that's good." Beckett took a long pull on the beer. "You look so excited, I was afraid for a minute you might of gone out and struck gold."

Roscoe finished drinking his beer while he watched me finish unloading the truck. It was a lovely early summer night, clear and cool, with the aroma of lilacs heavy as fog.

Roscoe said, "I'm on my way downtown." He crumpled the aluminum can and tossed it to me. Three or four nights a week, he plays a set on blues guitar with the house band at Angel's. Even on the nights he doesn't perform, Beckett usually stops in to regale the crowd and check the till. He asked if I wanted to go along, but I passed on the invitation.

The Pastor busied himself trying to squeeze behind the wheel of his white sixty-five Continental, one of those old heroes of the road with suicide doors.

"These people," I said absently, "they stay long?"

"About as long as it took to write that note," Beckett said. "I think it made them nervous, having their impressionable youngsters around an authentic piece of Americana such as myself."

Youngsters. Of course. I had forgotten about the youngsters.

"How old are they? The kids?"

"Early teens, maybe. Boy and a girl. Kids all look alike to me. Reminded me of Donnie and Marie."

"And the woman?"

"Yeah? What about her?"

I thought, all right, Banks, you crafty bastard, what about her? Then I said, "Christ, I don't know . . . just, what about her? You know."

Beckett started to laugh, and I was afraid he might injure himself on the steering wheel. Instead, his belly triggered a series of staccato blasts on the horn. "Ah, Leo, this sounds like one woman you never told me about."

"It was a long time ago. We were just pups."

"That's the worst kind. You want I should bring you a bottle of Glenlivet?"

"Not hardly."

Inside, I left all my gear stacked in the foyer. I shucked off my dusty clothes, and spent the next fifteen minutes standing in the makeshift shower I'd rigged above the old tub, which stood on four lion paws near the tall, gurgling toilet. Later, I found enough unspoiled ham in the refrigerator to make a half-decent sandwich, which I took to bed. The sheets were almost clean. I set the sandwich aside, closed my eyes, and tried to imagine how Gerry and Sarah Heyman and their two kids would look a couple of days from now, when they pulled their car to a stop under the sagging carriage entrance to the Hollingshead mansion.

I hadn't seen Gerry or Sarah for over twenty years. I knew them both at the University of Illinois in the late sixties. Gerry and I were roommates our freshman year, when I started seeing Sarah. She and I didn't waste any time deciding that we were the only two people in the world who really understood life, and we shacked up together on the sly for about a year. Sarah was from a working class family up around Chicago, and Gerry was from Mauvaisterre, a little farming town in southern Illinois, not far north of St. Louis. The name is pronounced *Movis-star,* and I remembered that Gerry had told me once it was French, and meant *bad place.* Gerry was a real hometown kind of guy, who thought the town's name ironic. I never went to Mauvaisterre, but I'm from a similar small town farther south, near the Kentucky line. Personally, I always thought the French had a way with words.

Unlikely as it now seems, we were having what passed for a revolution in those days. I was very intense about staying drunk and changing the world, so it didn't take long for me to flunk out of school, and it took even less time for Uncle Sam to get his hooks into me and prove just how hard the world can dig in its heels. I had what Sarah considered the bad social judgment not to resist. She moved out, and was spending a lot of time with Gerry even before I joined the navy. We all prided ourselves on being freethinkers. I did the best I could to be happy for them, and we stayed in touch after I left for Great Lakes.

Not long after they were married, Gerry and Sarah moved to St. Louis, where Gerry entered medical school at Washington University. Now, he was a physician back in Mauvaisterre. Thanks to irregular cards and letters, the odd phone call, I still kept track of my old friend and his wife in the clandestine, apparently coincidental way that has afflicted replaced lovers for centuries. I felt a flutter of excitement, as I wondered whether it was Gerry or Sarah who had thought to run their old friend Leo Banks to ground.

But it didn't take long before excitement faded into a sort of vague dread. I had already learned that leaving the job I'd had for over twenty years was a lot like throwing a rock in the ocean. The ripples last a few minutes, but the hole closes pretty damned fast. Sarah Heyman was a stone that had settled deep into the floor of my memory, and all the ripples had long since flattened into the far horizon. Sure they had.

Through the years, the picture of Sarah that remains strongest to me is of her sitting cross-legged on the floor of our tiny apartment back in Champaign, Illinois. She is barefoot, wearing patched jeans and a ragged T-shirt. The light from a dozen candles flashes in her long, braided hair and in her eyes as she looks across at me and smiles. Half a lifetime of carefully nursed sentimentality was invested in that memory. So when Gerry called on Monday night, and said they expected to be at my place about noon the next day, I

15

found myself feeling awkward and giddy. After hanging up, I took account of my apartment. Despite the high, formal ceilings and Ronald Hollingshead's elegant woodwork, it still looked like the kind of place where you found lonely middle-aged guys who'd blown their brains out.

I spent Tuesday morning vacuuming and dusting, stashing piles of books, papers and rocks in assorted closets, reminding myself that this visit was not a first date, but a haunting. Roscoe Beckett stopped off once for coffee, but was frightened away by the spectacle. By mid-morning, the place no longer resembled a landfill. By noon, I was sitting in a wicker chair on the spacious front porch, trying to look casual. At about one o'clock, Heyman's green Buick battle cruiser turned into the drive off Eau Claire Street.

The greeting was chaotic, and surprisingly unforced. Gerry was balding now, but he was still thin as a birch, with eyes that somehow managed to be soft and penetrating at the same time. The line of his face was concave below high, strong cheekbones. The handshake was immediate, warm and strong. Now, though, he radiated an authority I had never known in him. It was the air, I supposed, of a physician.

And then Sarah stepped out of the Buick.

"Leo?" Her voice was bright. "Leo, my God, it's really you."

"In the flesh." I stood my ground and offered my hand, which she stepped past to hug me. When I hugged her back, her ribs felt delicate and tense as a bird's. She was dressed in khaki climbing shorts, a lime green polo shirt and deck shoes. Her hair was cut short and, paradoxically, the very few flecks of gray made her seem even younger. Her eyes fastened on me, and did not waver. "Do you know how far Montana is from the rest of the world?"

"Pretty damned far," I said. And I thought, maybe not far enough.

"We decided you must be hiding out," Gerry said.

Sarah got the kids out of the car, and introduced them. Michael was thirteen, and obviously had better things to do than spend half his summer chained inside the car with Mom and Dad, traversing the Wild West, meeting old-timers like me, and probably being forced to listen to awful radio stations in the bargain. Michael had his mother's eyes, but his feet were huge inside a pair of Air Jordans, and I suspected that he would be tall, like Gerry. The girl, Lisa, was ten. Her teeth were still too big for her face, so when she grinned, which was often, her happiness seemed like the real thing. She wore a yellow T-shirt with an elk stenciled on the front, from Glacier Park.

I asked Lisa how she liked the park.

She looked at her mother, then at me. "We seen mountain goats."

"*Saw* mountain goats," Sarah corrected.

"How about you?" I said to Michael.

The boy shrugged. "It was okay."

For the next few hours, we kicked around inanities. I told them the story of Leona Hollingshead's house, and explained that Pastor Roscoe Beckett, while not exactly a pastor, was also not as dangerous as he might appear. Gerry and Sarah talked about their trip, about their life in Mauvaisterre, and, once Michael and Lisa were dispatched outside, about Michael and Lisa. Several times, Gerry took Sarah's hand, and it struck me that she seemed reserved toward him. But I chalked this off to too many days on the road.

Late in the afternoon, Gerry excused himself to go outside and see how much damage Michael and Lisa had inflicted on the neighborhood. A moment after he left the room, Sarah got up from the sofa and began looking through the group of geologic artifacts that I had set out for display on a built-in sideboard. Briefly, she handled the mastodon tooth from Canyon

17

Ferry, then looked over her shoulder at me and smiled nervously. I realized that this was the first time I had been alone with Sarah since she took up with Gerry.

"This is turning out to be harder than I expected," she said.

I don't know what it would have taken to make the situation easier for Sarah, and I wasn't inclined to start tossing out bromides. "You made a choice," I said. "We all make choices. You've got a decent husband, kids. Successful life. Isn't that what most people want?" I was surprised by how quickly we seemed to slip back into the conversation of a couple.

She went back to the sofa. "Answered prayers." She smiled and toyed with her hair. "Yes."

"You told me once," I said, "you couldn't abide sharing your life with someone who didn't have the strength to follow his conscience."

She folded her arms and crossed her legs. "And you said only a fool confuses love with politics."

"I said that? I must have been pretty desperate."

"We both were," she said. She took a deep breath, and stared off to her left. Then she looked back at me with a self-conscious smile. The smile I remembered through all that candlelight.

At that moment, I could have gathered her in my arms and kissed her and begged her to send her husband and children on their way. And I could have beaten her senseless for making me want that.

"Ever since we got to Montana," she said, "I find myself thinking almost constantly about you. All these endless mountains and forests . . . or the empty prairies . . . We drive through those places, and I imagine you just around the next corner, over the next rise . . . imagine you hiding, and Gerry and I have found you out."

"And you wonder when I'm going to grow up and come home."

"I didn't say that."

"No. No, you didn't." Sarah didn't know anything about my life in Montana. Not a thing. She was a tourist. I wondered how long it would be before Sarah and her brood rounded the first corner on the way out of town. I was ready to ask just that, when Gerry and the kids came back in. Michael's expensive Nikes were soaked, and I knew they had been down by the river.

Sarah shrugged, then laughed too quickly and glanced at Gerry. "Sweetie," she said, "maybe we'd better go find a place to stay."

Gerry looked at his watch. "Maybe a little longer?"

Sarah suggested that they get settled in for the night, then meet me for dinner. I recommended Stevie's, a white-tablecloth restaurant with lots of glass, which is along the Holt River not far upstream from my house. A few moments later, I stood on the porch and waved at the green Buick pulling away. As I watched, I thought about Leona Hollingshead, who had died alone and barren, after waiting nearly ninety years for the one perfect person to make her life complete.

Rozette, Montana, is not an especially formal place, so despite the golden orchid centerpiece, and the sprinkling of French entrees on the menu at Stevie's, I was acceptably dressed in tan slacks and a plaid shirt. Gerry looked the part of a physician in his blue blazer, white shirt and tie. Sarah was trim and lovely in a yellow cotton dress, simple enough that I was sure I had owned pickup trucks that cost less money. An ivory-colored cameo hung from her neck on a thin, gold chain. She didn't need the soft light inside Stevie's, but it didn't do her any harm, either.

Dinner came off without a hitch, at least until the food started showing up. The grownups had grilled salmon, while the kids were forced to make do with shrimp cocktail, steak Diane cooked in brandy flames at the table, and chocolate double fudge sundaes, each specially ordered with *two* cherries on top. Lisa was as genteel as any human could be with such a load of food to dispose of, but Michael ate like a turbine. Afterward, when he asked the astonished waiter for a toothpick, Sarah pummeled him with one of those motherly looks. You know, the kind that reminds you of candy-coated death. Once in a while, I caught myself staring at Sarah, wondering how it would feel if she were directing those do-something-with-the-kids looks at me instead of Gerry.

Across the river, the evening light fell easily among the pale green trunks and branches of a grove of young cottonwoods. About halfway out, a fisherman made long casts in fluid yellow arcs, which settled onto the water and rode the current downstream. As he watched the fisherman, Gerry Heyman toyed absently with his blue and red tie, and seemed to become lost in the delicate, hypnotic twirl of the yellow line.

Sarah smiled at me and put her hand on Gerry's arm. "My husband could empty an L.L. Bean warehouse."

Gerry glanced down at his wife's hand, then at me. "It just looks so perfect out there."

I said, "You've never tried it?" Perhaps he could use his children for bait.

Okay, so I was not in the best humor.

When I knew him in school, Gerry talked a lot about moving west, about the kind of harmony that people in the late sixties thought derived from a certain geography. While Sarah was actively political, Gerry in his calm, deliberate manner always wanted a world that made sense and, above all, was compassionate. It was that kind of thinking, I decided, that probably drew him to medicine. Not such a bad thing, really. I mean, the world could always use more doctors. But when it came to the West, Gerry's was the kind of thinking that twenty years ago made John Denver the Caruso of hot tubs, and today caused some people to believe that the relationship between wolves and deer is painless simply because it's pure.

"Time." Gerry shook his head and sipped a glass of wine. He looked at me and blinked his eyes, as though trying to bring them into focus. "You know how it goes, Leo. Just ordinary old time."

"There's almost always somebody out there fishing about this time of day," I said. "I've heard people say he's hired by the restaurant. But that's not true. That story came from a book. There was a guy wrote a novel about this hippie living in Rozette. The hippie gets a job as a scenic fly-fisherman outside a fancy restaurant. That's where the story comes from. About ten years ago. A few people read the book and talked about it, and now everybody thinks that guy out there in the river is nothing but an actor."

With the nail of his little finger, Michael gouged a piece of food from between his lower incisors. "That's the kind of job you should of got, Dad." A few moments later, I sensed the boy staring at the scar on my throat.

"A moment of stupidity," I said lightly, brushing a finger against the scar.

Sarah rushed to correct him. "Michael—"

"No," I said. "It's okay."

"Mom told us you were in the navy," he said.

"I was. But I didn't do anything risky enough to get this. This was from a bad dope deal. When I was working undercover a long time ago. I wasn't smart enough to know I could get hurt. So a man did me a favor and taught me."

"I still can't believe you became a cop," Gerry said, refilling his wine glass.

"We're the perfect generation," I said. "We started

the drug revolution, and now we've turned it into the war on drugs."

"Schizophrenics," Sarah said. Her tone was acidic. She pursed her lips, as though tasting a bad kiss, then folded her napkin and laid it over her plate, which was still half full. "We were convinced we knew what we wanted, then had the bad luck to get it."

Gerry shrugged an apology for her, then looked back out at the fisherman.

I thought fondly of the moment when I could refile this artifact from my past life where it belonged, under *O* for *Over*. When Gerry said he'd like coffee and cognac, I suggested something called a Nick's Special, a blend of Amaretto and Metaxa that a friend of mine in Montana had learned from some drug coppers in L.A. Sarah protested that she and the kids were worn out. After some discussion, Gerry and I decided to stay on for a while. She would go back to the motel with the kids, and I could give Gerry a ride back later on.

After she was gone, Gerry tossed back his drink and nodded appreciatively. "I'm sorry, Leo." He scowled into the empty snifter. "This seemed like a good idea back when we were in the middle of South Dakota."

I laughed. "Lots of things seem like a good idea in the middle of South Dakota."

"I always thought this would happen the other way around," Heyman said. "You know, sometime when you'd come back to Illinois to visit your hometown, you'd just pop in on us."

I laughed again. "You might have needed to wait another twenty years."

"You've never been back?"

I shook my head. "There's no traumatic reason for that. It's just the way things worked out." That wasn't quite true, but given Gerry's mood, it was all the truth I wanted to be responsible for. In fact, I had been back several times, and always made it a point to avoid Mauvaisterre. The reasons, which seemed obvious to me, had nothing to do with Gerry or Sarah alone, and everything to do with them together. If he wasn't smart enough to have figured that out on his own, what was the point in telling him now?

The air of assurance I'd seen in Heyman before was gone. "I guess the way things were back then . . . with the three of us—"

"Gerry," I said, "it's okay. It's done. As far as I'm concerned, two old friends stopped in for a visit, a nice dinner beside the lovely river, a couple of slots in the slide tray for the neighbors back home. End of story."

He shook his head and frowned. "Sarah's smarter than me about some things. It turns out I'm maybe not as grown-up about this as I expected."

"Then why are you here?" Without warning, I felt myself slip into an investigative frame of mind. What did this man, old friend or not, want from me? I sat waiting, and as I waited I felt my face go blank.

"Am I that transparent?"

"Everybody wants something, Gerry. That's the reason we keep on getting up in the morning. It's lying about it that gets us in trouble."

He motioned to the waiter for another round. "And you think I've been lying?"

"Well, it's a cinch you didn't come here to improve your marriage."

Gerry arched his eyebrows and whistled softly between his teeth. "No. Not for that. The truth is, I think I need an investigator of some sort, and I couldn't think of anybody but you."

"You're in trouble?"

"Me? Oh Christ, no. You forget I'm Dr. Heyman, healer of the sick, pillar of Mauvaisterre, Illinois. And before that I was little Gerry, the nicest boy in town. Hell, Leo, I couldn't get into trouble to save my life."

The waiter arrived with our drinks. I pushed mine aside, while Gerry dipped his fingertip into the drink, then touched the finger to his lips. "I'm sorry, Leo. I just thought, you know, if we could get together and decide we were all still friends, maybe then you'd be more likely to help me out." He drained off the second Nick's Special. "Sarah told me it was a rotten thing to do."

"She was right," I said. "Maybe you should tell me why it is you need my kind of help."

Outside, the fisherman had waded to the shore. The wind had begun to roll out of Bride's Canyon, tearing fine shreds of spray from the churning, slate-colored river.

2

Tell the right kind of ghost story and you get a haunted man. That was Gerald Heyman's particular brand of trouble. In the nearly empty restaurant, I could hear the wind drawing under the eaves. Heyman polished off his drink, then mine, then waved for another. I watched the shadows from the young cottonwoods play across the water.

"You were smarter than me," Heyman said finally. "About leaving home, I mean. Going back, you know, it's been like slipping my neck inside a noose of cobwebs."

"It's not a matter of smarts," I said. "It's easy to mistake luck for a plan."

"I was a farm kid," Heyman said. "Remember?"

I nodded. "And your dad was a schoolteacher, too. English?"

"History. Our farm wasn't very big, so he was able to teach and run the farm both. He's retired now, of course. Neither my sister nor I had any interest in taking over the farm, so he sold it. That was about ten years ago. Now he and my mother live in Florida. She plays bridge, he plays kamikaze golf."

Heyman's face took on a wistful light. If he was waiting for me to reciprocate with some news out of my own deep, dark past, he was wasting even more of my time.

Finally, Gerry got the point of my silence and went on. "When I was a little kid, my father told me about a murder that happened on the farm next to us. I ever tell you that story?"

He hadn't.

"This murder happened in 1937," he went on. "Otto Turk—that's the name of the neighbor—was married to a wealthy woman, a kind of heiress, I suppose you'd call her, from St. Louis. They had a son, Matthew, who was something like fourteen or fifteen that year.

"On his own, Turk was just another small-time farmer, like most of my people were, too. But like I said, Grace Turk had money. After they were married, they built a huge stone house on his farm, and he started buying up more and more land.

"One afternoon in late May, the boy comes home from school, finds his mother floating face down in a pond not far from the house. Deader than last year's celebrities. The Turks had this hired hand living with them. A retarded kid named Mickey Cochran. Not a kid, really. He was almost as old as Otto. But my father always called him a kid."

Heyman studied the gold-colored orchid in the center of the table. "Kind of funny, isn't it?"

"How so?"

"Cochran. He's probably ten years older than my dad, but he's still a kid. That's what we do to retarded people, you know? Stop counting years when their minds stop growing."

"I guess there are all kinds of calendars," I said.

Heyman extended his hand and gently touched the

petals of the orchid with his fingertips. He scowled, as though considering a diagnosis.

"Otto Turk immediately accused Cochran." Heyman withdrew his hand and rubbed the fingertips against his thumb. "I guess justice was easier in those days. The sheriff impaneled a coroner's jury that same night at the Turk house. Cochran was arrested and in the county jail by midnight. It was bad enough that Grace Turk was murdered. A pretty, young wife and mother, decent woman from a well-off family. But there was also some evidence she'd been raped. Put all that together, and you've got a real ugly crowd outside the jail."

Late that first night at the jail, according to Gerry, the local prosecutor and the sheriff had a talk with Cochran. By the time they were through, he had confessed to both murder and rape. A few months later, he tried to recant the confession, but the judge wasn't having any of it. And that fall, while the jury was still being selected for his trial, Cochran changed his plea to guilty. Because of his slow-wittedness and the fact that he pled guilty, he was sentenced to life in prison, rather than to death in the electric chair. A few days later, he was sent to the Menard State Prison at Chester.

It was nearly dark now, and the evening wind had brought clouds down from Bride's Canyon. Rain began to nick at the large window. Heyman stared into his empty snifter, looked around for the waiter, then changed his mind.

I said, "Lots of people have a story like this, Gerry. Something that came to them very young."

He laughed. "That sounds like you're leading up to asking me what all this has to do with you."

I settled back in my chair and waited, thinking that it must be quite a luxury to be haunted by only one murder.

"Do you have a story like that, Leo?"

Now I laughed. "I guess I probably do. Or did, anyway. If so, it's gotten all mixed up since then with too many other stories." Old friend or not, I wasn't inclined to give him more than that. And anyway, the story I might tell would be the story of me and his wife. I doubted he was in the mood to hear that.

"Grace Turk taught me about death," he said. "I know, she was dead a long time before I was even born. But just the same, I learned from her."

Grace Turk was buried in a small family cemetery that joined the Heyman farm. When Gerry was a kid, he went on to tell me, he discovered the place on his own. It was all grown up with weeds and brush. Some of the graves were over a century old, and were now marked only by the shallow depressions left by collapsed coffins. Grace Turk was the last person buried there.

"In some places," he said, "animals had burrowed down into the graves to use the coffins for dens. I used to go there and play. That was the place I first realized things happen in the world. Things outside your own life, I mean. Terrible things you might never understand but you have to try. That must sound pretty crazy."

"Nothing's truly crazy about death," I said. "We're not that lucky."

"I knew you'd say something like that. That's why I knew you were the only person who might help."

"You still haven't told me what kind of help it is you want."

Heyman slowly ran his hand back and forth over his high forehead, as though trying physically to sort through his thoughts. He said, "I've done some reading about homicide convictions. You were a cop for a long time. You know the average time a guy serves in this country for homicide?"

"The last I heard, it was about seven years."

He pointed a finger at me and dropped his thumb

like the hammer of a gun. "Very good. That's the same figure I read. Well, last month I went to see Mickey Cochran. Where do you think I saw him?"

Pakistan, for all I knew. I wished that my old friend hadn't needed so many drinks working up to his big finish.

"Menard," he said. "That's where I saw him. Still in Menard."

"Not a bad stretch," I said.

"That's over fifty years." He shook his head incredulously.

"What do you want me to say, Gerry? You want me to say fifty years is too much, just because seven isn't enough?"

He ignored me. "Cochran was an orphan. He ran away from a foundling home in Missouri when he was nine or ten. Somehow he ended up around Mauvaisterre, where different farm families more or less passed him around, until he landed with the Turks. In all those fifty plus years inside Menard, Cochran never had a visitor. Never had a letter, never wrote one. No phone calls. Nothing. As if he'd been dropped into a black hole."

I was personally acquainted with some murderers who could use a hole like that. In twenty years of policing, I had never known a life sentence actually to mean forever. I said, "What about parole? Like you said, seven years is the average ride. Sooner or later everybody gets paroled. He must be a real peach for them to hang onto him that long."

Heyman shook his head abruptly. "Never asked. The people at the prison say there's no reason for it, except the poor dumb shit never asked."

"So you appointed yourself his first visitor."

He waved me off. "Give me a break, Leo, okay? I may be obsessive about this thing, but I'm not dysfunctional. Sure, I knew the story from when I was a kid, dug out the old newspapers and all that. Some reporter called him a *fiendish brute of the field* and a *beast,* can you imagine that? But it's not like I've made the guy my life's work."

Heyman went on to explain that Cochran was dying, and the State of Illinois in its wisdom had decided that he should die on the outside. So whether Mickey Cochran wanted it or not, he was getting kicked. Since he'd been convicted out of Mauvaisterre, that was where they would send him to die. Gerry Heyman was the only medicine show in town, which meant that once Cochran was moved into the local nursing home, he was bound to be Gerry's patient. Gerry had been asked to check Cochran's medical record in advance of the move. Because of his childhood interest in the case, Gerry took the opportunity to visit Cochran while he was still in the joint.

"The thing is, Leo," Heyman said, "I don't think this guy did it. We talked for a long time, and he says he didn't. I believe him. Simple as that."

I didn't want to patronize my friend, but I was sure I knew more about cons than he did. "There's something you should understand, Gerry. A lot of these guys behind the walls, guilt is something they check at the gate with their street clothes. The guy confessed, for Christ's sake, pled guilty. Saying you're innocent doesn't make it so. Is this what you want me to investigate? A murder that's half a century old and the guy rolled on it from the very start?"

"You don't have to make it sound so trite."

"I can't help the way it sounds. Look, you're a doctor. How much time do you spend trying to raise the dead?"

The haunted look in Heyman's eyes hardened into determination, perhaps even contempt. "I can pay you, if that's what it is. I came to see you because I remembered you as the kind of man who would help on a thing like this. I've got a successful practice—

damned successful—and I don't heal the sick for free. At least not all the time. Just tell me what you need."

I straightened, and wondered if it wasn't time to reach for the check and start calculating the tip. "I gave that up," I said. "The world doesn't need another ex-cop on a fool's errand."

"Then think about this," Heyman said. "Not long after he buried Grace, Otto Turk did a weird thing. He moved out of that big stone house. Got drunk as a lord, then smashed out all the windows, and after that he just left the place standing. The damned thing is still there, kind of like this great big stone skull."

"So what? I might have done the same thing. So might you."

"And Cochran's denial?"

I'd already told him what I thought of Cochran's denial, and I wasn't in the mood to tell him again. "Listen," I said, "if this job's so important to you, get somebody in Mauvaisterre to do it. Hell, do it yourself. There's no great trick to being an investigator. Just make yourself a pain in the ass." I didn't tell him that he seemed to be well on his way to learning that great trade secret.

"I considered that. It's not something a hometown boy can do. You're from one of those little towns yourself, Leo. You know how they are."

Yes, I knew. When I was in eighth grade we were taught about the "red menace" from a book by J. Edgar Hoover. Some parents complained that Hoover's text was a little soft. And when John Kennedy was killed, folks were sorry that the president was dead, but if a president had to go, well, this one was better than some others they could think of. And then with Bobby . . . ditto. In Mauvaisterre, I figured, convicted murderers were probably just one notch above big city liberal Democrats and Soviet agents. Thinking about Gerry Heyman's part of the world made me feel all cramped up inside, the way I felt

31

whenever I dwelled too long on any of my bum marriages.

Gerry's shoulders slumped now, as though he were sinking with a huge anchor of sadness tied to his ankles. I didn't like feeling that I was part of that weight, but I liked even less the thought of perpetuating his delusion by telling him lies.

"Maybe," he said, "I've read *To Kill a Mockingbird* too many times. You always want to believe that some heroic man will stand up against the town, rescue the misunderstood innocent."

I'd already spent more nights than he could imagine trying to shore up my own character. "It's worse than that, Gerry. You want to *be* that man."

"Doesn't happen like that, does it?"

"It's a great part," I said, "but Gregory Peck already played it."

Quickly, he reached for the check, and then for his wallet. "We'd be better advised not to misunderstand in the first place."

A better man than I would have argued harder over the check. But when Heyman pulled out his wallet and started culling out the twenties from the fifties and hundreds, it didn't take me long to surrender to my lower instincts. Screw him, I thought, he had ended up with Sarah and two nice kids and a Buick. That had to be worth at least dinner and the bar tab.

I had parked my truck under a large blue and white canvas awning, so we managed to avoid the rain. The downpour was in earnest now, one of those sudden, explosive storms that can drop out of the mountains without warning in early summer. The air was cool, and I could smell the nearby spruce trees, along with the willows and lilacs that crowded the parking lot. I started the truck, and headed for Heyman's motel.

"You said your father told you this story, Gerry. You didn't say what he thought about it."

"He was a better teacher than that," Heyman said. "He never came right out and told me what he thought. He said he learned about the murder while he was chopping weeds along the road. Another neighbor came walking by, on his way to the Turk place. The neighbor had a rope coiled over his shoulder."

"So what'd your pop do? Stay at home, or go along?"

"He never said."

"You're right, he was a good teacher," I said.

"Maybe," Heyman said, but he didn't sound convinced. "Maybe he just never wanted me to know."

"You ask him again. Chances are he'd tell you now. Now school's out."

Heyman looked across at me. He was smiling and the shadow of the windshield wiper passed back and forth across his face. "Maybe I just don't want to know."

"We have a hard enough time living with our own sins, Gerry. All of us."

I turned into the motel, and saw the Buick parked at the back of the court, near the low brick wall that surrounded the pool. The heated water gave off steam, and the underwater lights cast a rippling, aqua glow across the two-story fieldstone structure that rose behind the pool. When Heyman opened his door, I could smell the chlorine. I asked him if he wanted to meet me for breakfast in the morning. He was both polite and firm in saying that they needed to get on the road very early.

"I wish we were leaving in this old car I want to buy. A Corvette. A red, sixty-two Corvette. A real cherry. A serious traveling car."

"That depends," I said, "on what kind of traveling you've got in mind."

The look on Heyman's face said he wasn't looking

for the kind of route they give you at the auto club. He went on: "This old guy back in Mauvaisterre, he's got it stashed in a shed behind his house. I really want to buy that car, Leo. Buy it and just, you know, just go for a drive. A nice long drive."

"You're a rich doctor, buy the sonofabitch. Rich doctors can do anything."

His grin was crooked. "Yeah. Yeah, sure they can."

I don't know why—maybe because of the sadness I heard in Heyman's voice—I said, "You've got good kids, Gerry. I'm glad I got to meet your kids." When Gerry didn't say anything, I decided that the remark must have sounded as lame to him as it had to me.

We finished up an elaborate set of good-byes, which had the ring of forever about them. It was almost as though we had both maintained our long-distance friendship for twenty years just to see how we would handle this moment. As Heyman was about to close the door, he stopped and leaned unsteadily into the truck. "You still remember why you became a cop, Leo?"

"I needed a job."

"I'm a doctor because Sarah said she always wanted to be married to a doctor. Way back when we were in school at Illinois she said that. She ever tell you that? You ever know her as well as you thought?"

"No."

"Yeah . . ." He took in a deep breath and let it out, filling the cab with the sticky odor of stale booze. "That's what she always said. I used to think about you, you know, when I'd get a letter or something, and I tried to imagine what your life, your work must be like out here." He hesitated while he loosened his tie. "I guess I always kind of envied you. Living a life you invented to suit just yourself."

"Then you were a fool," I said.

"Yeah, well big fucking deal." He pulled the tie

from his neck and wrapped it around the knuckles of his left hand. "And fuck you, too. See you around." He slammed the door and walked away into the steam and the rippling blue light.

3

Gerry Heyman may have been honest about the real reason why he'd looked me up, but he hadn't come close to giving me a reason why I should share his crusade. During my career on the police force, I had first learned to thrive on suspicion and anxiety, and finally been poisoned by them. I was far from ready to shoot up again on the misfortune of others.

After Gerry and Sarah Heyman and their two kids left town, I did not sink into a fit of melancholy. No, I went fishing. Not in Stevie's scenic fisherman spot, but in the deep, emerald pools of the Holt River, where it breaks through Smithson Gorge into Bride's Canyon east of town. Trout, though, turned out to be harder to catch than criminals had ever been.

I answered all my mail. But I didn't make the finals in a single sweepstakes.

I kept up with my laundry.

I got a haircut.

"You gonna decompose, Jim," Pastor Roscoe Beckett said one day. "You keep this up, you gonna just start from the feet up and rot clean into the ground."

I went shopping for a new truck. But Buick doesn't make a truck.

Thomas Cassidy, one of the detectives I used to work with, had a new book come out. He's been hacking out thrillers for a decade or so. Last year's *Ninjas of Christ* had nearly gotten Cassidy cooled out by a bunch of radical Christians from south of Missoula, folks who couldn't warm up to the concept of Jesus as a Bushido mercenary. Cassidy's latest epic, *The Truth Warrior,* was billed as his autobiography, the true story of the Rozette, Montana, Police Department.

"You read it yet?" Red Hanrahan asked me one night. Hanrahan was my old partner. He had stopped by the house after working late on a stabbing.

"Too deep for me," I said. "I only read westerns. Only westerns where they put a horse on the cover."

"I found a copy somebody left in the restroom," Hanrahan said. He tugged at his drooping red mustache and shook his head. "I always thought you got along with Cassidy."

"It was Cassidy got along with me. That's not the same thing."

"That explains it," Hanrahan said.

"Explains what?"

"He's got a piece in there about you. 'Arrogant and overrated, about as sharp as a disposable razor after a hundred shaves.' That's what he called you, Leo." Hanrahan dug into the large sack he'd brought from Burger King and pulled out a Whopper.

"Maybe he's right," I said. Maybe a guy who wasn't arrogant and overrated would have spent a few days helping an old friend look into a pet case.

Hanrahan didn't argue with me. He chewed on a mouthful of hamburger. The mayonnaise on his mustache looked like the symptom of a horrible disease.

In early August, I got a call from Sarah Heyman. It

37

was nearly midnight, and I was dozing through the rerun of a political talk show. Pat Buchanan was yelling at some half-wit about the ungrateful poor.

I heard the faint long distance crackle. "Leo?" When she said my name, I knew instantly it was Sarah.

"What is it?" I felt my breath shorten, and my hearing seemed to turn inside out in the momentary silence.

"It's Sarah."

"I know." After seeing her and Gerry just a few weeks ago, I could think of no good reason for her to call.

"Sarah Heyman."

"Sure, I know. What is it?" She was leaving him. What else could it be? Twenty years, and the embers blown back to life by one short, tense meeting. Jesus Christ almighty, what was I going to do now? How soon could I get her to Montana?

"It's Gerry," she said.

Gerry? Oh yeah, the guy who stole you away. Too bad. He'll get over it.

Her voice sounded flat and coarse, the way people sound when they've had too much of a bad thing. "I have to tell you, there's no other way to do it, Gerry's dead."

At that moment, Buchanan's target fidgeted with his tortoise-shell glasses and made some practiced, well-reasoned statement, like he really believed Pat Buchanan gave a shit about well-reasoned statements spilling from the mouths of guys like him. By the time this poor chump was done, Buchanan was practically drooling with anticipation. That's because Buchanan has chumps for lunch. Things like Chumps on the Halfshell, or Chumps Rockefeller. God, I love Pat Buchanan. He can take your mind off anything awful.

To Sarah, I said, "That's crazy."

"Gerry's dead, Leo. He was murdered, somebody killed him."

"What happened?" I felt as though my whole body had begun to shrivel as I sat there listening, mummified by guilt.

"They aren't really sure. He had a flat tire one night. Somebody . . . it was with the jack handle, somebody hit him in the head and killed him. They hit him a lot of times, Leo."

"*They.* Who's *they,* Sarah?"

"Nobody knows. The sheriff says there's hardly any evidence. Just nothing. They don't know who *they* are." Her laugh was short and bitter. "Don't even know if it's a they, a he, a she, or an *it.* I don't think the sheriff knows anything at all."

"When did it happen?"

"Sixteen days ago."

A homicide case can get colder than the body after forty-eight hours. After sixteen days, the grass on the grave already needs mowing, and you start to tidy up the file.

"I feel terrible," Sarah said. "Not calling sooner, I mean. For some reason, after seeing you this summer, I knew it wasn't enough just to write you a letter, I had to *tell* you. Then I'd start for the phone, but just couldn't face it."

I remembered the young woman who had seemed to have no trouble giving me the air when we were both barely twenty. What stroke of daring had led her to call me now? As always, she had perfect timing on the punch line.

"I think I need your help," she said. "I have to know, Leo. Know what happened to Gerry. And if you think about it, about when we were together all those years ago, and even about this summer, you think about all that, Leo, and you'll have to know, too. Please."

"You want me to come back there? That's it?"

"Yes."

I started to ask her some more specific things about Gerry's death, but backed off. A long time ago, I went on a call where a guy had taken himself off by laying his neck across a train track. When we put the guy in the body bag, one of the cops balanced the guy's head on his buttocks. *So he can kiss his ass good-bye,* the cop said. When I told Sarah I'd think about helping her out, I felt like I'd just puckered up.

She said, "I know it's maybe awkward—"

I stopped her. "No. I'm more grown-up than that. I've got a whole life, Sarah, a life you don't know anything about." And the funny thing about that guy on the railroad track, the really funny thing, was he hardly bled at all. Somebody said the train must have pinched all the vessels closed at the same instant his blood pressure disappeared. Presto, no muss, no fuss. Just kiss your ass good-bye.

"I'm sorry," Sarah whispered.

"There's nothing to be sorry about. It's not a bad life. I'm not some kind of walking wounded." I tried to think of how to explain to Sarah how I felt. I wasn't even sure I could explain it to myself. "Gerry was my friend, and I'm sorry he's dead. You were my lover, I'm sorry about your hurt. But I'm *outside* that trouble. You want more from me than grief. I'm not sure I can give it." I wasn't even sure how much grief I was good for. For a long time, I'd made a living off dead and hurt people, and life in the margins beyond grief was something I had unwisely consumed like cholesterol. I was getting too old for that kind of diet.

"Can give it, or *will* give it?"

"Suit yourself. I'm telling you I'll think about it. That's the best I can do right now. Anyway, it's not as cut and dried as you make it out."

"I don't understand."

"You've got people there who are paid to do these things, investigate crimes." The last thing any investigator wants is some hired gun from out of town breathing down his neck.

"We have a sheriff. A man named Pointdexter. But he isn't any good."

When we broke up years ago, Sarah had given me a speech about right and wrong, then cut me loose and never looked back. Through all that, she expected me to understand. And the really crazy part was that I did. Something in me got older at that point, and it all made sense. But no matter what she said this time, it was going to be damned hard to choke down the sixteen days it had taken her to give me this bad news. If Gerry were the victim of a coronary, instead of an unsolved homicide, would she have troubled to call me at all?

I said, "You could always try the yellow pages."

"I beg your pardon?"

And there was Gerry, disillusioned and drunk, walking away from my pickup into that lousy blue light outside the motel. "Nothing," I said. "Forget it."

After a few more moments of give and take, I told her I'd call her back the next afternoon with an answer. Then I hung up the phone and went into the kitchen for a can of beer. It didn't bother me at all that a more decent man—a man, perhaps, like Gerry Heyman—would not need to make Sarah wait just to prove that he could do it.

The next morning, I was up by six o'clock. Beer at midnight had been a good anesthetic, but my middle-aged bladder was an even more effective alarm clock. Standing bleary-eyed in front of the toilet, I heard the Pastor on the stairs. A cool breeze off the river was blowing through the house, and I began to feel distressingly human as I heated a mug of water in the microwave, then stirred in freeze dried coffee. Through the window, I heard the sound of a guitar from the backyard.

The Pastor sat on a wooden bench near the river. He was wrapped around his big Martin D-24. His shoulder-length black hair was tied back and shiny in the early morning sun. He was playing blues, playing hurt, and he didn't look up when I opened a folding lawn chair and sat down beside him. My feet were wet and cold from the dew-soaked grass.

"Your belly gets much bigger," I said, "you'll have to grow longer arms to reach that guitar." The Pastor took up every bit of space inside a giant-sized Grateful Dead T-shirt. He was barefoot, and the cuffs of his voluminous khaki pants were dingy and frayed. The stub of a burning cigarette was about to set his beard on fire. Despite his ravaged appearance, the nails on his right hand—his picking hand—were long and well-manicured.

"Mornin', Jim." His eyes were closed tight, and his crow's feet glistened with sweat.

"You're up early," I said.

"Sometimes it's early, sometimes it's late."

I noticed the Johnny Walker bottle propped against his right ankle. I said, "I take it in your case we're talking late."

"'Bout as late as it gets, Jim. Late . . . as . . . it . . . gets."

"Chastity?"

"Young women, Jim, what can you say?"

Chastity, who could seem both younger than tomorrow's newspaper, and older than the Bible, was a stripper at Danny's Club, a neon- and strobe-lighted cave at the edge of town. Chastity was her stage name. Her real name was Tiffany.

"It was probably a felony, an old guy like you carrying on with a gal her age. What was the attraction? You give her lunch money?"

"You got no appreciation for love, Jim, absolutely none." The Pastor clawed at the strings, making music that was an eloquent, discordant plea. How could those fingers, thick as sausages, be so delicate and quick? His left hand, mangled years ago by a woman in Philadelphia, was so deformed it seemed impossible that he could chord, let alone race through a lead.

The Pastor went on. "I figure it was all that seventies disco music she has to listen to out there at Danny's. You know, that shit, it ain't music for humans. They make half that music on computers, Jim. Howya supposed to think that it's music? Turn you into an alien space monster cannibal."

"I guess that explains it," I said.

"What you talking about?"

"How that gal Chastity just ate you up."

The sun was beginning to streak through the haze above Bride's Canyon. Although I couldn't see the river, which lay just beyond the grass-covered levee at the back of the yard, whenever the Pastor paused between guitar phrases I could hear it churning through a nearby riffle. And, whenever the breeze picked up, I could smell it. The sky was pale blue and clean behind the mountains that rim Bride's Canyon east of town. God, I did not want to leave this place.

The Pastor sucked a last drag on the cigarette, then flipped it toward the levee. "Least I'm a damned good meal," he said, reaching for the Johnny Walker, then changing his mind. "So now you know how come I'm up late. How come you're up early?"

I told him about Sarah Heyman's call. After the way he'd seen me carrying on since her visit, I didn't have to explain further.

"I hope she don't like disco," the Pastor said. "She does, Jim, you're on the menu."

But Pastor Roscoe Beckett didn't understand any better than Sarah had. Sure, I could go there and moon around and feel bad, ask a few questions, maybe even get lucky on the homicide. The trouble was, I could do all that and not give a rat's ass about it one way or another. Over the years, I had acquired a great distaste for that part of me that relished another person's disaster.

I leaned back in the chair and looked at our house, which the Pastor liked to call a mansion. The back porch sat lopsided on a crumbling stone foundation, and the whole place was shedding paint like a big, ugly tarantula that had outgrown its skin.

"I always wanted to live in a nice, big house," I said. "Like one of those cribs over in the Defoe district." The Defoe district is an old, gilded neighborhood that begins about three blocks from our place on Eau Claire Street. Most of the houses there are what the Hollingshead mansion had been once, spacious and elegant. The people who live there keep perfectly groomed lawns under maple trees as lush as the neighborhood bank accounts. If you lived in the Defoe District long enough, you could vote in the presidential election and not think it was funny.

"You got a big house, Jim," the Pastor said. "Biggest damn house in town. Least, you got part of it . . . the part I ain't got."

"Place could use a good air strike," I said.

The Pastor shook his head. "Your problem ain't with the house, it's with your head. You want to belong someplace. But you can't belong because you're not willing to take money for selling people things they don't need, providing advice they already know but want to hear again. You got to be willing to tell folks dumb jokes they already heard, then laugh like hell when they tell 'em back to you next week."

I said, "My friend Gerry Heyman had a life like that." Maybe that's what I was afraid of, coming nose to nose with that kind of smug, secure attitude toward the here and now. Maybe I was afraid I'd end up crawling around inside myself wanting it. I listened to the river, and felt as though the river were running through me. That's sentimental, I know, but sometimes sentimentality is the most alluring bait.

Beckett was derisive. "You ask me, Jim, all this moonin' around, it's because of that woman."

"You always think it's a woman."

Pastor Roscoe Beckett negotiated his way to his feet, then gathered up his guitar and his whiskey. "'Cause it always is. That gal Chastity, you know what she said, Jim? Said I reminded her of her daddy. Lord God, that like to ruin me forever."

"When she tell you that?"

The Pastor's face went blank, like he'd just seen the Hindenburg go down. "You don't want to know, Jim. You just plain don't want to know." The Pastor started back toward the house, apparently on his way to bed.

I looked across the river, toward downtown. A huge flock of pigeons wheeled in the early sun around the top floor of the Dolby Building, which rose near the north end of the Defoe Street Bridge. The Dolby is the tallest building in Rozette, and it's not the sort of place you might expect to find in Montana. It's built of gray brick, with elaborate stone cornices. It needs a flashy restaurant, a marble swimming pool and a gymnasium with Indian clubs and medicine balls, an expensive cigar stand and a uniformed elevator operator named Jackie. People say the Dolby used to have all these things. All it's got now is a list of tenants that includes mostly pensioners, ladies and gents who remember the First World War, when the Dolby was built and the West was a place people tried to leave behind at the city limits. Looking at the Dolby and the green and tan mountains behind it made me even more uneasy about crawling back, after all these years, into small town life in southern Illinois.

I thought: Sonofabitch.

And then I went inside and called Sarah Heyman. I told her I'd do what she'd asked. I told her I'd fly into St. Louis the next day, then rent a car and drive to Mauvaisterre. And then I told her I had a condition.

"This is a job for me," I said. "It's what I used to do for a living, and I guess maybe it still is."

She didn't hesitate an instant. "How much do you need, Leo?"

I thought about the money Gerry had that night at the restaurant, and about the way he'd characterized his practice. I didn't hesitate either. "Fifteen thousand dollars."

This time, Sarah wasn't so quick. "Don't you think that's quite a bit?"

"Do you have that much?"

"That's not the problem."

"I didn't think so."

"I guess I should be glad you were our friend," she said. "Otherwise, I might have had to sell my children to afford you."

"If I wasn't your friend, you wouldn't have asked at all." I didn't need to remind myself again of those sixteen days. "It's a lot of money," I said, "but you're asking a lot. Let's say it's a way for both of us to stay on an even keel."

"Sure." Her laugh sounded awkward. "Maybe you'll donate it to charity or something."

I said, "I doubt it."

4

I came to live in Rozette, Montana, because one day
in late 1970 I fell off a freight train heading east,
and got arrested. This is not the way most policemen find their vocation. I was fresh out of the navy,
and on a rip, and I had every good intention of going
back home to Illinois. I really did. But a mind, like the
man said, is a terrible thing to lose.

Dave Johanson, an authentic, old-time street bull,
had the biggest hands I've ever seen. Public drunkenness was still a crime in those days, and it didn't take
Johanson a minute to have me cuffed and stuffed. He
sat for a moment behind the steering wheel, reading
over my brand-new separation papers. His lips moved
while he read. When he was done, he looked over the
seat at me, and asked just what the hell I thought I
was doing. I told Johanson I really didn't know, and if
I did, what business was it of his? He thought for a
while, then got out of the car, dragged me from the
back seat, and unlocked the cuffs.

"I give you forty-eight hours to figure it out," Johanson said. "Then I break your leg. Time I get to your arms, maybe you'll have an answer."

Twenty minutes later, I was wolfing down burgers at Roosa's Cafe with Johanson and a couple of the guys he worked with. Even from that first encounter, I was put off by the military elements you find in any police department. But listening to those old coppers talk, I felt myself being swept away by a part of life that most people never experience, the part that goes on backstage, behind closed doors, under the skin. In 1970, nobody my age wanted to be a cop, so a few months after Johanson put the arm on me, I had little trouble landing a job. Dave Johanson and I went our own ways a long time ago, but his question was still as good as ever: "Just what the hell do you think you're doing?"

When I was a kid, my best friend in high school was a guy named Andy Shane. Andy had a pilot's license, and his father owned a little Cessna. By the time we were seniors, it occurred to Andy and me that the best way to pass a spring afternoon was to ditch school, scare up a sixer of Schlitz, and go flying. Through some miracle of youthful craziness, we were not killed. Sometimes we hugged the green hills overlooking the Mississippi valley. Others, Andy would take us up to eight or nine thousand feet, and do hammerhead stalls. Pulling back on the yoke, he would urge that little airplane into the steepest climb imaginable. Then, at the instant the wings lost purchase, he would kick the rudder hard, stand the plane on a wingtip, and roll it into a plunge that left your belly somewhere up there on a cloud.

The flight in from Montana to St. Louis was not, thank God, as eventful as a flight with Andy Shane and a six-pack. Wasn't as much fun, either. I have rarely flown in a private plane since leaving home. And I hadn't seen or heard from Andy Shane since I was back in Illinois after my mother died. That was maybe fifteen years ago now. Andy and I stood outside in a cold November drizzle, while an auctioneer used his gavel to pound nails into the last of my material connection with that country. We talked about flying. My sister was there that day, too. She talked about her husband, a contractor down in Knoxville, who was all wrapped up in a big condo deal and too busy to have kids at the moment. Every five years, I get a questionnaire for my high school reunion. Someday I should fill one out and send it back.

As soon as I stepped outside the terminal at Lambert St. Louis airport, I felt suffocated by the heat. But as the sprawl of suburban St. Louis fell away, I began to feel more at ease. The air conditioning on my rented maroon Chevy kept the climate at bay. Traffic cooperated. My map was accurate. On the radio, I ran the dial through livestock reports, pop music and a breath of unlikely Mozart. I was in the heart of a dense, green country fed by great brown rivers and crammed with radio stations. A long, long time ago, I might have said I was home. I settled on a Dexter Gordon set over an FM station out of St. Louis.

Crossing the Missouri that Monday afternoon, I tried to imagine its headwaters at Three Forks, Montana, where the Gallatin, Madison and Jefferson rivers braid together in cold, clear strands and start the long journey east. Not much farther downstream from the bridge west of Alton, Illinois, that journey is transformed into the Mississippi. Here, the water itself looked older than the mastodon tooth I'd dug from the sediment at Canyon Ferry just weeks before.

A few miles ahead, another bridge carried me across the Mississippi and dropped me into downtown Alton, an old, working class city built on wooded hills. The Mississippi is restrained at Alton by a locks and dam, which look like a huge cement and steel comb extending across the channel.

Not far upstream from Alton is the confluence of the Illinois and Mississippi rivers. There, I turned north along the Illinois, and headed for Mauvaisterre on a two-lane blacktop highway.

I didn't have any more facts about Gerry Heyman's death now than I had learned during that first call from Sarah. When I'd phoned her earlier that morning, just before I left for the airport, she'd tried to tell me about a powerful man in Mauvaisterre, a guy with whom Gerry had been at odds recently. The man's name was Matthew Turk. I remembered that Turk was the son of the woman whom Mickey Cochran had confessed to killing.

I said to Sarah, "Gerry told me about that old murder."

"I know," she said. After the perfect hesitation, she added, "He wanted you to help him with something."

I smiled now as I listened to Alberta Hunter sing of tragedy and love. You had to give Sarah credit for knowing how to set a hook.

The country all around was languid in the heat. The floodplain of the Illinois was flat as a sheet of paper and several miles wide, and the highway ran along the base of steep hills and cliffs that marked its eastern edge. The long fields to my left were planted in corn and soybeans. The tall stalks of corn bore yellow tassels, the beans were lush, like long, rolled cushions. To my right, the mixed hardwood forest crowded the roadway, and the dense undergrowth seemed to exude heat. There were frequent limestone outcrops, but for the most part the hills were an unbroken tangle of trees and brush. The whole country was a trembling, sonorous green, blending at the horizon with the margins of a tight, gray sky. Ahead, the highway dissolved in the sunlight into a shimmering silver mirage.

Mauvaisterre was about seventy miles north of Alton. Because of the quality of the road and my mood,

I took nearly two hours to make the trip. I passed either through or near little towns with names like Eldred and Hillview. Would I meet, I wondered, a white fifty-eight Impala with my father behind the wheel, on his way to another cup of coffee with another prospect? Would I see my mother standing in the shade of a porch, waving while I sped on by? Nothing a man might find in yesterday ever helps. Nothing. That much I knew for sure. The farther I drove, the more my belly felt as though sometime, somewhere, I had done something wrong. I had run away from home.

Finally, the floodplain narrowed and the highway made a broad turn away from the limestone hills, toward the river. The road began to rise as I neared Mauvaisterre. It was that quirk of geography, I decided, that distinct elevation, which had made the town possible.

I braked at the city limits. The sign that welcomed me said that the population was two thousand, and the streets were radar patrolled. I passed a gas station, then an old schoolhouse that had been converted into a secondhand store. A few blocks farther on, I found myself in a neighborhood of small bungalows with neat yards, and gardens full of sweet corn and tomatoes. Ahead, I saw the corrugated steel cylinders of a grain elevator, which rose behind a brown, single-story train station. When I drove through the crossing, I saw that the station was closed, and the tracks in both directions had been pulled out. Just past the crossing, a big brown dog lay sleeping in the street. He didn't even look up as I made a wide, slow detour around him.

Three blocks farther, I came to my first stop sign. Beyond the sign, the street broadened into an asphalt parking lot. A fractured cement boat ramp descended into the river. There was just one outfit, an old orange Dodge pickup and boat trailer, in the lot.

Following a sign that gave directions toward the business district, I turned right. Three blocks, then another right, then two more blocks and I found myself making a circuit around the town square. The courthouse filled the block at the northeast corner. There was a bronze statue of Abraham Lincoln in the center. Lincoln sat on a stone chair that could have been a throne. Judging from the look sculpted on his long, haggard face, he might have been contemplating power. Or, he could just as well have been weeping. The statue was guarded by a World War II vintage artillery piece. A few people wandered from store to store. Were they really watching me, studying my unfamiliar car?

On my second circuit, I pulled into a space in front of the tiny old Hotel Mauvaisterre, which sat on the corner opposite the courthouse.

The Hotel Mauvaisterre was built of red brick, which had turned chalky with age. The place was only two stories high, with white-trimmed windows. Some of the windows sported small air conditioners. A sign near the rear of the hotel advertised a dining room and tavern.

It took my eyes a moment to adjust to the dim light inside the lobby, which smelled of fried chicken and cigarettes. The furniture amounted to a broken-down leather sofa, a newspaper machine offering the *St. Louis Post Dispatch,* a television, two sunken armchairs, and a pay phone. People were noticeably absent. I was about to rap my knuckles on the green formica counter, when a wiry old man pushed aside a beaded curtain behind the desk.

"Whadya want?" He finished wiping his hands on a faded red dish towel, then draped the towel over his shoulder. He had on blue pants and a white shirt, with the sleeves rolled up above elbows nearly as round and polished as billiard balls. Except for a few wild hairs around his ears, he was completely bald. He looked about a hundred and ten years old, but I might have been wrong. He might have been only a hundred and five.

"A room," I said. "Single."

"You out of your mind?" He hunched forward and squinted up at me, as though I were expected to give some serious thought to my answer.

"Maybe," I said. "Probably."

"We don't really rent rooms, you know."

"Must be my mistake," I said. "The sign says *hotel*, I figured—"

"Easy mistake," he said. "People make it all the time."

I said, "What's your name, anyhow?"

"Mike," he said, "it's any your business. Big Mike."

"You got rooms, Mike—"

"*Big* Mike."

"Right. Have you got rooms you *could* rent, Big Mike? If you were of a mind to?"

"Who the hell are you?"

"Leo Banks."

"Where the hell you from?"

"Montana."

Big Mike nodded, as though everything were suddenly clear. "Place belongs to my great-granddaughter," he said. "Most of the business comes from the restaurant and tavern. Got fried catfish that won't kill you outright. Cold beer. Stuff like that."

I said, "What about that room?"

He squinted at me again. "There's better places to stay."

"I don't care."

"Fine by me. I just want to make clear on that. Don't want you down here whining later on, claiming I didn't warn you."

"Just a room. A single."

"You want a air conditioner? Look like you could use one."

After just ten minutes outside the car, my shirt was soaked.

"Why not," I said.

Big Mike's eyes brightened. "I figured you for a high roller." He was about to hand over my key, when the phone rang from under the counter. Big Mike held the black receiver to his ear.

"Whadya want?" He listened for a moment, then said, "Yeah, it's him . . . Hell yes, I'm sure. How many people from Montana you think we got in this town? You want to talk to him yourself?" He listened again, then hung up the phone.

"That was the sheriff," Big Mike said. "Wanted to know if the guy in that strange car out front was the one here to help the Heyman woman."

"What else he have to say?"

Big Mike used the red towel to mop the sweat from his forehead. "Said he thought a big shot detective like you could find a better place to stay."

My room was at the front of the building, overlooking the square. There was a single bed with a pink chintz spread over a mattress that turned out to be not half bad. The remaining furniture consisted of a wobbly dresser and a wooden armchair with an upholstered foam pad tied in place on the seat. No TV, no phone. Big Mike had pointed out that he was giving me a deluxe room, one with a private bath, which turned out to be a private shower. And the air conditioner worked. I adjusted every switch I could find to either "High," or "Cold," then unbuttoned my shirt and went about some serious cooling off.

Sarah Heyman—Sarah Crey when I first met her— used to daydream all the time about traveling to Paris, about spending a month living in a small flat with a view reminiscent of the nineteen-twenties. Or her conception, at least, of what Paris was like in the twenties. Cobblestone alleys . . . soot-smudged buildings . . . romantic shadows cast by ancient streetlamps. A regular bohemian wine and cheese extravaganza. Complete, I suppose, with some buckaroo in baggy white pants and black beret.

Several times, Sarah and I took the bus from Champaign to Chicago for long weekends. One night in Old Town, we laughed at transvestites, and watched a man leading a lion down the street on a leash. And here she was today, sloshing around in exactly the kind of backwater she used to deride. As I looked down from my hotel window, there was certainly nothing Parisian about the view. Pickup trucks and big Chevrolets slowly lapped the square, and a scattering of men and women wandered in and out of mom-and-pop stores that looked out onto the park.

All in all, the Hotel Mauvaisterre was the kind of place where John Dillinger might have holed up. I could imagine him here at the window, edging aside the lace curtain with the muzzle of his .38 to check the lazy, innocent street below for G-men, then becoming more and more lost in languid contemplation both of his legendary exploits and the bleached blonde sprawled across the bed. Well, there was no blonde on the bed, and nothing legendary in the vicinity. But I did have a .45 Colt Gold Cup and three loaded magazines in my suitcase. And in my own way, I was still lugging around my own version of romance. I made a note to knock that nonsense off. If living in Montana teaches you anything at all, it is that, in the end, romance and myths will always break your heart.

I was enjoying the cold blast of the air conditioner across my belly when I saw a big white Ford with a set of overheads pull into the space next to my rented car. A man wearing a tan uniform, gunbelt and mirrored sunglasses got out of the Ford, hitched up the gunbelt, then walked into the hotel. Not long after that, there were footsteps in the hall, then a solid knock on the door.

Dillinger probably wouldn't have buttoned his shirt before answering.

"Freddie Pointdexter," the uniformed man said, walking on into the room without offering his hand or being invited. Well over six feet tall, he had probably thirty pounds on me, and not all of it through his middle. He had thinning brown hair, and his florid face glistened in the heat. His upper arms filled the short sleeves of his shirt, and his forearms weren't much smaller. His hands were thick too, and looked made for grappling. I noticed that there was no badge on his shirt. Maybe he figured that the mirrored RayBans he wore were the closest thing to a badge a man needed in Mauvaisterre, Illinois.

"Howdy," I said.

Pointdexter pulled off his sunglasses. The flesh behind the lenses was untanned, which made his blue eyes look larger than they were, and intensely innocent. I could also see now that he was about ten years younger than I.

"Howdy?" Pointdexter almost laughed. "By God, you are from the wild West." When he walked by me toward the air conditioner, I saw that the back of his shirt was saddled with sweat.

"Name's Leo Banks," I said. "I was standing there when Big Mike talked to you on the phone."

Pointdexter laced his fingers together, then inverted his hands, flexed, and cracked his knuckles. "Mike's the oldest guy in this county."

"*Big* Mike," I said.

"Right." Pointdexter was looking at my two suitcases. "Just plain Mike to his friends. Old boy used to be a club fighter in St. Louis. Least that's what people say."

I said, "You got a badge or something?"

Pointdexter raised a meaty hand to the two empty grommets above his left shirt pocket, where a badge normally would be pinned. Then he shrugged. "I put on a fresh shirt at noon. Must've forgot the damned thing. Happens sometimes. Hell, everybody around here knows me, anyhow."

It didn't seem to faze Pointdexter that I didn't know him. "Surprised you'd stay in a dump like this," he said. "Sarah Heyman know you're here yet?"

"What's that got to do with where I stay?"

"Sarah called me yesterday afternoon. Said she had an old friend, friend used to be a cop, coming to look into Gerry's death. Case you were wondering why I was waiting for you, now you know."

I went into the tiny bathroom and drew a glass of water from the lavatory. "So, is this the beginning of a turf battle?" The water was tepid.

Now Pointdexter laughed outright. "Not unless you plan to run for election here in Big Sandy County. I don't know what Sarah Heyman told you about Gerry's murder and my investigation. Or me."

I decided there was no need to alienate Pointdexter, at least not until I knew everything he was willing to tell. "She said it's been slow going," I said.

"Did she now? I'll just bet she did. You sure you're not runnin' for election?" Pointdexter looked at his watch. "What we ought to do, Banks, we ought to head downstairs and get us a couple of hamburgers, maybe a slice of pie. Close enough to supper time for me. What do you say?"

When I told him I should probably head over to Sarah Heyman's first, Freddie Pointdexter put his arm around my shoulder and started for the door. "Let's choke down some hamburgers instead. Hell, we might as well beat the rush. Know what I mean?"

A woman named Michelle brought us each a glass of iced tea. Michelle, the sheriff explained, was Big Mike's great-granddaughter. She was a petite woman in her early thirties, who wore a snug denim skirt and a red cotton blouse with short sleeves. Her black hair was short, and tightly curled.

"You want to fry us up some hamburgers, Mike?" Pointdexter said. He looked at me and swung his chin toward the lobby. "You already know Big Mike." He reached out and stroked Michelle's forearm, while he smiled up at her. "This here's Little Mike."

Little Mike took Pointdexter's hand and studied the palm. "I'd read your future, Freddie," she said, "but you haven't got one."

"How about getting married?" he said.

Her lipstick was almost as red as her blouse, and when she spoke, her lips seemed adroit enough to pick a lock. "Sorry," she said, "I got a hair appointment that day."

Pointdexter appeared to be lost in a daydream as he watched Little Mike waltz toward the kitchen. He took a sip of tea. "I already married her a coupla times," he said. "Wasn't as bad as Big Mike said it'd be."

"I guess you were lucky there."

"Not really," Pointdexter said. "He said it'd be trench warfare. As you can see, I am still alive."

"Sometimes, divorce can do you more good than eating fruit and vegetables," I said.

"Mine sure did. We just live together now. Lot simpler that way. Hell, I should've known I was in trouble when she made the preacher leave out the 'obey' part. You know, Love, Honor and *Obey?* Hell, once you start tampering with God's law like that, you might as well just shack up."

There were about a dozen tables, each draped with a white cloth, in the dining room. The walls were covered with pale green paper. It was about half past five in the afternoon, and Freddie Pointdexter and I were the only customers. At the rear of the room, an arched doorway led into the bar, which was a jumble of dim light from neon displays advertising beer. On the jukebox, Merle Haggard was deeply involved in a musical study of the sociology of depression. The bartender was nowhere to be seen, and the lone customer sat on a stool, while his head lay atop arms folded upon the bar. The guy was either passed out, or he deserved a decent burial.

Pointdexter cleared his throat. "So Doc Heyman was a friend of yours."

"Long time ago," I said. I gave him the short version of how I'd come to know Gerry. By short version, I mean I left out the part about my romance with Sarah. I went on to tell him about seeing Gerry and Sarah earlier that summer, but I decided that Gerry's story about the Turk family and Mickey Cochran could wait until I had a clearer read on Pointdexter. Then for good measure, I said that I'd recently retired from twenty years of policing.

When I stopped talking, Pointdexter rocked his iced tea glass absently on the table, while he chewed an ice cube. "Upstairs," he said, "you mentioned something about a turf battle."

I shrugged. "Just a precaution on my part."

"I understand. You might say this is just a precaution on my part, too. See, if I was Sarah Heyman and had an old friend like you, I might do just what she did. And if I was the old friend getting the call, no way would I be able to turn her down. I just want to make sure you have a full understanding of that word *retired* after your name, Banks."

I looked at the place on Pointdexter's shirt where a badge belonged but was not needed. "I figure, Sheriff, it means about the same as *out of town.*" Or, I thought, if worse came to worst, *get out of town.*

"Don't get me wrong," Pointdexter said. "What happened to Gerry Heyman is a terrible thing, and I want the truth as much as anybody. I don't care if the truth comes from you or the man in the moon, or even the FBI, God help me. But I don't play games, and I don't want to wake up and come to find out one's been played on me. You learn something, I want you to trust me enough to tell me what it is."

"You care to explain that?"

"No. You just remember that when you start asking around."

"I thought you said you don't play games."

Pointdexter looked toward the kitchen, where Little Mike appeared with our order. Then he looked back at me. His teeth were large and white. "I lied," he said.

"Sarah told me your evidence is pretty thin," I said.

Pointdexter bit off about half the hamburger, then wiped his mouth with a paper napkin. "About as thin," he mumbled, "as you'd see on a TV movie." He swallowed. "Bad TV movie."

Gerry's body was found on a country road at about six-thirty on a Tuesday morning. The discovery was made by a young farmer named Kenny Agle, who was on the way to his second job at the Mobile Chemical plant in nearby Jacksonville. Heyman was lying face down on the ground behind his car. His feet were in the grader ditch, while his head was at the very edge of the gravel roadway.

I said, "Sarah told me he was beaten to death."

"That's right," Pointdexter said. "With the jack handle from his own car." The left rear tire was flat, and the trunk was open when Agle found the car.

"Was the car up on a jack?" I asked.

Pointdexter shook his head. "Jack was still in the trunk, along with the spare tire. Looks like he was just getting ready to change the tire, when somebody came along."

"What about his injuries?"

"Four blows to the left side of his head, all of them striking between the ear and the crest of the skull. All of them causing fractures. Then there were three more blows on the right rear of the skull, this time behind the ear. All of those caused fractures, too."

"What about other injuries? Non-lethal ones?"

"His nose was broken, and the inside of both upper and lower lips were lacerated."

"Like he'd been punched a couple of times?"

"Exactly. And his left forearm was broken. About two inches up from the wrist. Seems pretty clear he got that trying to block some kind of blow."

"How sure are you," I asked, "about the jack handle?"

"Sure as you ever get about anything," he said. The jack handle had been found in the grass about four feet from the body. It was smeared with blood, hair, bone chips and other tissue. Pointdexter went on, "We sent that handle to the autopsy. It was consistent with all the injuries on both sides of the head. With the broken arm, too. All the blood and other muck came from Heyman."

"What about—"

"Prints." Pointdexter started to laugh.

I started to laugh, too. "You'd have been disappointed if I didn't at least ask."

"I been in this line of work seven years, I never had a case turned on fingerprints."

"Someday you will," I said. "I had one once. Maybe twice. Makes you feel like a real detective."

"Well, it won't happen this time," Pointdexter said. "No prints on the jack handle. And as long as we're on the subject, there weren't any identifiable footprints or tire tracks."

I said, "You told me he was found at about six-thirty. When do you think he was killed?"

"The best estimate is sometime around midnight."

"Rigor mortis?"

"Fully formed," Pointdexter said.

That meant that Gerry had probably been dead for at least six, but less than twelve hours.

"When was he last seen?" I asked.

Pointdexter pulled a cigarette from his shirt pocket and tapped the end against the crystal of his watch. "He had dinner at home the night before. Sarah says about eight o'clock. Couple of hours later, he left the house."

"She know where he went?"

Pointdexter shook his head, and pursed his lips as he lit his cigarette with a disposable butane lighter. "He got a phone call, left a few minutes later."

"Any idea who the call was from?"

"No. Heyman was one of those old-fashioned kind of doctors. Wasn't unusual for him to be gone in the evening. It's a better than even chance he was out checking on a patient that night."

"And you've checked his patients."

From the look on his face, I knew Pointdexter was enjoying our game of cat and mouse as much as I was. "As a matter of fact, I have. No luck. At a little after ten o'clock, Gerry Heyman bought a tank of gas at Cletus Porter's station. That's the last anybody saw of him."

I chewed on my last bite of hamburger, while I thought about what Pointdexter had told me so far. Pointdexter took a long draw on his cigarette, then said through a cloud of smoke, "That's a *Chevron* station, you understand. Topped off his tank with unleaded supreme." I ignored the sarcasm in his voice.

I said, "What about livor mortis?"

"You conducting a test, or what?"

Livor mortis, a function of gravity, is the settling of blood into those parts of the body nearest the ground. This turns the tissue a deep red, which can be mistaken for a bruise. If livor mortis is in place, and is inconsistent with the position of the body, that means the body has been moved from the position it occupied at the time the livor was formed. This makes livor mortis an important element in determining whether or not a body has been moved to a different location after death. Maybe Pointdexter was right. Maybe I was conducting a test.

Pointdexter stubbed out the cigarette on his greasy plate. This time, the patience in his voice was as heavy as a pair of cement overshoes. "This here's the smallest county in the state of Illinois, Banks. Folks used to think that Scott County was the smallest, but then the government did some new surveying and rechecked some old surveying, and damned if it didn't turn out that Big Sandy County was the smallest. Besides me, I got three part-time deputies. The city of Mauvaisterre doesn't have its own police force, so we got to work the town, too. I expect I pay those deputies less than what your pension is. I usually put in about fourteen, fifteen hours a day—that's if I don't count the dumbass phone calls I get at home all hours of the day or night. I'm at the end of my second term, and I plan to run for election again next fall. Now, none of these things I've told you means I'm stupid. Unless, of course, you consider the fact that only a stupid man would put up with a bullshit job like this. But then, you were a cop for twenty years, weren't you?"

I drank off the last of my ice tea, looked across the room at Little Mike, smiled, and nodded toward my glass. Then I looked evenly at Freddie Pointdexter, and said, "What about livor mortis?"

Pointdexter's fair eyes didn't waver. "On the bottoms of his arms, his belly and groin, his legs. Most pronounced in his lower legs and feet. He was lying uphill, remember? Everything just like it should be."

When Little Mike came to the table, Pointdexter's eyes broke away. He sat back in his chair, like a curious bull thinking about a charge. When Little Mike filled his glass, she absently laid her hand on his shoulder, a faint gesture that seemed charged with indescribable affection.

Pointdexter took a deep breath. "Thanks, sugar."

"It's just a glass of iced tea," she said. "I do this all the time." She started back to the kitchen.

"Sure," Pointdexter said. "Where was I?"

I said, "You were describing the livor mortis."

"No." He folded his arms across his huge chest, then reached up and scratched the corner of his mouth with a fingertip. "No, I was being a shithead. I don't have call to do a lot of heavy investigations. My insecurities are my problem. Sorry."

If Pointdexter was willing to overlook the fact that I'd baited him, then I was willing to let him. If he already understood the insecurities that all good cops face, then there was nothing more to be said.

As Pointdexter went on to explain the scene, it looked as if someone had come upon Gerry Heyman while he was fixing a tire. For whatever reason, the killer punched Heyman several times, apparently backing him into the ditch, then began bashing him with the tire iron. When Heyman fell, he fell forward, face down along the bank of the ditch.

"That accounts for all the injuries on Heyman's face, his arm, and the left side of his head," Pointdexter said. "Then, once Heyman was on the ground, I think the killer went down into the ditch, kneeled down and whacked him a couple more times. That gives you the other two fractures on the right side."

Both Sarah Heyman and Freddie Pointdexter had said there wasn't much evidence. But Sarah had led me to believe that Pointdexter wasn't capable of making the most out of what he had. I decided that I wouldn't make the same mistake—if mistaken was what Sarah had been.

5

They teach you in police school that every criminal leaves evidence of himself at the scene of the crime. Fingerprints, footprints, hair, fibers. Cigarette butts. Chewing gum. Blood, sweat or tears. Something. But the only thing this killer seemed to have left behind—the only thing, at least, that Freddie Pointdexter had found—was Gerry Heyman's corpse.

"If you're like I was," I said to Pointdexter, "you get it in your head that there had to be something there, you just missed it, you weren't good enough."

Pointdexter squared his shoulders and cleared his throat. "If you're asking, did I screw it up, the answer is no. If you want me to elaborate on that, I guess we could always take this little talk outside."

"We don't need to go outside," I said. "But you don't need to waste time trying to convince me that the possibility doesn't eat on you."

"I got no secrets," Pointdexter said. "This's the first murder I ever worked on. I've worked it hard as I know how. And I was smart enough to get help."

Most of the work at the scene and on the Cherokee, it turned out, had been done by a team of technicians from the Illinois Bureau of Investigation. "I took one look at things," Pointdexter went on, "and I said, whoa, hold the phone. Left everything just like I found it, called in the cavalry."

"The body?" I said.

"Even the body. Left the poor bastard lying there in the ditch for nearly four hours."

I have confidence in a guy who understands that a body is evidence and the dead have no need to hurry off to the morgue.

I told Pointdexter that if there wasn't any physical evidence to prove who killed Heyman, then there also wasn't any physical evidence to clear anybody. "You're a hometown boy," I said. "So was Gerry. Who do you think might have wanted him dead?"

"Who said I was a hometown boy?"

I shrugged. "You wouldn't have been elected if you weren't."

"You sound like some kind of goddamn sociologist, some kind of *liberal* like that. All right, smart guy, what makes you think I suspect anybody at all?"

"That's easier still. You ran for reelection. That means you're probably suspicious and contentious by nature. Unless you're lazy and a crook. Maybe I'm wrong, but you don't seem like a lazy crook."

Pointdexter's upper lip twitched, and he shook his head. "Just what I need, a vote of confidence."

"A small town doctor," I said, not rising to Pointdexter's bait, "he's usually a kind of heroic figure."

"Gerry fit that for most people. Hell, he even made house calls. When's the last time you heard of a doctor'd do that?"

"And what's the mood around town?" I doubted that a murder would rest easily in a small, isolated community like Mauvaisterre.

"Well, people are scared some," Pointdexter said. "Like you'd expect. But kind of resigned, too. The other day, somebody told me it fits that the one person who'd get killed in a dying town would be the doctor. People aren't much on irony around here, but that's one even country people can get."

The supper crowd was beginning to wander into the Hotel Mauvaisterre dining room. Pointdexter pretended to be distracted by a pair of old ladies who took the table nearest us. Then, when Little Mike stopped off with our check, Pointdexter gave her hand a squeeze and thanked her for the good eats.

"Little Mike here still makes her pies with lard," Pointdexter said. He finally let go of her hand as we stood up from the table. "That's how come they're so good. Bad for your coronary arteries, but hey, everybody's gonna die sometime, ain't that right?"

Little Mike nodded toward the drunk sleeping on the bar. "You'll take care of Tory?"

Pointdexter sighed. "Don't I always take care of Tory?" Pointdexter closed his eyes dreamily, while he flexed his shoulders and turned his head from side to side, as though trying to work out a kink in his neck. "Just hope to God he don't send me to the chiropractor again."

Out of curiosity, I followed Pointdexter through the low archway into the dim, cool reaches of the bar.

"Tory McDade," Pointdexter said over his shoulder. "Every other day or so, he comes in here, starts knocking back vodkas, been doing it for years. He's got so bad his ears are like bookends with no books between them."

I wondered if that lack of bar business was because of supper-time, or because of McDade hacking and gasping as he slept.

Pointdexter stopped better than an arm's length from the old man, then looked at me and winked. McDade was wearing a crumpled brown suit. Next to an empty shot glass on the bar lay an equally crumpled brown felt hat, the style of hat that men used to wear in the late forties and early fifties.

"Watch this," Pointdexter said. He leaned forward and nudged McDade's shoulder. "Tory . . . Hey, McDade."

McDade stirred slightly, and Pointdexter didn't waste a second drawing back.

"Wha . . . What!" McDade snapped upright and swung his arm in a wild arc toward Pointdexter. "What's the goddamn problem?" McDade glared first at me, then at Pointdexter. "You again . . . you still sheriff, Pointdexter? Can't believe I fought a war just to get you for a goddamn sheriff."

As McDade caught his breath, he used the flat of his hand to rub away the streak of spittle that had run from the left corner of his mouth. The flesh hanging from his cheeks and neck seemed loose enough to stretch and cover the faces of two younger men. His gray hair was thin, disheveled and cut very short. The large pouches below his dark, close-set eyes looked as though they had been storing up tears for decades, and the inflamed vessels at the margins of his nose were a map to places where nobody in his right mind wanted to go.

McDade jabbed a stubby finger toward Pointdexter and said in a loud voice, "You goddamn fascist!"

To me, Pointdexter said, "See what I mean?" Then he moved closer to McDade, wrapped his hands around the old man's shoulders like a tight end gathering in a pass and eased him off the bar stool. "It's democracy in action, Tory," Pointdexter said. His voice was louder than McDade's had been, and his mouth alarmingly close to McDade's ear.

McDade was unimpressed. "My hat . . . get my hat, ya Nazi." Now he was glaring at me.

I scooped up McDade's fedora and balanced it on his head. By that time, Pointdexter had him halfway to the door.

"See you tomorrow, Tory," Pointdexter said. He pushed open the padded red Naugahyde door and ushered McDade out into the startling light.

McDade wrenched himself away. With ponderous dignity, he adjusted first his green knit tie, which he wore with a black and gold plaid shirt, then his suit jacket and finally his hat.

"Tomorrow," McDade muttered. "Sure, yeah, tomorrow, what's that?" As he walked away down the sidewalk, he began an extended coughing fit, which ended when he hawked twice and spit on the curb.

I walked Freddie Pointdexter back to his car.

"You have guys like that in Wyoming, or wherever it is you come from, Banks?"

I started to correct Pointdexter about where I was from, but let it pass. "Nothing geographic about the Tory McDades of the world," I said.

"He gets worse this time of year." Pointdexter hesitated at the corner and glanced back at McDade, who seemed to be managing all right. The vent from the hotel kitchen poked out of the brick wall like a dull, silver-colored goiter. The fan groaned and stubby gray stalagmites of grease hung from the metal.

"How's that?" I asked.

"We got this big town picnic coming up in a few days." Pointdexter stepped around the puddle of grease on the sidewalk under the vent. "Local VFW puts it on every year. They make this great soup called burgoo, have a parade, a horse show, the whole shootin' match. Kind of a town holiday. Something to keep us from being a complete ghost town. For some reason, that picnic causes old Tory to go plum hog wild. Don't ask me to explain it. Hell, I don't understand it at all. Nobody does."

When we got to Pointdexter's cruiser, I held him up a minute. "I guess you've got a file on this case," I said.

Pointdexter nodded. "I do. But you can't see it. I

don't mind telling you what I know, but I'm not fool enough to turn over the file to somebody I just met. Especially somebody stays in a hotel like this." He jabbed his big thumb in the direction of the Hotel Mauvaisterre.

I understood about the file, and asked him about his crime scene photos.

"Got a ton of those. Nice eight by ten colors."

"And?"

Pointdexter thought for a moment, before hitching up his gunbelt and opening the car door. "I'll get them to you tomorrow. That soon enough?"

It was. I changed the subject then, and got directions to Sarah Heyman's house. Once we had that down, Pointdexter turned serious again.

"I told you earlier to trust me with things," he said. "I hope you took that to heart."

"As much as I take anything to heart," I said.

Pointdexter's blue eyes narrowed and he covered them with his RayBans. "I find that very comforting, I certainly do." He opened his car door, got inside and rolled down the window. "Whether you realize it or not, I think we can help each other on this murder business, and I'm just trying to get across that I'm not too big a man to admit that. Now, you'll probably find out some things that will make you want to clam up with me. That would be unwise. Of course, there's a chance you won't find out at all what I'm talking about. If that happens, it just means you're too damned dumb, and none of this matters. That make sense, bud?"

"Not a lot," I said.

"Don't worry," he said, starting his car, "it will."

"About those possible suspects," I reminded him. "You never gave me your short list."

"Nope." His smile was wide and innocent, crammed with teeth. "I must've forgot." Then he ad-

justed the air conditioner, rolled up his window, and
drove off.

Not long after Pointdexter left, I struck out for
Sarah Heyman's house in my rented Chevy. It was
getting along toward dusk, but there was still plenty of
daylight left. The air was dead calm and swampy,
while huge, steel-colored thunderbusters were beginning to top off in the southwestern sky. There was
hardly any traffic. The sidewalks and front lawns were
empty of people, and as I drove with the air conditioner on and window down, I caught the occasional
odor of a barbecue.

Mauvaisterre is cradled in a bend of the Illinois
River. With the exception of the boat ramp, which I
had seen earlier, a thick earthen and cement retaining
wall runs along the western margin of the town. Most
of the houses are small, frame bungalows, the kind
that I remembered from my childhood farther south.
I pulled to a stop in the parking lot of the boat ramp. I
watched the river glide by in muddy whorls, and
smelled the dead fish and the coming storm. Across
the river, a dense green wall of trees stretched lazily
through the dusky heat. The longer I drove, the more
I realized that the time I had spent with Freddie
Pointdexter had been a welcome evasion from meeting Sarah.

The Heyman place was on North Water Street. Un-
like the majority of the town, North Water is lined
with large, stately old homes. Overhead, the inter-
twined branches of huge oak and maple trees cast the
evening light in mottled shadows. No eaves needed
paint here, no brickwork bore a rough edge. The rhododendrons and magnolias were waxy and green, and
the most serious threat to the neighborhood seemed
to be that the roses might break down the trellises.

I found the right address at North Water and Douglas, and pulled to a stop at the curb in front of an

imposing two-story yellow house, which sat on the corner. A long, curving porch ran along the sides facing each street. The porch roof was supported by pairs of Corinthian columns. On the second story facing the cross street, Douglas, I saw the tall, narrow windows of a sleeping porch. The entire house seemed to fan out around a circular turret that overlooked the intersection. I tried to remember how much I had last paid a doctor to tell me I wasn't getting any younger.

Sarah Heyman was out on the porch before I had made it to the front steps. She was dressed in a teal cotton blouse and white shorts. Her legs looked tan and sleek.

"Leo." She held her arms open. I managed not to run the distance from the curb to those waiting arms. The silver bangles on her right wrist jangled softly.

"Sarah, I'm really sorry." I couldn't remember, maybe I'd already told her that on the telephone. But you know how it is, a woman's husband gets murdered, you say you're sorry more than once. What can it hurt? When we embraced at last, I felt as though she were squeezing years out of me. I stepped back and looked at her. "Maybe—" I said.

"No." She touched her fingers to my lips. "No maybes."

Sarah took me through the tall, double front doors, which were filled with leaded glass. "The kids are staying with friends tonight. I thought it would make it easier for us to talk."

Inside, the foyer was dark and cool. The crepe soles of Sarah's brown flats made delicate, squeaky noises on the hardwood floor, which was laid in a herringbone pattern. My own snakeskin ropers sounded like the drum of an approaching army as we walked deeper into the house, and turned finally into a bright room furnished with a plush yellow sofa and two matching love seats arranged in a U around a large, oak coffee table with a glass top. There was an ornate, antique table with a marble top under the window, and a comfortable looking antique rocking chair beside the table.

"Let's get this out of the way first," Sarah said. She went to the table under the window and brought back a check. "Fifteen thousand dollars."

I folded the check and put it in my shirt pocket, then sat down on one of the love seats. From the start, I had looked upon the money as a buffer between Sarah and me, something to keep the lines of demarcation clear. That moment on the porch now made the money seem like one hell of a good idea.

"I still feel bad that I didn't call you sooner," she said.

I waved her off. "You told me that the other day. There's no need to make a career out of it. I'm sure I'm not exactly part of your day-by-day thoughts."

"It wasn't that," she said, turning away. "If anything, since we saw you back in June, I've thought about you more lately than any time in the last ten years."

"We should have had a better visit," I said. Sarah had an instinct for the right mood, the way a chameleon always finds the right color. This was going to be harder than I thought.

"No, the delay had nothing to do with you. Really," she said. "There was the funeral, of course, and Gerry's parents and sister were here for nearly a week. To tell you the truth, nothing really settled in on me until they left. And then it had been so long and nothing was happening with Pointdexter, and it all started to seem—"

"It's okay," I said, stopping her. So far, her excuses seemed legitimate, but they might start to bleach out at any moment. That's the way it is with chameleons: the leaf always cooperates by maintaining a constant

73

color. "Are you getting along any better now? You and the kids?"

"Not particularly." She gazed off through the window, then looked down at her hands. "Not well at all. Michael wants to spend all his time in his room with the stereo headphones glued to his ears. He acts like this house is a concentration camp and I'm the boss guard. I think all the music he listens to is satanic. Lisa doesn't say much at all. Three or four times, I've thought she's run away, then found her curled up asleep on the couch in Gerry's study."

"And what about you?"

"I clean the house." A streak of color rose along the side of her neck. "How clean do you suppose a house can get?"

"How clean do you need it?"

Sarah's laugh was brittle. "Good point. Gerry used to say you get through life like any old plow horse—by putting one foot in front of the other until somebody pulls in the reins. I just never thought he'd be pulled up this short."

"I met Freddie Pointdexter," I said. "We had a hamburger uptown."

Sarah's face broke into a thin, quick smile. "Then you know what I'm up against."

"Not exactly," I said. "He seemed like a policeman trying to be honest and fair." For the moment, I ignored the fact that policemen such as that can create some dandy disasters.

"You think he's all right at first," she said, nodding. "I know I did. But as the days went on and on and nothing happened . . . not even a hint that I would ever know . . . that's when I started thinking about things that just didn't add up."

"Pointdexter told me what he had in the way of evidence," I said, then went through the information I'd heard earlier from the sheriff. "If that's all he's got, I'd have a hard time pressing him to do more with it. He hasn't got much."

"A mystery," Sarah said.

"Exactly that. A mystery."

"But you were a policeman for twenty years."

"That's right. A policeman. Not a magician or a movie actor. Not even for fifteen thousand dollars. I'm still not sure what you think I can do that Freddie Pointdexter can't."

"It's not so much what he *can* do as what he *will* do. I know Gerry told you that story about Mickey Cochran and the Grace Turk murder." She looked away, then made a fist and rested her forehead against it. When she looked back at me, her smile was apologetic.

"And I know," she went on, "Gerry told you that was the only reason we looked you up. I'm sorry."

"No need to be sorry for the truth."

"No, I'm sorry because that wasn't the truth. Well, maybe it was for Gerry, but not for me. I suppose it was okay to let him think so, but not at your expense."

Terrific, I thought. Murder and old times, and now a dash of romantic innuendo. Was it too late to demand more money?

"Then you probably know," I said, "Gerry thought Cochran was innocent, said he wanted me to come back here and prove it."

"And you told him he should give that a try himself."

"Yes?"

"Willing, he said you told him. You just have to be willing. Well, that's just what Gerry decided he was."

Willing, she seemed to mean, to try his hand in my world, and get himself killed for his trouble.

According to Sarah, Mickey Cochran had been tossed out of the joint and installed in the Big Sandy County nursing home about two weeks after the Heymans returned from their scenic tour of Montana.

Gerry didn't waste any time or diplomacy in stirring up the old case. He never made any secret of the fact that he believed Cochran had been railroaded, and his loose talk around town hadn't exactly endeared him to Matthew Turk, who was the son of Grace and Otto Turk.

Sarah's voice grew defiant. "Matthew Turk has Big Sandy County—including Freddie Pointdexter—in his pocket. Once Gerry started asking questions in public, it didn't take Turk long to decide he didn't like it."

"Are you saying you think Turk killed him?" I said.

"Maybe. I think there's a better than even chance of it. You said Pointdexter told you Gerry was killed on a country road. Did he tell you, too, he was killed at the gate to that little cemetery where Grace Turk is buried?"

"No. He didn't tell me that."

"And did he tell you that this was less than half a mile from Matthew Turk's house?"

"No."

"Well," Sarah said, "imagine that."

"So what's the story with this Matthew Turk guy? Besides being from a family that's part of the local legend, what's his claim to fame?"

"Money," she said. "Not just money, really. Money and land. When we moved here and Gerry set up his practice, the first thing I noticed was that everything seemed to lean in Matthew Turk's direction."

"You make it sound like we're talking about a feudal lord."

"In a way, we are. At last count, the Turks owned something like twelve thousand acres. Matthew's father—Otto—is really the owner, I guess. Matthew's more like the boss man. He drives around in a Cadillac and makes sure the work gets done. He lives in this big old red brick house with lots of gingerbread hanging on it. The kind of house that would give Edgar Allan Poe nightmares."

Gerry had told me, I remembered, that all of Otto Turk's money came from his wife's family. "Otto, then, I take it he's still walking around above ground."

"Slithering around would be more like it, as far as I'm concerned. He lives in another big old house down in St. Louis. Somewhere near Forest Park. His poor wife, I've always heard, was an only child. So Otto ended up with everything."

"And how is it that you think all this ties in with Gerry's death?"

"It's pretty simple, really. Not long after Gerry started asking questions about the Mickey Cochran business, he started getting phone calls from Matthew Turk. Very ugly calls. At one time, they got so frequent and so bad we started using an answering machine to screen our calls. And he sent Gerry a letter once, too. It was the same as the calls, all full of threats."

"Did you save any of that stuff? The letter, or the tapes?"

"No." Sarah got up and started for the door. "I think I'd like a beer. Can I get you something?"

I told her beer sounded fine. With Sarah out of the room, I was able to take a closer look around. Along with the love seats and the marble table, there was a large maple hutch crowded with framed photographs. Photographs of the Heyman family. I got up to take a closer look. Everybody was younger, of course. Gerry, Sarah, the kids. There were also photographs of older people, whom I assumed were grandparents. In one photo, Doctor and Mrs. Heyman and the two kids were bundled together inside a horse-drawn sleigh. It was snowing. The kids' faces were barely visible above a red and black Hudson's Bay blanket. Gerry and Sarah wore broad smiles, the kind of smiles grownups affect when they are documenting happiness. I went back to my seat.

Waiting for Sarah to return, I thought about farming twelve thousand acres. While that might make a decent-sized summer pasture in Montana, twelve thousand acres in southern Illinois was enough to need a boss man in a Cadillac.

"I know we should have kept the letter and the tapes," Sarah said, coming back into the room and handing me a cold bottle of St. Pauli Girl. "But what good were they? There certainly wasn't any point in complaining to Freddie Pointdexter." She sat back down on the sofa, and began using her thumbnail to peel away the label on the bottle. "And of course we never thought we'd be needing evidence of a motive to murder Gerry." Between her thumb and forefinger, she rolled a small piece of label into a tight ball, then dropped it absently onto the carpet.

"Talk around town is one thing," I said. "But all this seems like a pretty thin reason to kill somebody."

"It wasn't just talk." Sarah tipped the bottle to her lips. "About a week before Gerry was killed, he went to see an old man named Alfonse Leake. Leake was the lawyer who prosecuted Cochran. After that he became a judge. But he's been retired a long time now. Gerry said he got the impression from Leake that there was something not exactly right about Mickey Cochran's confession."

"Did Gerry ever tell you what it was?"

"No. He said it was nothing specific, just Leake's reluctance to say anything. It sounded like Leake more or less threw him out."

"Have you talked to Leake yourself?"

"No."

"Has Pointdexter?"

Sarah finished her beer and set the bottle on the floor beside her foot. "Get serious, Leo."

"Okay, so Gerry finds a loose screw in the erector set. What in the hell did he think he was going to do? Score himself some points in the hereafter?"

"Even crazier than all that," Sarah said. "He decided he was going to write a book. An exposé. Like anybody would give a damn what happened fifty years ago in this burg. Jesus, Leo, this town doesn't even attract enough attention to keep grass from growing in the streets."

I shook my head. "Murder always draws a crowd."

"Excuse me," she said, "while I go have somebody start making up the T-shirts. 'Death Down On The Farm.' With a nice graphic showing the Grim Reaper tooling around on a John Deere. How does that sound? Next stop, Geraldo Rivera."

"You got an agent?" I sipped on my beer to keep from laughing. "I'm sorry."

But Sarah was laughing, too. "No need to be sorry. It's all so stupid you can't help it. Stupidest damned thing anybody ever heard of." And then she was crying.

I remembered the young woman with braided hair who believed that all she needed to do to make the world operate correctly was to will it so, the young woman who would have gone so far as to help Gerry write his precious exposé. The Sarah Heyman I remembered would wag her finger at God Himself. Hell, she might even be willing to acknowledge the truth about the Reagan Administration. It made me almost unbearably sad to hear her express the same ridicule toward Gerry and his naïveté that I felt.

I watched her cry for a while, and then I said, "Do you remember that weekend you and I went up to Chicago? And spent the afternoon at the Art Institute?"

The lines around Sarah's eyes softened, and when she spoke the years fell away. "All those French painters. Seurat. Degas."

"And Renoir," I said. "Don't forget Renoir."

"No. No, I didn't forget Renoir. That was your favorite, wasn't it? *Two Sisters*?"

Yes, that had been my favorite. How often, over the years, had I thumbed through coffee table books about French Impressionism, looking for *Two Sisters*? It was the expression on the older girl's face that drew me, an expression that I could never manage to describe. Now, looking at Sarah, I realized that it was the eyes, innocent eyes that had seen everything. Sarah's eyes.

"I liked the Monet landscapes," Sarah said. "Everything composed, but not quite precise. And the light absolutely alive. I can't imagine how it must have felt for those painters—seeing the world in an absolutely perfect way, and knowing you'd invented it, too."

"That's why the Cubists had to take it all apart," I said. "Otherwise, there was nothing left to paint." I didn't know much about art history, but I did know that.

"No." She licked her lips and lowered her dark eyes. "Nothing left at all. Thanks."

"For what?"

"Don't be coy." When she looked up, her face was brighter, slightly embarrassed. "For changing the subject on me. For making me think about a better time."

"It was easy," I said, and decided to change the subject again, before I began to feel guilty about taking her money. I got up and went to the window. It was dark out now, and the streetlight filtering through the trees cast the neighborhood in a lime-colored glow. Three boys rode by on bicycles, trailed by a big yellow dog.

"I'll start digging around tomorrow," I said. "Maybe early in the morning, when I won't sweat to death in this miserable climate. You'll be home then?" I wanted to talk to her in detail about Gerry's last day.

"I should be here all day." Sarah got up, too, and walked toward me. "I made up a room for you." She folded her arms and rubbed her hands nervously against each biceps.

When she asked about my bags, I told her I had already installed myself within the palatial confines of the Hotel Mauvaisterre. I knew how a little town worked. She'd catch enough flak just for having me around, to say nothing of keeping me under her murdered husband's roof. And there was certainly no guarantee that I wouldn't find myself tiptoeing down the hall at midnight. It didn't seem necessary to explain any of this to her, so I was surprised when she began to insist that I stay at the house.

"This is business," I said.

Her expression was flat. "Fine. I guess I'm paying you enough so you can afford to rent a room."

Now she was getting the idea.

On our way to the front door, Sarah asked me what I planned to do first. I told her I'd start out by talking to a few people. I didn't tell her which few, because just then I didn't know. I told her I would probably do a lot of the same things that Gerry had done. If there was no evidence pointing to his killer, then perhaps the best bet would be to retrace his path, see what flushed out of the bushes along the way. And, perhaps, by looking into the Turk homicide, maybe I wouldn't feel quite so bad about denying my old, dead friend a favor.

Sarah pulled up in the foyer and looked at me evenly. "Your plan doesn't sound very earth-shattering to me."

"That's what I told Gerry."

"I hope," she said, "that doesn't mean you'll end up like he did."

As I left Sarah Heyman's house that night, the wind began to gust, tearing at the leaves, causing the light to ripple along the street. I was about a block and a half away when I saw a pair of headlights flash on behind me. I drove slowly along the darkened streets, and made four or five pointless turns on my way back to the hotel. The lights stayed with me. For a moment, I thought about seeing how long I could make this little game of tag last, then changed my mind and headed for the hotel. Several times, I saw lightning flare across the river. My shirt clung to me like damp skin, and I felt beads of sweat seep out of my hair, behind my ears and down my neck. The tall clouds pulsed, and seconds later thunder rolled across the water.

Behind me, the car slowed as I rounded the square, but speeded up when I pulled into a parking space in front of the hotel. When the car was maybe twenty feet from my back bumper, I slammed the transmission into reverse and mashed the accelerator. The tires on the tail car were still squealing when my feet hit the pavement. The hot asphalt tugged at the heels of my boots as I walked to the driver's door.

"What're you, crazy?" He was a barrel-chested man, about my age, with a full head of blow-dried hair. He was driving an older tan Mercedes sedan.

I said, "Get out of the car."

"What're you talking about, you almost hit me."

"Get out of the fucking car!" I jerked open the door, then reached inside and grabbed both of his ears. People teach all kinds of ways to get guys out of cars, all kinds of akido kung-fu bullshit. No one I know of teaches ears, but a lot of guys use them. Hair works just dandy, too, but sometimes the guy turns out to be bald and you pull back a handful of rug, which is the same as a handful of nothing. "You got something on your mind, slick, let's hear it."

It turned out the man was big enough that I could have wrenched my back dragging him out of his car. But that's the nice thing about ears—people scramble to keep up with you. He quit shrieking once I got him stood up against the side of his Mercedes, which happened to be a diesel and was smoking up the street like the aftermath of an air raid.

"I don't know what the hell you're talking about," the guy said. He grimaced as he held both hands against the sides of his head. "I'll have you in jail over this." Now that he was out of his car, my eyes were just about level with his Adam's apple. I was deciding if I should hit him or something before he decided he was big enough to break me in half, when I heard the short blast of a siren, and what I thought was Point-dexter's big white patrol squealed to a stop behind the Mercedes. It wasn't Freddie Pointdexter, though, who got out of the car.

The deputy who stalked toward us was about my height, but not much bigger around than a fence post, and he was dwarfed by weapons. A revolver with an eight-inch barrel, and a black, side-handled nightstick —the kind called a PR-24—both flopped from his gunbelt, and as he neared, I could see that he also carried a second handgun, an auto, in a shoulder hol-ster under his left arm.

"Reach!" he shouted. He wore a uniform shirt identical to Pointdexter's, but blue jeans instead of brown uniform pants. His head was covered with a brown baseball cap that bore a cloth sheriff's star above the bill, and a cheesy brown mustache dripped from the corners of his mouth. The heels on his black cowboy boots were high enough to give most people a nosebleed, but what really caught my eye was the Rambo-style survival knife lashed to his right calf. His tiny, black eyes narrowed. "I said reach, asshole!"

As far as I was concerned, the guy from the Merce-des was the asshole, so I stood my ground.

"Grab sky!" he said, not clarifying anything at all, "or eat cement!" This time, he whipped the nightstick from the ring on his gunbelt, and began slapping it against his palm.

"You've got the vocabulary down, son," I said, "but I think your tone's a little shrill."

"Deputy Wiesel," said the guy from the Mercedes. "Thank God you're here."

So now it was clear that I was the asshole. I figured I was on my way to jail, but I sure as hell wasn't going to get beaten on by any stringbean with a nightstick. When he cocked his arm, getting ready to swing the stick, I stepped into him, grabbed his gunbelt with my left hand, and jerked him into a near embrace. When our hips collided, I put my right hand on the pistol under his arm and gave it a short tug, not enough to clear the holster, but enough to let him know I had it. The sudden blank look in his eyes told me that he'd gotten the point. His breath smelled as if he'd been eating last week's roadkill.

"Let's talk this over," I said quietly, holding him close. If he slipped away, and the gun stayed behind in my hand, we'd be well on our way to making the nightly news. "Just settle down."

"Fuck you, asshole," he said. I could feel him fumbling for the revolver.

There was a blast of music from the side street, and over the deputy's shoulder I saw Freddie Pointdexter, who wasn't wasting any time heading our way from the tavern door. I immediately let go of the gunbelt and the gun, and stepped away, raising my arms in a gesture of submission.

The deputy drew the nightstick back again, and there was a loud *smack* as Pointdexter grabbed his wrist.

"Otis, what in the goddamn hell is going on here?" Pointdexter sounded like a man who should be lugging around a set of stone tablets.

"Gonna bust this scumbag," Otis said.

Pointdexter pulled the stick from Otis's hand, then stepped back and surveyed his deputy from head to toe. "Otis, what'd I tell you about carrying all that shit on you? I'm surprised you haven't got a shotgun, too."

"Stuck in the rack," Otis mumbled.

"What?" Pointdexter said, tilting his head, aiming his ear at the deputy.

"I said it's stuck in the goddamn rack," Otis said. "Back in the car. That's a grievance, you know. Officer safety. I could file a lawsuit, Freddie."

"He's right, Sheriff," said the guy from the Mercedes. Everything had happened so fast, he'd gotten lost in the shuffle.

Pointdexter rolled his eyes. "Jesus, Joseph and Mary." Then he looked down at the smoking exhaust from the idling Mercedes, pulled a face, and tossed the nightstick onto the trunk.

Mister Mercedes looked alarmed. "Goddamnit, Freddie, I—"

But Pointdexter stuck up a hand big enough to palm a watermelon. "What's goin' on?" he said. He was looking at me now.

"This guy here followed me from Sarah's house," I said. "I just want to know the score, that's all."

"Nick?" Pointdexter said, looking up at the other man.

By now, the man named Nick had recovered himself. You couldn't tell which had hurt him more, getting his ears mangled, or his trunk lid dented. "I'm driving along minding my own business, this goddamn maniac backs out in front of me, then assaults me right here on a public street. I want him arrested."

"That figures," Pointdexter said. Nobody sounds more bored than a cop who's trying to decide if he wants to arrest some poor dumb schmuck.

"You know this guy?" I said to Pointdexter.

"Shut up, pus bucket," said the deputy. "You got the right to remain silent. Use it."

"Otis . . ." Pointdexter said. "Otis, please don't do that right now."

Otis seemed to sag under the weight of his weaponry.

"Leo," Pointdexter said, "this here's my chief deputy, Otis Wiesel. Otis, this's—"

"The *detective*," Otis Wiesel snorted. "I bet that's who he is." He hooked his thumbs behind the buckle of his gunbelt, and cocked a hip. "Well, big fuckin' deal."

A clap of thunder rolled down the street.

"And him?" I nodded toward the guy with the ear problem.

"Go ahead, Freddie," the guy said, hitching up his pants, "go on, tell him."

Pointdexter started to laugh. "It just so happens, pard, this here is Nick Serette. He's the state's attorney in this county. Get it? I make up my mind to boot your sorry ass off to jail. Mr. Serette here's the guy gonna be telling his buddy the judge what a thoroughly bad human being you are."

I decided to make the most of my freedom while I still had it. "That doesn't explain why he was tailing me."

The lightning was much nearer now. Each flash seemed to freeze us in the street, and the explosion of thunder was almost immediate.

Pointdexter looked back at Serette, as though he were following a tennis match. "Nick?"

"Not that it matters," Serette said, "but Sarah Heyman is a friend of mine. I knew she'd asked you to come here, Banks. And I knew you told her you'd only come for money. Too damned much money. I know all about your past with her and Gerry, but twenty years is a long time. I plan to make sure my friend doesn't get scammed by some smiling piece of shit from South Dakota."

I started to say I was from Montana, just to keep the geography organized, but Freddie Pointdexter was talking again. "Now Nick, let's not be calling Leo here a piece of shit just because he's from out of town and didn't vote for us. Hell, I didn't vote for you either, and I don't consider myself a piece of shit." Pointdexter clapped Serette on the shoulder, knocking him off balance. "Do you?"

"I still want him arrested," Serette said.

"I'm sure you do, Nick." Pointdexter walked behind me and surveyed the two cars. "Looks like a traffic problem to me," he said. "Something I should caution you boys about. Banks, I don't know how they drive wherever the hell it is you live out West there, but we try to have a care here in Mauvaisterre."

"What about the assault?" Serette said.

The force of Pointdexter's shrug could have rearranged mountains. "No witnesses, Nick. Your word against his. You're a lawyer, you know how these things go."

"What about you?" Serette said to the sheriff. "You're a witness."

"Me?" Pointdexter said, "Sorry, Nick, not me."

"Otis, then. He was right here, he saw it all."

"He didn't see a thing," Pointdexter said.

Otis took a step forward. "Well, now, I—"

"Shut up, Otis," Pointdexter said. None of Otis's weapons could protect him from the look Pointdexter fired his way.

"Who called you, then?" Serette said. "Somebody had to have seen and called you, you got here too fast."

Wind whipped around the buildings, and the first few drops of rain came crashing to earth around us.

Pointdexter nodded. "Big Mike called me. He was sitting in the lobby there watching kickboxing on TV. You ever watch kickboxing, Banks? Mean sport. *Mean.* Worse'n Australian rules football."

"There's your witness then," Serette said. "If you won't make the charge, I will."

"Suit yourself," Pointdexter said, walking toward the hotel door as the rain kicked up. "But I was you, I wouldn't waste my time. Believe me, Nick, Big Mike never seen nothing, either."

6

Nick Serette was half right about the money. The rub wasn't so much the amount, as it was that money had not been an issue for Sarah at all. While I might demand a fee as a means of keeping distance between me and Sarah, I couldn't help but wonder why she had so readily agreed. Sure, it was possible that her reason for paying might be the same as mine had been for asking, but somehow that didn't quite fit. For all she knew, she could have been hiring the worst investigator in the world. If it were true that a decent friend might not have demanded money for what I was doing, was it also true that an honest friend might have raised at least a little fuss before writing out the check? What was it that Sarah Heyman hoped to buy?

I swung my legs over the side of the bed and sat up. All night, the air conditioner had kept awakening me with tubercular gasps, and the heat had made getting back to sleep one of life's more memorable struggles. My pillow felt like a damp sponge.

For the next twenty minutes, I stood under the

tepid shower, trying to work the kinks out of my neck. When I dressed and went downstairs, I didn't feel anymore worth fifteen thousand dollars than I had the night before, when I'd taken Freddie Pointdexter's cue and acquired enough sense to come in out of the rain.

Downstairs, I found Big Mike sitting on a worn hassock in front of the TV. He was watching a golf tournament on TV.

"I love cable TV," Big Mike said. He turned his head toward me, but his eyes stayed focused on the cool, green links. "Hate golf, though. Silliest game you ever saw."

"What would you expect from a game invented by Scottish misogynists."

"Scotch what?"

"Misogynists. Guys who don't trust women."

"Scotchmen, huh? Figures." Big Mike nodded toward the rolling, televised fairways. "Looka that pasture. Those Scotchmen should've stuck to raising sheep."

I said, "How old are you, anyway?"

"Ninety-five," he said, still studying the TV. From time to time, he tilted his head one way, then another, as though looking for a new perspective.

"Then you must remember a guy named Otto Turk."

"Otto?" He met my eyes now, and his wrinkled face hardened. "Hell, I knew Otto Turk when he didn't own no more'n a pair of bib overalls and didn't have nothing better to do than stand around and scratch himself."

"Sounds like you were real pals."

"You're gonna ask me about his dead wife, ain't that right?"

"Chances are," I said.

"Can't help you. I wasn't here then. Kansas City, that's where I was. Me and Little Mike's great-grandma, we was split up for a while and I was off trying to conquer the world." His laugh was a high, sharp cackle.

"What about a guy named Alfonse Leake?" I said.

Big Mike cackled again. "Now there's a guy never had to have a go at Kansas City."

"I heard he was a main hammer on the Grace Turk case."

"You heard right."

"I also heard that guy Mickey Cochran took a bum rap on the deal."

Big Mike's face was momentarily blank. The heavy shelf of bone above his eyes could have shaded a million secrets. "I used to pay Mickey Cochran two bits to spar with me. Back when we was kids and I was taking the train to St. Louis to fight in the clubs."

"I thought he was retarded."

Big Mike shifted his hips on the hassock and crossed his arms. "He was strong as an ox and he wouldn't quit for anything. That seemed like enough."

"You figure Cochran had it in him to murder that woman?"

Big Mike turned back to the TV. "Mickey Cochran had it in him to do most anything, long as it didn't take more than muscle to get it done."

Back in the dining room, there was no sign of Little Mike. A woman with a blue beehive hairdo never let me see the bottom of my coffee cup. She was pushing the outer limits of middle age. Whenever she wandered back with the coffee, she left her cigarette smoldering in an ashtray on top of a long glass case containing a dozen or so pies. I was about ready to go hunt up Freddie Pointdexter, when Pointdexter himself strolled through the front door and found me. He waved the waitress off before she'd even pulled the cigarette out of her mouth.

"Got the caffeine shakes already," Pointdexter

said. He pulled off his sunglasses and hung them from his shirt pocket. Today he was wearing a badge. "That's part of the law enforcement business, isn't it, Banks? Got to maintain that razor sharp edge between too much coffee and not enough." He spread his hand in a balancing gesture and grinned.

"You look excessively official," I said, pointing to the heavy gold star that tugged at his tan shirt. "Serette send you over here to drag me off to jail?"

Pointdexter shrugged. "You know how it goes, son. One day you're whipping up on a prosecutor, next thing you know you're hearing big doors slam behind you. Then again, some days you whip up on a prosecutor with nothing inside his pants but a rumor."

"I take it that means I'm a free man."

"Don't exaggerate," Pointdexter said. "It just means you don't get any broken bones resisting arrest. Not today."

Without wasting any more time on male bonding, Pointdexter gave me directions to the place where Gerry Heyman was killed. Take the highway back out of town, he told me, then turn off on the first gravel road to my left. Follow the gravel road back up into the hills, away from the floodplain, for about three miles. Past a big old stone house, the one I remembered Gerry telling me about. About a half mile on past that house, and I would see a little cemetery— the Turk cemetery—off to my right, maybe a hundred yards south of the road. It was right there at the turn-off into the cemetery, just east of that turnoff, where Gerry got it. I would see all the grass torn up from when they hooked his car.

I asked Pointdexter if he wanted to come along.

"I've seen it, thanks," he said. "Seen it a hundred times. Seen it enough to know there's nothing there to see. Unless you're a big fan of weeds and tombstones. You get back to town, stop in at my office if you want to see the photos. I'm in the basement of the courthouse."

I left too much money on the table, and followed Pointdexter out into the sunshine, which was already bringing the street to a slow boil. I was about to ask Pointdexter about Heyman's car, when we both turned simultaneously toward the noise of a speeding engine. From our right, a jacked-up black Toyota pickup came slamming down the street. Behind the wheel sat a boy wearing black wraparound sunglasses, his black hair shaved in a Mohawk. When he turned to face us as he passed, an earring made of blue feathers fluttered in the wind. The kid's face was flat. He gave us the finger.

I said, "You folks allow that kind of stuff out here in the heartland?"

"'Scuse me," Pointdexter said, smiling as he slipped his face behind his RayBans, "while I go kick that boy's ass."

Once I left the highway, the gravel road began weaving up between limestone bluffs. I found myself expecting at each bend in the road to encounter some face from my own past farther south. Ghosts, I thought. Ghosts. I remembered a county fair over thirty years before, when a man whose name I never knew suffered a heart attack in the heat and we all crowded around and watched him die on a makeshift bed of baled wheat straw. I could still see the look on his face as he stared up at us, a look of haunted recognition and regret, the kind of look I could feel on my own face that morning as I drove through the oak and maple forest. I reached for the radio dials, but changed my mind. Bullshit. Just bullshit. What in God's name ever made me decide I needed to learn about killers?

At the top of the bluff the countryside cleared for a short distance, then made a dip along a small creek running slow, brown water. I recognized the rich, honeyed odor of pig shit. Then the road rose again and I drove past thirty or forty small, portable sheds strung out under the trees. Maybe a hundred and fifty Hampshire hogs—Hampshires are the black ones with white belts up their front legs and over their shoulders, like a snazzy pair of golf shoes—all of them wandering around, lying in the dirt, squabbling about whatever it is a couple of hogs find to squabble about.

The road straightened again and the trees began to thin. I glanced down at the odometer, but realized I hadn't checked the mileage earlier when I turned off the highway. When I looked back up, I saw it, the great, abandoned house of pale stone. The empty windows seemed to follow me as I drove slowly by.

Before realizing what it was that I was looking at, I saw the cemetery off to my right, just as Freddie Pointdexter had described. The stones sprouted from a dense, green island of grass surrounded by a field of clipped, yellow wheat stubble. I pulled the car into the turnoff to the cemetery, stopped and got out. The air was still, with an almost fleshy texture to the heat. Insects buzzed about their careless, voracious business, and far off I heard the groan of a farm tractor. The smell of the wheat straw reminded me of high school days spent bucking bales and puking up too-cold beer.

So what did I expect to find? Clues? God, I haven't believed in clues since that day over twenty years ago when a beautiful woman shredded my cover and a criminal cut my throat.

Answers? Answers are what you get when you call people on the telephone.

It was easy to see why Pointdexter didn't want to waste his time with another trip out here to the boondocks. Any tire tracks that may have been visible at one time were now gone. As Pointdexter said, there was a gouge in the yellow clay, but even that was starting to heal over. The grass along the ditch was covered with a fine coat of dust, which had settled behind the passing traffic. I crouched and brushed my hand through the coarse bluegrass and wild oats.

Sometimes—this sounds crazy, but it's true—sometimes a murder is a thing that you can, I don't know, almost inhale. Or absorb through your skin, the way a cell feeds itself by osmosis. You don't solve mysteries like this, but now and then, if you're lucky, you learn precisely what mystery it is that requires a solution.

I knew that there must have been blood, my dead friend's blood, but by now it had all been worn or washed away. Maybe licked up by wild animals, or even by some nice family's wandering collie dog. Nature isn't especially fussy about human misfortune. I took a long look around at the flat, obscure horizon, which was already beginning to shimmer with heat. As I got to my feet, creaky knees reminded me that I was prematurely retired.

When I reached the maroon Chevy, I kept on walking down the tight lane to the cemetery. The lane was grown over with grass and weeds, but appeared to have been mown several weeks before. I kicked up a storm of grasshoppers as I walked.

There were perhaps a hundred stones, many of them so weathered that they were no longer legible. Often, as Gerry had said, the old graves were marked only by grim depressions indicating where coffins had long ago collapsed and the earth settled in an even tighter, more determined embrace. The oldest date I could make out was 1817.

Grace Turk's stone was easy to find. I just went to the biggest of the lot, a tall spire of polished black granite. A small vase of plastic flowers hung from a skewed shepherd's crook. From that vantage, I could see the vine-covered remains of the stone house, sitting about five hundred yards away across a shallow draw. Along the bottom of the draw ran a marshy reach of willows and cattails. Several dozen starlings and redwing blackbirds were working the wheat stubble between the cemetery and the willows. Overhead, I heard the bray of a crow tormented by a small squadron of sparrows.

I remembered Gerry Heyman telling me that he grew up on a farm not far from the Turk cemetery. Again, I looked out across the broad, flat fields, but saw no sign of any house except the old Turk hulk.

You could be looking at your own life, I thought. At the days running out and back like row after row of rustling green corn. At gasoline and diesel fuel, herbicides and pesticides and dying soil, at balance sheets and bills, at machines, wives and kids. No, not wives. I'd tried three of them. Just one wife, and in twenty years you've never turned the light out on a fight. And your sons play football and your daughters lead cheers.

Sure they do.

And what about me? Am I a man who is not so prideful, arrogant and curious that he lets it all slip away just to see what's inside the darkened room behind the next door?

The weeds, some higher than my knees, snagged my pants as I neared the edge of the cemetery on my way back to the Chevy. Near the last row of graves, I almost put my foot down on a large blacksnake. My right hand shot to my hip for a gun, before I realized that I wasn't carrying one. Jesus Christ, I hate snakes. It's lucky I didn't have a gun, because I might have shot myself in the foot. Hell, I could have picked up a gravestone and crushed the sonofabitch just to teach him a lesson.

So maybe I didn't connect up with any mystery of my own, maybe I was just a hired hand doing chores for Sarah Heyman. Or, I thought as I scuffed along the lane back to the car, maybe I had a sense of what the mystery had been for Gerry. Maybe, for the kind of wages I had demanded, I could do more than one chore. And who the hell knew, maybe Grace Turk's murder and Gerry Heyman's murder were really just the same big job.

Before heading back to town, I decided to have a look around the old Turk house. There was no turn-out, so I parked along the road, hopped the ditch and walked the fifty yards back to the house. The weeds were even thicker, more tangled than in the cemetery. Morning glories and mullen and button weeds, lambs-quarter, and hundreds of lovely purple flowers bobbing at the ends of tall thistles. In no time, my pants were bristling with sticktights and cockleburrs.

The house was surrounded by a stone wall, which looked as if it were once about four feet high, but was now crumbled in many places. Wild rose and black-berry brambles tugged at the wall in a prickly green net. I stepped over a rusty, precarious gate.

The large roof slumped in the middle, and was bracketed on each end by double chimneys built of dull, aging red brick. I didn't see a single pane of glass still in place, and the ivy was heavy enough in places that the stone walls were obliterated. The sagging front porch, which ran the breadth of the place, looked as though it might collapse of its own weight into a heap of kindling.

I tried the spongy boards on the porch, then stepped gingerly toward the front entrance. I ran my fingertips over the ochre-colored limestone, and studied for a moment the faint impressions of fossilized mollusks. It struck me that the house was built of the corpses of a multitude of tiny marine plants and animals. I could smell the rot sighing toward me from its cool, dank insides.

I heard a car on the road, coming hard from the direction of the cemetery. When I looked back, I saw a plume of dust rising above the trees, and an instant later the car, a big white Cadillac, appeared. The car was nearly past the house with no sign of slowing down, when the driver dynamited the brakes and the Cadillac came to a stop in a chaos of skidding tires and spraying gravel. The door flew open, and the driver didn't waste any time wading toward me through the weeds.

"What in the goddamn hell do you think you're doing?" he bellowed. He was a beefy guy, with wavy white hair combed straight back from his broad forehead.

"Who wants to know?" I shouted back.

"*I* do." He kicked aside the rusty gate and made it to the edge of the porch in less time than it takes James Worthy to go to the hoop. For a man his age—about sixty-five—he was either in pretty damned good shape, or pretty damned mad. From the pace of his breathing, I guessed he was pretty damned mad.

"*I* do," he said again. He was wearing starched khaki slacks, a Western-cut white shirt with short sleeves, and tan ostrich skin boots. A tuft of white hair bristled from the collar of his shirt. "And if I have to ask you one more time, I'll come up on that porch and do it. Then I'll have 'em send out a goddamn ambulance after I get to town."

"I guess I'm a tourist," I said.

"That's no answer."

"Then why don't you step on up here and get a better one." He was right, maybe some people would have to drive out here in an ambulance. "You must be Matthew Turk."

"What makes you think that?" He still hadn't come onto the porch.

"Because you're herding around that big road hog out there. And you're acting like you own everything in sight. Both descriptions fit what I heard about you."

"And you must be that shithead from New Mexico

the Heyman woman hired. Nobody but some dumbass from out of town would be standing where you are right now. I do own everything in sight."

"Not exactly everything." I looked at him evenly for a moment before stepping down off the porch. "Quite a house," I said, dusting my hands on my pants.

"Oh, it's a great house, all right." Turk's voice was coarse and throaty, and now the anger seemed blunted by fatigue. "Thing is, we stopped indulging curiosity seekers around here back in about 1945. When I got home from the war."

"Can't say as I blame you." If he was willing to step back from the brink of mayhem, so was I. "I was out this way on a little business. Saw the house and stopped on a whim."

"I expect you went back to the cemetery, too."

I shrugged. "If a man's going to trespass, he'd just as well get his fill."

"You come out here to see where that nosey sonofabitch got himself killed," Turk said. "Now you're acting just as nosey as him."

"His wife got it in her head I could find out who put him down."

"That woman's got a lot of things in her head. So did that silly kid she married." Turk's watery blue eyes drifted off somewhere in the vicinity of the horizon.

I said, "Heyman thought that guy in the joint for killing your mother was the wrong guy. Thought he was just some poor dumb retard got himself shoved in front of a judge while the kangaroos were being fed."

"That was over fifty years ago," Turk said. "You know, I never slept in this house again after that night."

"What night would that be?"

"What night? *What night?*" Turk shook his head and smoothed back his hair with both hands. "And that poor woman's paying you fifteen grand?"

"Who says she's paying me fifteen grand?"

Turk folded his heavy arms across his chest. "Gimme a break, huh?"

"You mean the night they found your mother's body."

"Yeah, yeah, you got it now, smart guy. Only it was *me* found her. That grove of willows down the ditch behind the house?" He waved in the direction of the willows and the cemetery. "That used to be a pond. Then between the pond and this house there was a big barn, a bunch of outbuildings. But that's all gone now, all them buildings burned down and the pond silted in. There used to be a *life* here, you understand? Anyway, it was down there in that pond I found her."

"Heyman came almost two thousand miles," I said, "to try and get me back here to look into that whole mess. He must have put at least some stock in what Cochran told him."

"It might look like that," Turk said, "unless you knew better. Unless you knew how bad Gerry Heyman wanted a piece of me and my old man."

"What's that supposed to mean?"

"Oh, that little farm over there." Turk waved his arm toward the east.

"The Heyman farm," I said.

"Ah, the Heyman farm, he says. Well, now, that would be right."

According to Turk, he and his father had bought the Heyman place about ten years ago from Gerry's father. The land was good, but there wasn't much of it, three hundred and twenty acres. Financially, the Turk operation could absorb the Heyman farm without much of a ripple, and it was a good chance for them to pick up a piece of property that was contiguous to their main holdings. The sale was a good deal for Gerry's father, too, who was ready to fold his tent and migrate to a climate that offered twelve months of golf.

"Gerry never was a farmer," Turk said. "Same time, he couldn't abide the place being sold. Sentimental."

It so happened that I knew something about sentimentality and farming. The lobbies of banks are littered with the bones of farmers who needed just one more loan, one more round of financial CPR to keep their backbreaking dream alive. My father was a man like that, his pride tough and rare, like a bad steak.

Turk went on. "I don't think he was ever exactly thrilled about the place being sold. But it was probably the fire that did it."

Not long after the sale closed, Matthew Turk stopped off one day at the Heyman place and started setting fires. A couple of days later, he brought in a bulldozer and began leveling out the rubble.

"That gave us twenty acres more to farm," Turk said now, "plus got rid of the headache of all those buildings."

"Even the house?"

Turk shrugged. "I'm in the agriculture business, Banks, not the housing business. So I rent the house for a few hundred bucks, spend all my time trying to keep some renter happy. Big deal. Nobody eats one peanut if he knows it's gonna give him a bellyache."

Turk went on to tell me that the Heyman family had been on that land since the county was settled in the eighteen twenties. The house itself was over a hundred years old, a real artifact.

"I can see how he might feel," Turk said. "But Christ, I can remember when he was a kid, he hardly turned a tap on the place. Couldn't wait to get away, from what people always said. Hell, he wanted the place so bad, he could of bought it himself. So you tell me, Banks, what's his problem? Huh?"

I didn't have an answer for Turk. Crazy, I thought, the way you investigate a guy's death and end up being the custodian of his life. Happens every time. I was interested in what Turk had told me, I had to be, but I wasn't about to let him use it to sidetrack me.

"Funny," I said, "you'd make such a big deal out of getting another twenty acres out of the Heyman deal, but this heap—" I made a sweeping gesture with my arm toward the house. "You let this heap stand here, twist a knife in your guts every time you drive down the road."

Turk sighed and looked around, as though taking a new account of the ruin. "Kind of like a monument, isn't it?" he said. He drew in an even deeper breath and let it out slowly. It was only mid-morning, but I could smell the whiskey on him. He licked his lips. "Her hair—she was blond, you know—her hair looked like a bouquet of cut wheat all fanned out on the water. Jesus Christ, I still can't get over it." A drop of sweat gathered on the tip of his chin, then dropped onto the front of his white shirt. Then he went on talking.

After Matthew Turk pulled the body of his mother from the pond, he sat down beside her and waited. His father was off working somewhere on the place. So he sat down and waited. He was still waiting when Otto Turk showed up nearly half an hour later.

"Nowdays they'd say I was in shock," Turk told me. "We got head doctors today know all about stuff like that. Explain it in ways that make sense. Ways that people believe."

"But you don't," I said.

Turk shrugged. "Doesn't matter anymore. Not after all these years."

Otto Turk summoned the sheriff, a man named Denton McCool, whom everybody called Buckshot. By the time Buckshot McCool showed up, there was no shortage of bystanders. Otto Turk told everybody it was plain as day that Mickey Cochran was the killer. Hell, anybody could see it, for despite all the turmoil —to say nothing of the fact that it was suppertime and

the half-wit always took his meals with the family—
Mickey Cochran was nowhere to be found. Besides
that, Grace Turk's blouse had been ripped open, and
Mickey Cochran had been acting funny around her
for weeks. *Ain't that right, boy?* Otto Turk said, and
the boy nodded, Yes.

"And it was true," Turk said now. "Everything I
told them that day was true."

The men spread out over the countryside in the
gathering dusk, but still no Cochran. They were still
searching when Alfonse Leake, the state's attorney,
drove up in his big gray Packard, and not long after
that they caught Cochran trying to sneak up into the
barn loft.

"That night," Turk said, "Cochran told the coroner's jury he didn't know anything, which they all took
to mean he just wasn't saying." Turk pulled a blue
bandanna from his hip pocket and mopped his forehead and his florid cheeks. "Then they hauled him off
to jail. Leake and Buckshot talked to him some more,
and somewhere along the line he confessed. Then he
went off to the state pen down at Menard."

"And now he's finally out."

"Yeah. Now he's out."

"And he's just about dead."

"Yeah. That's a shame, ain't it."

"What kind of evidence did they have on him? Besides his confession?"

"Evidence?" Turk snorted. "Hell, I was a fifteen-
year-old kid and that sonofabitch just killed my
mama. What'd I know about any fuckin' evidence? Or
care, for that matter."

"So it's just, case closed."

"You got it, Toyota. Case closed."

"And the house?"

"Sure. The house. That's how all this line of bullshit started, isn't it?"

Otto and Matthew Turk followed the procession

back into town, where they spent the next several nights at the Hotel Mauvaisterre. After the funeral, they moved out of the stone house and back into the little frame house on the original Turk farm, where Otto and Grace Turk had lived briefly just after they were married. They had built the stone house for one another, and now that she was gone Otto seemed to have no heart for it. One night in the fall, not long after Mickey Cochran had pleaded guilty and gone off to prison, Otto Turk got supremely drunk. He burned down the barn and all the outbuildings, then went through the house in a rampage, smashing out every window in the place.

"After that," Matthew Turk said, "he just let it go, let nature have it back. We lived in the old place, him and me, till I went in the army. Then he bought a big old house just down the road—you can't see it from here. Spent a mint on the place. I got back from the war, he moved to St. Louis. That's where Mama's folks lived, and they were all gone by then, too, so he had that big house down there."

I smiled. "Quite a story."

"I got no secrets about the tragedy," Turk said.

"I guess not," I said. And then I told him I was surprised at how easily he'd told me, a stranger, the story.

"Don't get me wrong," Turk said. "It doesn't bother me that Heyman's dead—no love lost, none of that shit. But it was a murder. A man ought to take note of that, make allowances."

"Cooperate any way he can," I said, prompting him.

"Whatever you say."

"Maybe," I said. "But I figure there's a better than even chance you told me all this because you don't want me poking around on my own. I've talked to a lot of guys like you, Turk, guys who spill just enough, they figure, to keep you from finding out more on your own."

"You're a goddamn idiot," Turk said. He turned away and walked the short distance to the stone wall, where he turned his back and unzipped his pants. "You figure I killed him, then? Because he was asking questions that got too close to home?" I heard Turk's water splatter against the stones.

"I believe what I can prove," I said. "Maybe someday I can prove that. Maybe I can't."

When he turned back toward me, Turk was still fiddling with his zipper. "Gerry Heyman was like a little mosquito keeps biting you on the ass. He doesn't really hurt you, but after a while you mash him just because he doesn't have brains enough to leave you alone."

"I think it was more than that."

"I don't really give a shit what you think," Matthew Turk said, laying a warm, heavy hand on my shoulder as he smiled. His top eye teeth were discolored and edged with gold. "Long as you know enough to stop nibbling on my ass before I get tired of it."

I stared languidly down at Turk's hand, then back into his pale eyes. He pulled his hand back.

"Give me a couple of reasons," I said, "why I shouldn't believe you beat Gerry Heyman's brains out back down the road there."

Turk's face was like the sun sliding from behind a cloud. "Why, I don't have to, Banks. This is America, remember? Plus, I'm a rich man. Now get off my place, before I start acting like a real American and throw you off."

7

By the time I got back into Mauvaisterre, it was late morning and the day was starting to cook. I longed to be home in Montana, panning for sapphires, say, or splitting ammonites out of limestone. Maybe if things got too slow, I could mosey down by the nearest trout stream and drown a brace of yuppies. There are more yuppies in Montana rivers these days than there are trout. Hell, I even heard about some California transplant down in Bozeman, Montana, who made a rule you had to have an out-of-state ID and a gold card just to set foot in his tackle shop. Or rather his gallery of trout fishing equipage. I swear to God that's what he called it. Well, that's Bozeman for you.

I was on my way to see Sarah Heyman, but as I neared the big yellow house with the curved porch, I saw Nick Serette's Mercedes parked on the side street. It was a lovely scene, wasn't it? First Freddie Pointdexter's cryptic remarks about trust, then Serette's monkey business last night. And now here he was this morning, calling on the grieving widow. You didn't have to be Sigmund Freud to be more than a little curious. No, in the absence of pure genius, a corrosive mind would do.

Without slowing, I drove past the house on North Water Street, then turned at a four-way stop with a gas station on one corner, a Baptist church on another, and a ragtag mechanic's shop on a third. The fourth corner was taken up by a large corrugated steel shed, which looked empty.

I made a loop around the town, including a swing past the boat ramp, and soon after that the courthouse. The courthouse was a massive two-story red brick building with white stone trim around the windows, the eaves and cornices. The front doors were flanked by two white statues of idealized women dressed in flowing robes and helmets, each holding a sword in one hand and the scales of justice in the other. The building was topped off by a huge, square cupola, with a clock face on each side. As I circled the building, I noticed that all four clocks registered a different time, and none were correct. A pall of dust hung over the lot. Small town courthouses are similar all over America. Wooden floors creak under the weight of justice and political appointees, and the air grows dull with the odor of flaking calfskin law books and ledgers.

I thought about stopping in at Pointdexter's office to have a look at his photos. But there would be time for that later. There's always time to look at pictures of dead guys.

Back at the four-way stop, I kept going straight instead of turning back onto North Water Street. In short order, I passed first a Methodist church and then an Assembly of God church. I thought I'd surely run out of churches, when up ahead I saw the false buttresses of the Roman Catholic church, which was accompanied by a rectory. Like the other three churches, the courthouse and the hotel, the Catholic

107

church and rectory were built of red brick. Sturdy, American red brick. I looked at the street sign on the corner. I was on Church Street. It made so much sense I thought I must be nuts.

I kept going. The trees and homes began to look less well tended. There were more dogs in the street than motor vehicles. Just before the edge of town, the street turned to gravel, then came to a dead end at a low, white cinderblock building, which was flanked by a long warehouse, and maybe half a dozen large storage tanks. Parked in the lot were three spray trucks outfitted with oversized balloon tires and large tanks. There were also four delivery trucks, two-ton Chevys with box beds. Everything in sight had *Turk Seed and Chemical* painted on it in green block letters, along with the company logo, a stylized shock of lush green corn topped with golden tassels. Half a dozen men stood just inside an overhead door at a loading dock, watching me. As I made a slow U turn in the lot, I saw Matthew Turk's white Cadillac parked behind the cinderblock building. Parked next to it was a sheriff's patrol car.

Back at the four-way stop, I glanced at the corrugated steel shed and saw that it wasn't really empty at all. There was a sign on the door announcing that Christ Bible Brotherhood met there. I wondered how long it would take for the brotherhood's coffers to have enough money for a supply of red bricks.

I don't know why, but seeing that ragtag church made me think about the Gold Cup languishing in the suitcase back in my room. What a waste of a perfectly useful weapon. I headed back to the hotel. I wasn't quite ready to start strapping the Colt on my hip again—an old habit easily surrendered—but keeping it under the seat of the car seemed like a good compromise. All those churches just gave me the willies. I swung by the hotel and picked up the .45.

When I went by Sarah Heyman's place again, Serette's car was gone, so I stopped. Rather than go to the front door, I walked around the side of the house. I had turned up a fieldstone walk toward a bank of rhododendrons, when I heard a soft, electronic click behind me. After twenty years in the policing business, I instantly recognized the sound as someone keying the microphone on a patrol car's PA system. When I looked back, Freddie Pointdexter made a thumbs-up sign, then gave the car a short burst of gas, squealing the tires as he pulled away. I wondered if he had tagged me when I passed through the lot of Turk's business, and if he was on his way back there with a report.

The rhododendron leaves rustled softly as I eased through the narrow green gap into the backyard. There was a glassed-in sun porch on the back of the house, and outside that a large redwood deck, which was flanked on either side by red, white and yellow rose bushes climbing trellises. The remainder of the backyard was filled by magnolias, more rhododendrons and a large sycamore tree. Sarah Heyman, wearing large sunglasses with ice blue frames, was sitting on the deck at an umbrella-covered table with a glass top. As I neared her, I saw a green BMX bicycle near the door to the sunporch. There were two coffee mugs on the table, one a solid blue, the other decorated with pictures of whales. We exchanged good-mornings, and then without explanation, Sarah excused herself, collected both of the cups and went inside. When she returned, she was empty-handed.

"Looks like one of your nomads came home," I said, nodding toward the bicycle, and taking a seat beside her at the table.

"They're both back," Sarah said. "But Michael's cool now. Too cool to ride a bicycle anymore."

I told Sarah that I had seen the place where Gerry

died, and also that I had met Matthew Turk. I didn't say anything about my brush with Nick Serette the night before, or the fact that I had just seen him parked at her house.

"I think about Gerry all the time," Sarah said, adjusting the sunglasses. I could see her eyes only faintly. She wore sandals, and I noticed that her toenails were painted. A light coral shade. Very nice. "Lying all alone out there in the dark. In the country. The medical examiner said, you know, that he can't tell exactly the time when he died. And of course we don't know when he was attacked. So I can't help thinking of him lying there hurt. Dying. Maybe knowing for hours what was happening to him, aware in a way a doctor would be that his body was shutting down, and there was nothing he could do."

"There isn't any evidence that he suffered," I said. "At least not like you're implying." Survivors always want to be sure that a loved one's passage into death was beyond knowledge and pain. I know that when I was nearly killed all those years ago, I was sick with fear and grief. I hurt like hell, too. I said, "How did you find out he'd been killed?"

"It was a Thursday night. He had worked late at the office." She went on to recount what Pointdexter had already told me about the family having dinner near eight o'clock, then Gerry receiving a call and leaving at about ten.

"Pointdexter said he might have left to visit a patient."

"Maybe," Sarah said. "But sometimes he would just go for a drive when he felt unsettled."

"Was he unsettled that night?"

"That's hard to say." She tugged at her ear, and thought for a moment. "The last month or so, since we got back from Montana, he seemed unsettled most of the time. So it's hard to say what was on his mind that night."

"What had him unsettled? Cochran?"

"Yes."

"What else?"

She frowned. "Why should there be something else?"

"No reason. But you usually don't find out if you don't ask. When did you start to get worried?"

"A little after midnight. I called the hospital over in Jacksonville—that's the nearest hospital, where Gerry sent most of his patients. I thought maybe while he was out, he'd stopped in just to check on someone, then gotten sidetracked from letting me know. He did that quite a bit, too."

"I take it, then, he wasn't called in."

"No."

"And what makes you think it wasn't a patient who had him unsettled?"

"Nothing in particular, really. It's just the way he was about those things. He'd been in practice here for a long time. He'd learned to keep office problems at the office."

"Do you know who his patients were on that last day?"

"No."

"Does Pointdexter know?"

"He said he checked into all that." She crossed her legs and looked up into the sycamore branches. "But I'm never sure he's done the things he says he has."

As I looked at Sarah, I remembered the dinner we had shared at Stevie's that night out in Montana. The Gerry I had seen that night, a man who had dissolved into a melancholy, boozy haze, might well be the sort of man who would leave the house for no apparent reason, and spend the next several hours trying to drive his troubles away.

"I can tell you," Sarah went on, "about one patient Gerry saw that day. Mickey Cochran. I remember at dinner he said he'd stopped off at the nursing home early that afternoon."

"How long has Cochran been back in town?"

"A little over a month. There was some delay while all the government agencies decided who was going to pay his nursing home and medical fees. It's not cheap to die of cancer."

"What's been the reaction around town?"

"You mean to having him out of prison and back here?"

I nodded.

"Not much, as far as I can tell. There's Matthew Turk, of course. He's not happy."

I told her that I had met Turk that morning. "If anything," I said, "his attitude toward Cochran seemed more or less restrained."

Sarah smiled and shook her head. "You're in the backwater of backwaters, Leo. We manage to keep our hatred on patios and porches, keep it all strictly among friends around the kitchen table."

"Did Gerry say anything specific about his visit to Cochran that day?" I asked. "The day he was killed?"

"Just that he had seen him. He really didn't say anything much at all that night. I thought I told you that already."

"Not in so many words."

"Well, yes, that's the way it was. He was just very taciturn and restless. Didn't eat much of his dinner. Then he watched the Cardinals and I think the Phillies on TV. He hated baseball, really, but he always tried to watch because there are so many Cards fans in town—the whole damned town, it seems like—and Gerry liked being conversant with them about how the season was going. And then he just took that phone call and said he was leaving." She braced her left elbow on the table, then turned away and leaned her mouth into her fist.

"What was he driving the night he was killed? That

hunk of Buick you two had when you came to see me in Montana?"

Sarah shook her head. "The Buick is really my car. Gerry was driving his Jeep Cherokee. His back-to-nature car, I called it. It has four wheel drive, so it makes . . . made him feel like an environmentalist, and an air conditioner so he wouldn't forget he was a doctor."

I remembered the light in Gerry's eyes as he'd watched the fisherman that evening we had dinner at Stevie's. And I remembered all the glasses that the waiter had brought to the table full, and carried away empty.

"Where's the Jeep now?"

"Pointdexter still has it. Locked up in a garage somewhere."

Nearly three weeks after the homicide, keeping Gerry's car on ice seemed like an extraordinary step for a hick sheriff who, if I were to believe Sarah, wasn't much more than a waste of clothes when it came to investigating crime.

"I've tried several times to get the Jeep back," Sarah said. "But Pointdexter just smiles and tells me it's evidence. It's the same with *all* of Gerry's things. His personal effects, everything. Pointdexter's keeping it all. He says it's all evidence until the murder is solved. At the rate he's going, we'll all be dead of old age before I get Gerry's things back."

Pointdexter was starting to sound as thorough as me.

There was a crash, and when I looked back toward the sun porch, I realized that Michael had used one of his Air Jordans to kick open the aluminum door. His black jeans were shredded, and his black T-shirt hung on his thin frame like a tent. He was holding a sandwich in one hand, a portable tape player in the other. His ears were covered by headphones turned high enough that rap leaked out. And, most surprisingly of all, both sides of his head were completely shaved, with the crown left growing in a long, stringy mop. Pastor Roscoe Beckett would have welcomed him with open arms.

"I'm afraid," Sarah said, "my charming little boy was murdered along with my husband. This all started, you know, just a few days after the funeral."

Michael, his brain pinioned between the headphones, was oblivious. He sat down at the table, but didn't look at either his mother or me.

"Michael?" Sarah reached across the table and shook his elbow. "Michael!"

"Whaaat." His voice was a whine, which shifted octaves somewhere in that wasteland stretching between the word's beginning and its end. When Michael continued to look away, Sarah reached across again and jerked the headphones from his ears, then dropped them, squawking, onto the table. "What's your problem *this* time?" the boy said.

"You remember Mr. Banks?"

"Yeah, sure."

"We went to his house in Montana, then had dinner with him that night?" Her voice had that singsong quality that mothers everywhere employ with children they would love to strangle.

"Yeah. You mean the night Dad came back to the motel drunk and we're all going, like, whoa, I'm asleep."

I started, however lamely, to tell Michael that I was sorry about his father, and that I wanted to try to catch the man who had killed him. I had spoken maybe half a dozen words before he replaced the headphones, then got up and left the yard by way of the sidewalk through the rhododendrons.

Sarah needed a moment to compose herself. "I'm sorry. He was raised better than that, but the last few days, you really couldn't tell it. You know, he uses

Gerry's electric razor every morning. To shave half his head. Dear God."

By now, Sarah was completely distracted, and I couldn't think of anything to say about her son that didn't hinge on a platitude. I said, "The night Gerry was killed, did you ever call anybody and report him missing?"

She shook her head. "It's always bothered me that I didn't do that. But I keep reminding myself, who would I have called? You know what kind of town this is, Leo. You call for help, you're telling the whole town you can't take care of your own problems. In a place like this, family troubles only exist if you're foolish enough to tell someone about them."

"Family troubles?"

She made two impatient fists and took a deep breath. "You see, that's just what I mean. There weren't any family troubles. But call Freddie Pointdexter in the middle of the night because you don't know where your husband is, do that and you've got family troubles for the rest of your life."

"So you get comfortable and make the best of it," I said.

"Exactly. And then some big dumb sheriff comes to your door early one morning and tells you this time you were wrong, you should have sucked up your pride and called somebody."

"This time?"

"Oh, *Christ,* Leo, what is it with you?" I couldn't see her eyes behind her sunglasses.

A small breeze, the tag end of the morning's freshness, worked its way through the trees. High overhead, the contrails of a jetliner, itself no more than a silver bullet, billowed into a broad, synthetic cloud, reminding me of that same Midwestern sky when I was fifteen and still believed that the sky was the home of heaven.

"One of my grandmothers was very religious," I

115

said. By now, I was leaning far back in the chair, still intent on the sky. "When I was a kid, we had a thunderstorm one day. One of those huge, beautiful storms with the clouds like yellow mother-of-pearl in the sunlight before it hits. I called my grandmother on the phone—they lived just down the road—and told her she should take a look at that cloud. Because that cloud was why I didn't need to go to church anymore."

"And what did she say?"

"She was polite."

Sarah laughed. "That's required of grandmothers. But you didn't shave your head, did you?"

"Not quite. A few years later, I grew a ponytail. But you—"

"Yes, I remember." There was another silence before she went on. "You haven't said anything about us. You and me."

I felt tired, hauling my eyes back to earth. "You can't be serious. How's this: We'll always have those college memories."

Her voice was low. "It isn't that trite, is it?"

I shrugged. "You tell me. All along, you had it exactly in your mind what kind of guy you would settle with, and you weren't about to be swayed off course. At least that's what *Gerry* told me. Christ knows, I never heard that from *you.*"

"No, you didn't."

"Then it was true?"

"It was the times," she said. "Vietnam and the sixties had us all confused."

"I think *fucked up* is the operative term. Anyway, I don't think our breakup was that historic. Gerry Heyman turned out to fit your specs. I didn't, and that was all she wrote. I've married and divorced three women. I figure you did me a favor by scratching me off your 'A' list. Otherwise it might have been four."

"So it's as simple as that," she said.

"It sure is."

"And all those years stuck way out there in the West?"

I started to laugh. "Sweetheart, you've seen Montana for yourself. If I still have to explain, you'll never understand, so what's the point?"

Sarah pulled off her sunglasses and squinted in the light. "The point is maybe I do understand. Maybe I understand a lot of things now that I didn't before."

I smiled and patted her knee. "How charming."

She reached far back with admirable fury, and I was lucky enough to catch her wrist before her hand got to my face.

"You sonofabitch." She jerked her hand free and stood up quickly, knocking over her chair. "You're nothing but a sonofabitch."

"Congratulations," I said, "you finally figured it out."

8

What the hell did I care, as long as Sarah didn't demand her money back? And even if she did, so what? One thing she'd learn about sonsofbitches is they always keep your dough.

The Big Sandy County Nursing Home was on the north end of town near the river, not far from a grove of ancient maples. The home itself, though, was built on an elevated, flat parcel of bare land, which looked as though it might have been reclaimed from a backwater after the levee was built. At first glance, the place looked like nothing more than an older two-story house sided with gray shingles, the kind of place that would have made a good setting for either a journalistic exposé or a horror movie. As I neared, though, I could see that a new, low wing stretched out toward the horizon behind the old house. The wing had a flat roof, and was built of those ubiquitous red bricks. But to get to the new wing, you had to pass through a reception area inside the old building. Long fields of tall, yellow-tasseled corn pressed close

 118

around the building and parking lot. The leaves on the corn stalks clattered and hissed in the fitful air.

There was nothing wrong with the air conditioning inside the home. I was chilled just a few steps through the door, and for a moment that chill distracted me from the odor of medicine and moribund dreams. In contrast to the drab exterior, the foyer was surprisingly bright. A couple of old women in wheelchairs were parked near the reception desk. A woman in her twenties with moussed-up blond hair sat behind a counter.

"Pssst!" In slow motion, one of the old women waved me closer with a gnarled hand. "D-don't give 'em your n-name."

"Now, Bessie," said the receptionist. Her voice was loud, elaborately patient.

"Why's that?" I said, bending close to the old woman named Bessie.

"Tell 'em who you are, they w-won't let you l-leave."

"Bessie, you know that is not true." The receptionist seemed to stop just short of wagging her finger. "You'll scare this poor man off." And then to me, she said, "Is there something I can do for you?" She had intensely green eyes.

I said, "You have the greenest eyes I've ever seen."

"Thanks. But they're not really mine. Oops, well, the eyes are mine, that's silly. But the color, that's contacts. I got them on special over in Springfield. At that place in the mall." Her smile was broad, not the least bit self-conscious.

"I want to visit one of your residents."

"Usually, my eyes are brown," she said.

I studied her eyes closely, and saw a thin ring of brown around the bright green discs. "They sure are," I said. And then I told her I wanted to see Mickey Cochran.

"Oh, him," she said.

"The murderer," said the old woman named Bessie. "He's come to see the m-murderer, Sue." She was talking to the other old woman, who appeared comatose. "Nobody ever comes to see you or me, Sue, us with kids and grandkids and great-grandkids and nieces and nephews. Even *preachers!* But that m-murderer, he gets all kinds of visitors, even s-s-strangers from out of town. My lord!"

I said again to the receptionist, "Mickey Cochran?"

"I'll have to go get the supervisor." She disappeared into the room behind the reception desk.

"What's he want to see that murderer for, Sue?" Bessie said. "He's c-crazy, I'll tell the world. You remember, Sue. Cochran. Mickey C-Cochran. The half-wit boy killed that rich girl Otto Turk married in St. Louis. Lord God, Sue, you almost married Otto Turk yourself."

I looked at Sue and frowned. I was about to ask her about Turk, when Bessie said, "Don't waste your time. She can't answer. Can you, Sue? I just talk to her as a kindness. But it's like I told you years ago, Sue, it's just lucky you didn't have enough money to keep Otto T-Turk interested. Might of been you that half-wit murdered, instead of that poor woman from St. Louis. Young man, why do you want to waste your time on that c-crazy old m-murderer?"

Before I was forced to answer, the supervisor stepped out of her office. She was a middle-aged woman with steely hair arranged in a bun, and a white doubleknit smock worn like armor. "I'm Miss Detweiller. Was there something you needed?" There was a beauty mark near the left corner of her thin mouth.

"Mickey Cochran," I said. "I want to see him."

"And your name?"

I told her my name.

"And the nature of your business?"

"I'm selling life insurance."

Miss Detweiller's nostrils flared. "There's no need to be smart."

"I apologize," I said. "I'm really selling tombstones. Easy credit, but a pretty short payment schedule."

"You must be that man I heard about." Her face looked like she'd just bitten into something sour. "That man Sarah Heyman hired."

"Bingo."

"That detective from someplace out West."

"Anything you say."

"And now you're here to see that crazy old murderer," Miss Detweiller said.

Bessie said, "Last visitor that crazy murderer had was D-Dr. Heyman, and now he's dead. At least people say he's dead. Well, we haven't seen him around, have we, Sue, it must be true. D-Dr. Heyman . . . D-dead. And him such a young man." She gazed up at me with absolute wonder. "Young as you."

"It's this way," Miss Detweiller said. She led me through a set of double doors at my left, then down a long corridor. As had the reception area, the corridor bristled under stark light. Old men and women sat in doorways, or navigated the hall in wheelchairs or walkers. Soft moans, or fragments of speech were, I came to realize, replays of long-ago conversations with now-imaginary partners.

Miss Detweiller assumed the roll of tour guide, explaining that most of the home's residents were at a point in their lives where they needed—and would continue to need—constant care. I took that to mean that from Bessie's perspective, it made a lot of sense not to give them your name. Give them a name, they start a file. Start a file, assign a room. Assign a room, begin the wait.

Miss Detweiller said, "We weren't especially pleased about having this Cochran fellow. I mean, of all the places they could've sent him, this is the one place on earth—this facility—where people know who he is, *what* he is, and what he did."

"Maybe you won't have him for long," I said. If my sarcasm registered with Miss Detweiller, she didn't let on.

We stopped outside a closed room, the only closed room I had noticed along the corridor. There was a plastic fixture beside the door, with slots where tags with the name of the patient and the patient's doctor could be inserted. Both slots were empty.

"He's in here," Miss Detweiller said.

"Bessie said he has visitors all the time. Who else besides me and Doctor Heyman?"

Miss Detweiller shook her head. "Nobody. Nobody alive, anyway. Maybe he has a lot of ghosts come to see him."

"You don't seem like the sort to believe in ghosts," I said.

The softness in her gaze caught me off guard. "I've worked here too long not to," she said, then turned and started back down the corridor.

The room was cool and dim, nearly silent except for the mumble of a television set. The Venetian blinds were closed, casting the sunlight in dim bars across the bed. Cochran himself, lying partially on his right side, was absolutely still. His dark eyes, though, behind thick lenses mounted in heavy black frames, followed me from the moment I entered the room.

"Howdy," I said. "My name's Leo Banks. I was a friend of Gerry Heyman's."

Cochran cleared his throat as though he were about to speak, but he didn't say anything. He was completely bald, his large ears pressed close against his head. His chest rose slowly, as though against a great weight, and then collapsed under that weight, sending the breath whistling past his teeth.

I said, "You in the mood to talk to me for a while?"

Cochran shrugged his bony shoulders, rustling the sheets. His hands, startlingly large, lay spread across his distended belly. He was covered by a sheet and thin blanket, and despite the fact that his body was hunched and curled into a near fetal position, his large feet still hung over the edge of the bed. Nobody had told me that Mickey Cochran, whatever his mental qualities might be, was also a goddamn big man. And despite the fact that his body could have been stone, there was enough life bottled up behind those black eyes to give me the creeps.

I asked Cochran if he knew about Gerry.

He flicked his eyes toward the TV. "Heard it on that thing."

"Sorry."

"What for?"

"Well, for one thing, he believed you were innocent."

"Don't matter."

"Mattered to him. He came to see me a while back. Wanted me to investigate your case."

"You the cop from Texas?"

"In the flesh." Texas, I thought. Well, what the hell? The best detectives are all from Texas.

"Shared a cell once wit' a guy from Texas. A guy messed wit' little kids. I tried to stick his head through the bars one night. Goddamn almost did it, ha!" His mouth twitched into a grin, and the bottom seemed to fall out of his eyes. "Baby-raper. Messed 'im up good. Shoulda killed 'im."

"I told Heyman the joint's full of guys claim they're innocent."

Cochran didn't flinch. "Yep."

"What makes you so different?"

"Nothin'. Got any candy?"

"No."

"Sugar Babies? I like 'em."

"Sorry."

"That what *he* says, says he's sorry. Brings me Sugar Babies."

"Who says he's sorry?"

"Him."

"Sorry for what?"

"I ain't never killed that woman they say I did."

"But you told 'em you did."

"They gonna hang me."

"Who's gonna hang you?"

"Them."

I pulled a pale green institutional-style armchair to the bedside, sat down, and made a great show of getting comfortable. "Why don't you tell me what happened?"

"Hot," he said. "Hotter'n hell."

It took a while, with lots of questions and answers, lots of switchbacks, but after about an hour, I felt confident that I had the story in hand. Cochran claimed that on the day of the murder, he'd been at the far end of the farm, cutting weeds from fence rows with a scythe. He decided that the best remedy for the heat would be a swim, so he walked over to Big Branch Creek, which was about a mile and a half away. Walked a mile and a half, I thought, for a swim? With a pond right there at the house? Not a chance, not if everything was on the level. Cochran's brain might have thrown a shoe, but he wasn't altogether lame.

When Cochran got back to the house, he saw Buckshot McCool's sheriff car and Alfonse Leake's Packard.

"Everybody knew that Packard car," Cochran said. "Put that car with old Buckshot's car, meant trouble. Trouble always mean me."

Not taking any chances, Cochran went on, he tried to sneak into the barn, planning to wait out whatever was wrong. As it turned out, he was the thing wrong, and there was no waiting it out.

Once the crowd of men fell upon Cochran, it didn't take much longer than a heartbeat for them to start pointing fingers, and all the fingers pointed at him. He tried to tell them he'd been looking to hide because he was afraid.

Afraid? Afraid of what? Innocent men don't have to be afraid of anything. Innocent men walk right in and ask what the hell's going on.

Off to jail he went.

"Heard 'em outside," he said. "Heard 'em talkin'. Knew what they was sayin', they was sayin' I messed with that woman and they knew what you did with a man like that. Lots of light out in the street. Louder. They was drunk 'cause I'd be drunk, too, I was out there with 'em."

I said again, "You told them you did it."

"Got any smokes on you?"

"Gave them up."

"That mean old bitch runs this place won't let me smoke. How 'bout a chew?"

I shook my head. "Trying to keep my lethal habits to a minimum."

"Le . . . lethal?" Cochran made a face.

"Deadly."

"Oh yeah. Yeah," he whispered. He lifted his right hand, and studied the nicotine stains on his fingers.

"So tell me, Mickey, how come you said you killed her?"

His grin was filled with perfectly awful teeth. "You was a copper."

"Twenty years."

"Which twenty?"

"The longest twenty."

"Swore I'd never talk to guys like you again." Trouble passed over his face, as though he just realized he'd spent quite a while breaking that oath.

"Suit yourself, bud." This time, I made an equal show of getting myself up. "I'm making a lot of money just to hang around this lousy town. I've got a lot more time to waste than you do, and it really doesn't matter to me if you killed that woman or not."

"That boy," Cochran said. "He comes to see me all the time."

"Heyman," I said. "Dr. Heyman."

"No, no, no," he whispered, impatient. *"The boy.* Matthew. Come see me all the time, say he sorry."

I remembered being told that Cochran hardly ever had visitors. I was sure that Matthew Turk, of all people, would attract notice. Still, it made no sense that Miss Detweiller would lie about such an apparently insignificant detail.

"Sorry for what, Mickey?" I sat back down.

"Alfonse Leake, he says they was gonna hang me. That night they was gonna do it. And that Buckshot McCool, he says he gonna let 'em. And you was twenty years a copper. Shit." He drew the last word out, like a long, impatient sigh.

"So you told them."

"You're goddamn right I told 'em. Weren't any secret that's what it was gonna take to get me through to morning."

"And you never told anybody any different. Not in fifty years."

"Prison ain't so hard, no harder than sleepin' in some fella's barn, bein' his mule twenty-four hours a day."

"Or getting hung."

Cochran laughed. "Lot easier than gettin' hung. Anyhow, that boy keeps tellin' me he's sorry, so I guess it worked out, didn't it?"

"Sorry for what?"

"For what? Hell, I don't know for what."

"Mickey," I said, "I guess it just doesn't add up for me. I keep casting around for reasons why you wouldn't take that confession back. If it was all a lie, I mean. Why do all that time?"

The mangled grin reappeared. "Ain't like I never *thought* about doing what they said I done. Not killing her . . . but . . . you know, the other. *That.* I did used to think about that. A lot."

"You mean having sex with her."

He swallowed and glanced away. "Yeah. Yeah, that's what I mean." When he looked back at me, his expression was blank. The shadows seemed deeper under his heavy cheekbones. With apparent effort, he again raised a hand, this time his left, and wiped it down the length of his face. Then he took a deep breath and let it out slowly. "All the goddamn time. You never seen her, you wouldn't understand."

"Try me."

"She swims a lot in that there pond." Two or three times a week during the summer, Cochran told me, Grace Turk would slip away to the pond for a swim. "She had to sneak off, 'cause Otto, he didn't like her showin' herself like that."

"Showing herself? She didn't wear a swimming suit?"

"Most of the time she did. Sometime she didn't."

"How do you know?"

"Otto, he caught her."

"How do you know?"

"He'd get mad as hell, run around like a wild man."

"Mickey, how do you know that?"

"Sure wish they'd let me have a goddamn cigarette."

"She must've been a beautiful woman. A lot of times, women, when they're off alone like that, they'll sing to themselves. Did Grace sing to herself, Mickey?"

"Goddamn you!"

"Would she wade out until the water was about up to her hips, then squat down and push herself out into the deep water? Where it was cool?"

"You sonofabitch. Goddamn the whole bunch of you."

"How do you know all this, Mickey?"

"He caught me. You happy? Caught me."

"Caught you where?"

"Wasn't my fault she carried on like that."

"Where did he catch you?"

"In the weeds, okay?"

"What were you doing in the weeds?"

"Hah!"

"Mickey, tell me what you were doing in the weeds."

"Knew it's wrong even thinking about it, me bein' a half-wit like I was. Surprise you, me saying a thing like that? Folks think you're a half-wit, you don't know it, don't know you ain't like other people. Think you're too stupid to know you're stupid. Well, it ain't like that."

"How many times did Otto catch you?"

Cochran's answer was quick. "Once. Caught me that one time and that was the end of it."

"The end of the swimming, or the end of you watching?"

"End of swimming."

"How do you know, if you weren't still watching? Not all the time, maybe, not like before. But watching just a little bit. Maybe even just seeing her down there by accident."

"Couldn't help it," he said. "I lived there! And she never had no business carrying on like that."

"How long was it before she died that Otto caught you in the weeds?"

"Don't know. Couple of weeks, maybe."

With some effort, Cochran turned onto his back, and tried to rearrange his gangly legs under the sheet. "Listen, I says to Leake and McCool, I says, sure, I done it. Wasn't hard, 'cause I was real scared, see, and I figured, hell, I could always take it back."

"At your trial."

"Yeah. My *trial.*"

"But that didn't work out, either."

"Nah. My lawyer, he says nobody's gonna believe me. Says they'll convict me before lunch and give me the chair that afternoon."

"So you cut a deal."

"Yeah, I cut her all right, cut me a deal. Anyhow, it kept eatin' on me, the way I knew I done wrong, watching her like I did them times. Doin' what I was doin', you know, with myself, when I watched her. So I figure, ah, Christ, let her go. I didn't deserve nothin' for killin' nobody. But I was real wrong, so it was okay."

"And now it's not okay," I said.

Cochran shrugged. "Don't matter. That Gerry Heyman, he asked, so I told him. First time in all those years anybody asked. Ain't like I expected nothing. Ain't like I went looking for any of this. Just told a doctor what he wanted to know."

"You told Heyman everything you told me today?"

"Far as I know."

"What's that supposed to mean?"

"I don't know. Nothin'." Using both hands, Cochran took off his heavy black glasses and closed his eyes.

"I keep wondering, Mickey," I said, "how come you walked all that way to the creek for a swim. I mean, it's hot enough to fry up a slice of ham on a flat rock, a man sure as hell doesn't walk all the way across the country to do what he could do right there on the place. At the pond, you know?"

Cochran never opened his eyes. "I done what I done."

"That's what I'm afraid of," I said. "Why didn't you use the pond?"

"Couldn't."

"Why not?"

"Just couldn't."

"Why not, goddamnit?"

Now he looked at me, a look that made the backs of my ears tingle. "Cause she was in it, okay?"

"Dead?"

"No, hell no. Alive, swimming around, you know, like she was, like I told you. It's like you said, I wanted to use the pond. But there she was."

"Swimming around naked?" I said. "That's what you want me to believe?" I know that sex wasn't discovered in the sixties, but I would have to think long and hard before deciding whether or not I believed a young wife in the nineteen thirties would carry on in the way Cochran had described.

"That Otto," Cochran said, "he'd of caught me again down there around her in that pond . . ."

"So you walked to Big Branch."

"*Ran* there."

"Why didn't you tell this to the men that night? To Leake and McCool?"

Cochran's laugh disintegrated into a rasping cough. "They already thought I killed her. What they gonna think, they find out I watched her swimming around naked?"

They would have thought what I was thinking: Cochran had lost control, and now he needed a story. "If you didn't kill her," I said, "who did?"

"Beats me," he said, without opening his eyes. "I was you, I'd ask that kid comes to the window sayin' he's sorry."

Ask, he meant, Matthew Turk.

A moment later, Cochran's breathing settled into a rasping rhythm that sounded like sleep.

9

I was halfway into my second draft when Tory Mc-
Dade came strolling through the door of the
Mauvaisterre Hotel bar. Before that, I had been
the only customer. Little Mike stopped off every fifteen minutes or so to see if I was ready for a refill.

"How's it goin', Jackson?" McDade snapped his
fingers at me and walked directly behind the bar. His
fedora was cocked at a rakish angle, and his clothes—
the dark suit, the knit tie, the black and green plaid
shirt—were the same he had been wearing the day
before. He slid open the ice chest and pulled out a
bottle of Stolichnaya, poured a good three fingers
into a glass, then raised the glass in my direction and
winked. "Hair of the dog."

Little Mike was behind the bar herself in no time.
"Goddamn you, Tory, I'm calling Freddie right now.
You hear me?"

"Ah, Little Mike, just look at you." He smiled at
me and shook his head. "Just look at her. Ain't she
something? I was there in church the day she was
baptized." He poured another drink.

"That won't work on me anymore, Tory." Little Mike produced a telephone from a lower shelf and slammed it down on the bar.

"And who might you be, my friend?" He knocked back his second drink and poured a third. Clearly, he wasn't about to waste any time not drinking before Pointdexter arrived.

I told Tory McDade who I was.

"Ah, yes." As he paused to catch his breath between drinks, his eyes crossed slightly, then righted themselves. "The famous detective."

"Up yours," I said, hoisting my glass.

"And yours." Some more vodka vanished. McDade looked at Little Mike while he poured. "I guess maybe I insulted him already?"

"He's been here since yesterday," Little Mike said, "why put it off?"

McDade had apparently forgotten that he'd called me a Nazi the day before. Maybe he didn't consider that an insult. Carefully, as though handling fine crystal, he set his glass on the bar. And then he belched softly, and his mood darkened. "Here to find out who launched the sainted doctor off on his eternal voyage." His voice was heavy with sarcasm.

"You seem to know a lot about my business," I said. I finished off my beer, then leaned across the bar and refilled the glass from the tap.

McDade laughed. "Haven't you caught on yet, my son? That murder's the most interesting thing in town since they canceled *Gunsmoke,* and you're right in the middle of it. Hell's fire, you're a featured player. Christ, more than that even. You're the guest star."

"I'm honored."

"You should be! Yes, yes, the valiant avenger of the martyred physician. Great stuff, just great. Two and a half, maybe even three stars in the TV listings. No, just two and a half. My mistake. You only get three stars if the victim is a blond teenaged girl. Poor Gerry, he couldn't help it he wasn't a bigger ratings draw in the victim department."

Little Mike was hovering over the phone like a vulture contemplating its first bite from a bloated deer. I looked across at McDade and winked. "Why don't you step into my office?"

"Yeah? And where might that be?" He glanced down at the bottle of Stoly.

I pulled a twenty dollar bill from the pocket of my jeans and tucked it under the edge of the bottle. "Someplace outside."

"You got a car?" he said.

"It so happens I do."

"Air conditioning?"

"Do I look like a chiseler to you?"

"Not for a minute." McDade scooped up the bottle and slipped it into the side pocket of his jacket. "Nothing like a little drinking and driving. Let's go." He came quickly from behind the bar, took me by the elbow and started us toward the door. "I ever tell you about the time I was a war hero?"

"No, I don't believe I heard that one."

"Oh hell, yeah, Christ, sure. I'm an A-number-one patriot." With great affection, he patted his hand against the bottle. "Those commies, they weren't good for much, but they sure did make the best vodka in the world. This little product right here"—he slapped the bottle—"is the key to the door of a sound market economy."

For the fourth time, I shook off the bottle, then opened the car window a bit farther to get some relief from the cigarette smoke.

"Sorry this bothers you," McDade said, waving out another match and exhaling a cloud of smoke. "I quit once. Back in the fifties. But it didn't take." His laugh was loaded to the gills with good-humored resignation. He swallowed a short jolt of vodka, then took a drag off his cigarette.

"Back there in the bar," I said, "you sounded like you have an opinion about my friend Gerry Heyman. 'The sainted doctor?'"

"Well, we're all saints in our own way, aren't we?"

"That's not the way it sounded."

"No, no, it's true. Everybody's a goddamn saint. You can take that to the bank, pal."

"And what's your claim to sainthood?"

"Wouldn't you like to know."

We were on a gravel road running along the base of the levee south of town. In the rearview mirror, the island of trees marking Mauvaisterre faded through the plume of dust. To our left, the country was a nearly flat reach of farmland until it met the bluffs several miles away. From time to time, we passed a small, brush-covered mound.

"This here's a cradle of life, you know," McDade said.

"How so?"

"Indians," he said. "You wouldn't figure that, would you? In this part of the country? Not live Indians, you understand. Dead ones."

It turned out that the mounds were all considered archeological sites, where some of the oldest Native American artifacts and remains in North America had been found. According to McDade, back in the sixties some archeologists began to dig seriously at the Koster farm near Eldred, a little town to the south. Artifacts from that site have been uncovered from as far back as seven thousand years. Since the work at Koster, many sites have been identified all up and down the lower Illinois valley. Besides the mounds on the floodplain proper, scenes of ancient and extensive habitation had also been unearthed in the alluvial deposits wedged into the gaps between the bluffs.

"Surprised?" McDade said. His voice sounded distant, distracted. He looked wistfully at the bottle of vodka, which was nearly empty. "We bury our dead six feet under and think of it as forever. Now it turns out there's whole civilizations even deeper than that, resting down there in places we never even imagine." He finished off the Stoly, and tossed the bottle into the back seat. "Places where the sun used to shine and grass used to grow and the rain used to fall."

If I was surprised by anything, it was McDade's knowledge of the subject. "You sound like a poet."

"Yeah? Well, what's so fuckin' wrong with that?"

"Nothing I can think of."

"Then you ought to think harder." He looked distractedly out the side window. "And you ought not to of been so cheap you only bought one bottle of vodka."

I turned the air conditioner down a notch. "Let's say I'm using some consumer restraint. Doing my bit to help the balance of trade."

McDade's voice was suddenly bitter. "All I care, you can stick the balance of trade up your ass."

From time to time, the road crossed one of a network of large ditches, which ran torpid, brown water. The ditches, McDade told me, were part of a flood control system installed back during the Great Depression. Before that, the river bottom was largely uninhabited and unfarmed, not much more really than a large, open swamp. For ages, the river had cut its way back and forth across the floodplain, leaving behind rich, black sediment, which turned out to be just the ticket for growing corn and soybeans, once the government figured out a way to keep the river in its place.

"There's a sand ridge runs along under the bluffs," McDade said. "That's where most folks lived here in the bottom before the levee and the ditches. Kind of country where them Indians lived. Poor people. You

can't grow much on sand but watermelons and tomatoes. Hogs." He looked at me and showed his teeth.
"And extinct Indians."

A century ago, the prosperous farms were all on
the huge expanse of prairie beyond the bluffs, that
part of the country where Otto and Grace Turk had
lived, and the town of Mauvaisterre grew up as an
agricultural port on the Illinois River.

"I grew up on the sand ridge," McDade said.
"When I was a kid, we used to keep a john boat tied
to the back porch, case the river got out."

"I guess the Heyman family lived up there on dry
land," I said.

McDade nodded slowly as he continued to look out
the window. "Oh, they were *good* people. I went to
school with Gerry's dad. Leslie. That was his name.
He had his own car to drive to high school. I know
that don't sound like much today. But it was a real
deal in 1939." He looked at me suddenly, his face
bright with bogus cheer. "A real deal!"

I made a left turn onto a side road, and drove away
from the river. Within half a mile, we passed a newer
ranch-style brick home, which was surrounded by a
large metal building and perhaps half a dozen cylindrical steel grain bins. It was the first house we had
come upon since leaving town. Not much farther on,
there was a small white bungalow surrounded by a
grove of pecan trees. Not knowing where I was going,
I kept on driving just to give the two of us a cool place
to sit. If McDade had a destination in mind, he never
said.

"We were talking about war heroes and saints," I
prompted.

"Is that right? I thought you wanted to talk about
murder."

"Maybe they're all the same subject." I decided
that McDade had come into the bar that day looking
for more than booze.

"Could be."

"So when were you a hero?"

"Me? A hero? Yeah, I guess I said that, didn't I. Must've been sober at the time."

"World War Two?"

McDade nodded. "That was the first time."

When I told him I didn't get it, he turned and looked at me squarely, something he hadn't done for a while. The lines and bulges on his face seemed only a parody of good-natured drunkenness. "Neither did I. Not for a long time. Not till all these new Vietnam movies started coming out, and I started seeing little kids wearing army clothes to school. You know, them blotched green and brown things."

"Cammies," I said. "That's what they call them. Short for *camouflage*."

"Whatever. Anyway, I know there's been a lot of boys killed in clothes like that. Including my own."

"I didn't know you had a son."

"No, you wouldn't think that, would you? Town drunks don't have sons. And car salesmen weren't ever war heroes. So what? So big fuckin' deal."

"How old was he?"

McDade's laugh was a quick flare, like a match being struck. "How old were you in sixty-seven?"

"Nineteen."

"Close enough."

"Where's his mother?"

"You ever been married?"

"Once in a while."

"You figure it out." McDade straightened his tie, then tried to smooth down the wrinkled points of his shirt collar. "I have this dream, he keeps coming back to me, wanting to know how come I never told him what he was gettin' into, told him not to go, it wasn't worth it, none of it, see? But I never said nothing. No, sir. I sucked it all in and toughed it out, so he'd be

137

able to do what had to be done. I figure that's what makes me a hero in two wars."

"What about the other war?"

"That? That was Guadalcanal. Lots easier than the second time, eh? I was stupid way back then. Easy to be brave when you're nothin' but a young dumbass."

"So tell me, Tory, why do I get the feeling this has something to do with a not-so-sainted sainted doctor?"

"Let's just say I'm narrow-minded, how about that? Let's just say it's too bad he got himself killed the other night, but at least he had them twenty-five years or so after 1967."

Sometimes I think the last conversation I have on this earth will have something to do with that goddamn war and the goddamn so-called revolution that went with it. I said, "You know, Gerry and I met up at the university. That make me unworthy of talking to a hero such as yourself?"

"Don't be an idiot."

"I'll try. But I just want you to know I don't think you can be had for the price of a bottle of communist booze."

"That's where you're wrong, pal." McDade took a last drag on his smoke, then stamped the butt out on the carpet and spit the smoke out of the side of his mouth. "I can."

When I came to the next crossroads, McDade began giving directions. We turned back toward town, then crossed the highway and continued on to the north edge of Mauvaisterre on a road that was at first oiled, then gravel, then dirt. The car was thrown from side to side by ruts, while brush began to whip and scratch at the doors and windows. Finally, the lane came to an abrupt end at the base of the levee.

In the thicket off to my right, I saw a small house, a freestanding garage and a ramshackle shed. There was hardly any yard, but a large, well-tended garden filled the area between the house and the shed. The house and garage were covered with shingles made to look like tan bricks, while the shed was made of unpainted lumber. All three buildings were roofed with corrugated tin. There was a pen behind the shed, and the ground inside was all ripped up in deep, muddy ruts. When I saw that the heavy woven wire fence was mashed down, I began to wonder just what manner of animal might have escaped into the surrounding jungle.

"Home," McDade said. "Come on, son, I'll show you around."

"I suppose this has something to do with my business here," I said.

"Hell, I don't know. I'm just a drunk old man. What do I know about the doings of a big shot like you?" McDade made a short detour by the front porch, where he picked up, without explanation, an old wooden golf club.

The ground was spongy underfoot, the heat like a shroud. With McDade just behind, I followed a path, which led perhaps thirty feet up the side of the levee to its crest. Although the levee was grass covered, I counted five places where the grass had been ripped and rooted, leaving muddy trenches about the size of refrigerators. The path continued down the other side, and ended at the base of a long dock, which reached across the mudflats and backwater to the river proper. There were more areas of torn-up grass there on the back side. I took three or four steps onto the dock, then stopped when I noticed that Tory McDade, who was using the golf club like a walking stick, seemed to keep glancing over his shoulder, first one way, then the other.

I said, "Is there something you maybe ought to tell me?"

"Pharaoh," he snarled out of the side of his mouth.

I asked him what that meant, but he refused to say more.

The air sounded alive with insects, and smelled of dead fish, rotten leaves and mud, smelled like all the corruption and compost that ever was and ever would be.

I looked at McDade and shrugged. "I don't get it." A mosquito was busy as hell sucking blood out of my neck. I wasted no time smacking it, and another mosquito wasted even less time taking its place. I felt as if everything in the surrounding swamp were looking at me and thinking, Lunch.

McDade shrugged back. "You asked about saints, then you tried to get me drunk, now you're stuck. Come on."

I followed him across the warped planks to the end of the dock. Water edged past the pilings, and a length of heavy rope tied to a cleat disappeared down into the slow, brown whorls.

McDade noticed me staring at the rope. "Boat," he said. "Or what's left of a boat. My boy, his name was Bill. Him and your old friend the doctor used to be thick as thieves. But that was thirty years ago, before he was the doctor. He was just little Gerry back then.

"Lots of things different then. Me and the wife, we was still together. Had a house in town. Nice place. This out here was just a little fish camp where I used to bring the boys."

After Tory McDade taught them how, Bill and Gerry spent countless summer nights fishing on the river, hauling in big, wallowing catfish, buffalo and carp. It seemed to McDade, as he remembered it, that the moon was always full, the water always calm, the fishing better than it would ever be again. He would sit in a lawn chair at the end of the dock, keeping an eye on the boat as it rocked out into the channel through the moonlight. No matter how far out the boys went, he could always keep track of them by the secret glow of their cigars, which Tory understood the boys had boosted from Fielden's Grocery in town.

McDade said, "Every kid in town clipped cigars off old man Fielden. He kept a box of rum-soaked crooks in an out-of-the-way spot, you know, just so he wouldn't have to catch them at it."

And then Gerry and Bill weren't pals anymore. Heyman went off to the university, and Bill McDade went to war. One came back a doctor, the other in a box.

"They told us he got mortared," McDade said. "I knew firsthand what that was like. We never even looked to see what parts of him was in the coffin, what wasn't."

"That what got you to drinking?" I said.

"That? Huh? Nah, hell no." He waved me off and started back up the dock toward the levee. "Come on, lemme show you what this's all about."

As we walked back toward the levee, I heard an awful sucking noise coming from the green mire off to our right. The scrub brush began to quake and the sucking grew louder and then I realized that the quaking was on the move toward the levee.

"Pharaoh," Tory McDade said.

I was about to ask just what in the hell Pharaoh was, when the thing itself, a red leviathan covered with slabs of mud, heaved itself out of the backwater in a final, slurping lunge, and began climbing toward the crest of the levee.

"Just follow my lead," McDade whispered. "And whatever you do, don't make any sudden moves."

Pharaoh was the largest Duroc boar I had ever seen, and I had seen some Duroc boars.

As we made our way up the path, McDade began to whistle an old Glenn Miller tune, *Tuxedo Junction*, and by the time we reached the crest, I was whistling along with him. Pharaoh paralleled our progress. Just as we reached the top, Pharaoh let out a noxious grunt and squared himself in our direction. He was less than ten yards away, and his yellow eyes peered out from under floppy red ears. He had four tusks the size of bananas, which he ground rhythmically until his mouth began to foam and his breath chugged from his nose in twin clouds of faint, gray steam.

"I was afraid of this," McDade said. Without a single wasted motion, he planted his feet, raised the golf club in a surprisingly agile backswing and waited.

We didn't have to wait long, and when Pharaoh charged, he charged with alarming speed. At the last possible instant, Tory McDade brought the club down on the point of Pharaoh's nose with a queasy, hollow *thwack,* turning his head, and along with it, the charge. The boar let out an awful squeal, then stopped dead in his tracks panting.

"It's okay," McDade said. "Now he knows it's me. He doesn't see too good anymore. And when he gets in these moods, he won't listen to a thing I say." The peak of the boar's arched back was level with McDade's waist, and when McDade began to scratch him behind an ear, Pharaoh grunted softly, this time with apparent affection, rather than obvious menace.

"Jesus Christ!" I said.

"It's all in the club speed," McDade explained. "Getting your hips all the way through the swing, then rolling your wrists at just the right moment. And the follow-through, of course." He shrugged modestly. "Club speed."

"Jesus Christ," I said again.

"It's nothin'. Really." McDade polished the head of the club against his pants leg. "I used to be able to do it with a three wood. But as Pharaoh got bigger and I got older, I had to move up to a driver." He started down the levee toward the house. "Pharaoh! Heel!" he called, and the boar fell into step at McDade's left leg.

"I look at an animal like that," I said, following along, "and I see a lot of ham."

Pharaoh fell momentarily out of step, and I thought for an instant that I had made a tragic error.

"Snakes," McDade said. "This bottom country's full of snakes. Moccasins. Vicious goddamn things. Nothing'll keep snakes off a place like a good hog. Bite old Pharaoh a dozen times, doesn't matter. Hide's too thick and tough for the fangs. I've seen it happen lots of times. This hog sees a big old moccasin, all he thinks is, *chomp, chomp.*"

About ten years ago, McDade told me, he came across Pharaoh, just a pig then, living wild in the brush, escaped out of some farmer's pork factory. McDade fed him some table scraps and there, fifteen hundred pounds or so later, you are. The only problem was that he loved to root around on the levee, which now and then caused some concern among the Army Corps of Engineers, especially when the river was high. Other than that, he was a good protector against deadly snakes and other vermin, as well as halfway decent company.

"Voice commands," McDade said. "That's the real secret." When we neared the buildings, McDade ordered, "Pharaoh, kennel!" and the boar ambled off toward the shed with the beaten-down pen. "See what I mean?" He stood proudly with his hands on his hips. "Voice commands. Can't use a leash, the goddamn things ain't got any neck."

After watching Pharaoh wade through the strong wire fence as though it weren't there, he shouldered the driver and walked on. "Of course, the right club selection doesn't hurt, either."

10

A few minutes later, we were standing outside the rickety garage. McDade fished a key from his pants pocket, then snapped open the padlock and pulled open both sides of the double door. The car was covered with a clean white dropcloth. McDade gave the cloth a tug, whipping it aside.

The red Corvette was immaculate. The paint looked factory fresh, the wax job polished deep as an ocean. I walked a circuit around the car, and couldn't find so much as a scratch, while the white convertible top was stretched tight and true.

"A sixty-two 'vette," I said.

McDade whistled softly. "Ain't you the connoisseur."

I shook my head. "Not hardly. But I've heard the story of this car."

"From your dead doctor friend?"

"Yeah." I remembered the light in Gerry's eyes that night he'd told me about wanting to buy this car . . . *this car.*

McDade laughed. "Well, you might of heard about the car, but you haven't heard the story."

The Corvette was Bill McDade's high school graduation present to himself. He'd spent four years working odd jobs, saving money. Some kids saved for college, but McDade knew that wasn't his kind of life. In those days, the future was pretty cut and dried for healthy young guys once they turned eighteen. A green campus, or green fatigues. So Bill McDade bought himself a red Corvette and took his chances on the odds. It turned out the odds sucked.

"He wanted this car," I said. "Gerry did."

"Oh, wanted it bad," McDade howled, running his fingers lightly over the trunk lid, as though feeling for braille. "Worst kind of bad."

"I get the feeling it wasn't as simple as money."

McDade shook his head slowly, while pinching his nose and letting his breath out in a long burst through his mouth. "No."

When Bill McDade climbed on a bus for Fort Leonard Wood in the fall of 1967, Gerry Heyman had already been away at school for nearly two months. The two boys stayed in touch for a time, but it turned out there wasn't much time left.

"Billy was home on leave at Christmas," McDade said. "He got back once more before he went overseas. But that Christmas was the last time him and Gerry was in town at the same time."

"They get together a lot?"

"Did I sell the sonofabitch this car?" McDade's face went blank as the surface of that river on the other side of the levee. He busied himself putting the cloth back over the car. I tried to help, but he waved me off. "When a boy goes off to get himself killed, he shouldn't have to do it slinking out of town like he fucked up getting himself drafted in the first place."

"No," I said, remembering the look on Sarah's face the day I told her I'd joined the navy. "No, he shouldn't." Disgust, that was the look. A look of disgust that had brought me anger and shame then, and brought me too close to self-pity now. Why is it that sometimes you fall in love with people who make you feel like shit?

Once he had the Corvette safely covered, McDade dusted his hands on his pants, then lit another cigarette.

"So tell me," he said. The cigarette wagged between his lips, like the finger of a Sunday School teacher. "This Heyman kid, you say you and him was pals back then. He ever tell you about his best buddy back here in Mauvaisterre? He ever tell you about my kid Bill?"

"No. I'm sorry, but I don't think he ever did."

"Well then, now you know what I'm talking about." McDade closed the shed and snapped the padlock back in place. "*Doctor* Heyman. Rest-in-peace. The miserable fuck."

"Sounds like you might've killed him yourself."

"Me? Me!" For the first time since I'd known him, McDade laughed outright. He laughed so hard he fell into a coughing fit, which he tried to cure with his cigarette. "No, I never done that," he said, gasping. "Thing is, see, far as I was concerned, little Gerry, he wanted this here Corvette too bad to make it worthwhile killing him. You know what I mean? Diminishing returns, far as I was concerned. Me? Christ no, I never killed the little worm."

I heard the noise of an engine coming our way down the dirt lane. McDade frowned, as if he were listening with a lot of effort.

"Doesn't sound like somebody familiar," he said.

I laughed. "You know, Tory, you don't strike me as a guy people come to see." Nobody, I thought, except rich doctors looking for absolution and a car deal. And retired coppers with time on their hands.

"That's what I mean," McDade said. He drifted off and wandered into the house.

The outfit was close enough now for me to hear branches scraping along its sides. A moment later, a large four-by-four white pickup pulled into the clearing. The Turk Seed and Chemical logo was painted on the driver's door. After the truck ground to a stop, the two men inside exchanged words, then got out. The driver was tall and beefy, with dishwater blond hair combed in oily wings. His sidekick, a shorter guy walking around behind a beer gut, had a green baseball cap mashed down near his ears. Both men were young, in their mid-twenties, and both wore blue jeans, along with khaki work shirts that had the Turk logo sewn over the left pocket.

I said, "Howdy."

The two men looked at each other, then back at me.

"Yep," said the tall one, "that must be him."

"Yep," said the short one. He stood with his thumbs hooked in the front pockets of his jeans, rocking on his heels. "Must be."

"Yep," I said. "I've been me all day. Yesterday, too."

They looked at each other again. When they looked back at me this time, the tall one scowled, while the short one grinned.

"Idaho," said the short one.

The tall one nodded. "That detective Matt Turk told us about from Idaho."

"And you must be Bubba and Junior," I said.

They were right on schedule for another meaningful glance, when McDade came back. I doubt if anybody would have given the old man a second thought, except that he was carrying a side-by-side, double-barreled shotgun, and Pharaoh was at his heel. I thought about the .45 under the seat of my car, and wished idly that I had it instead in my hip pocket. I

147

probably wouldn't need it, though, unless Pharaoh got out of control.

"Boys." McDade's face was bright, but there was no smile in his voice. He scuffed to a stop, and it was very quiet there in the yard. Except for Pharaoh gnashing his tusks. "I was just cleaning this old gun." McDade raised the shotgun and looked through the barrels, first at the tall man, then the short one. "But it's already clean." He found two red shells in his pants pocket, fed one into each barrel, and snapped the action closed. "Birdshot. Case some dog comes around. What was it on your mind?"

While the tall man seemed completely distracted by Pharaoh, the short man looked squarely at McDade, and nodded toward me. "We seen you leave the hotel with this fella. Thought we'd look him up, ask about the elk hunting out there in the wild West."

The tall man stroked his jaw, and managed to take his eyes off the big red boar. "We're deer hunters ourselves."

"I've hunted deer, too," I said. "But you're right, I'd rather hunt elk. We've got a lot of elk where I come from. Hell, I've got a couple of ex-wives used to shoot elk."

McDade grunted and rested the shotgun casually on his shoulder. "I mostly just hunt fools."

I felt myself breathing steadily during the short standoff that followed. When the tall man raised his hand abruptly, McDade tensed and Pharaoh took a step forward. I was ready to lay my shoulder into McDade's ribs before he started shooting people, but these two bozos were on their own with the hog. Instead, the tall man flashed a grin and ran his fingers languorously through his hair.

"I guess that about does it, Dad," the tall man said to McDade. He glanced nervously from the shotgun to Pharaoh. "Whataya say, Wash?" he said to his sidekick.

"Yeah," Wash said, "sure. Just a little travelogue, get everybody's directions down pat." He had been staring at me ever since he'd come out on the short end of a comparison with my ex-wives. I would have felt better if he'd been looking at the shotgun. A man with normal mental processes would have attended very closely to a loaded shotgun. I know I was thinking about that shotgun, and I hadn't even had the pleasure of looking back down the barrels into McDade's drunken eyes. And a man with *sane* mental processes would have shown at least moderate concern about two-thirds of a ton of pork with an ill temper.

"We'll be headin' back to town," said the tall man. He took a couple of steps toward the truck. When Wash didn't move, he reached back and grabbed him roughly by the sleeve. "I said, we'll be heading back to town now." His voice was louder this time.

Wash was still staring at me as though I had stolen his girl at the high school dance. "Next time you see your boss," I said, "tell him I understand how tough it is to get good help."

Now blondie was looking at me, too. "Nobody wants to push this, cowboy. Especially Turk."

"That's good to hear," I said. "Far as I'm concerned, we're just a bunch of good old boys with some hunting stories."

Blondie nodded vigorously. "And now we all know where to hunt and where not to hunt." He opened the door and climbed back in the truck.

Wash, on the other hand, couldn't manage to find room in his brain for anything but an attitude. He walked slowly in front of the truck, glaring at me all the way. He stopped near the hood and pointed his finger at me, about to impart some wisdom, when Tory McDade said, "Pharaoh!"

The boar charged forward, plowing his head into the driver's door, and kept on charging until his tusks had ripped a gash about three feet long in the sheet metal. By the time Pharaoh had freed his tusks from the door and readied himself for another attack, Wash was inside the cab, the engine was running, and Blondie had decided not to wait around to see if Pharaoh was in the mood for dessert.

"Kids," McDade said sourly as the dust settled behind the truck. "Coupla dumb hammerheads."

"Who are they?"

"I thought I just told you."

"Not *what*," I said, *"Who."*

"Same thing. How the hell I know who they are? Some mama and daddy's errors in judgment, shoulda been left on the sheets. Name on the truck tells you who they are."

After taking a long, satisfied piss in the yard, Pharaoh waddled back to his pen without needing to be told.

I thought about the other night, when I'd bumped heads with Nick Serette. "What is it about this town," I said. "People keep trying to mess me up?"

"You ever think maybe it's you and not the town?"

"Me? Jesus Christ, you're the one carried a shotgun into this mess. You're the one with the homicidal hog."

McDade seemed to ponder what had transpired in the last five minutes. "Maybe," he said.

"Right," I said. "Maybe."

He broke open the shotgun, and the two shells kicked out onto the ground. "Like you said, nobody ever comes out here. Nobody. You got to understand, Banks, we ain't bad people around here. We just get scared sometimes so we talk tough, act stupid."

I asked him if he was talking about himself or Matthew Turk.

"All of us," McDade said. "I'm just talking about people. *Us.*"

I thanked McDade for his time, and he thanked me

for the communist vodka. When I said good-bye, he reminded me that his own car was still back in town. He was glad to accept a ride. He said he'd made the trip on foot before, but never when he was sober, and what need was there to start a new trend now?

McDade was nodding off when I saw the white pickup waiting at the first crossroads. He awoke with a start when the car swerved back and forth as I reached under the seat for the .45. The pistol was cocked and locked. I tucked it under my right thigh. McDade coughed discreetly, and looked as if he were trying to decide if the car was moving slowly enough for him to risk jumping out.

As I got nearer, Blondie and Wash stepped out and ambled toward the front of the truck.

"Maybe you ought to just drive on by," McDade said.

He was right. I could have smiled and waved and headed on down life's highway toward town. But that had all the markings of a long, dusty chase up and down bad roads. If the threat of a shotgun and a genuine hog attack hadn't dissuaded these two crackers, something had to be done.

"You ever drive a rented car?" I asked.

"No." McDade could have been contemplating biogenetics. "No, I can't say as I have."

"Well, I have. Take my word for it, the people who rent cars always give you shit when you bring one back all banged up."

"Yes, yes, I suppose they do." My sidekick had just discovered the secret of life.

When I got out of the car, I could see the uncertainty in Blondie's eyes. But if any part of Wash were ever uncertain, he had long since stomped on it.

"You ain't got no fucking hog here," Wash said. He was still moving my way when I thumbed the safety on the .45, and fired four quick rounds into the radiator of the truck. With that, everybody managed to stop in time.

"What the fuck was that!" Wash said. "What call you got—"

"It was an accident," I said calmly. I frowned down at the gun, then looked at Wash and shrugged. "It's a new gun. I never carried a gun like this before. You know how it goes."

"You're a fucking maniac," Blondie said. Green coolant was running in several steady streams onto the ground.

"I told you. It was an accident," I said, getting back into the car. "Honest." When I looked in the rearview mirror, both men were still standing in the road, looking after me. I was shaking, and screaming at myself for being a prime, living example of Tory McDade's theory of human behavior, a guy who talked tough and acted stupid. Then I remembered Tory McDade the man, who was sitting slackjawed beside me in the rocketing Chevrolet.

"I know several good people in the mental health field," McDade finally said.

I told him I'd keep his offer in mind.

Tory McDade was perfectly content for me to drop him off outside the Hotel Mauvaisterre bar. A few minutes later, I found Freddie Pointdexter gassing his cruiser at the station at the four-way stop. I told him what had happened. He wanted to know if I was making a confession. "I wouldn't be too hasty if I were you," Pointdexter said.

I told him I wasn't being hasty at all. "I come to you," I said, "it's a report. You come to me later on, that's when it's a confession."

"That's what I'm trying to say, son. You make a report, that means something happened, means I got to investigate. I thought you said you used to be a cop."

"I did. I'd have been pissed off, a guy did this in my

town. I'd just as soon not have you pissed off until it's really necessary."

Pointdexter topped off his tank and waved to the attendant inside. "That's a real healthy outlook," he said. "Let me talk to Matthew Turk before you go making rash statements to law enforcement, okay? Sounds like a couple of Turk's boys got overheated and you accidentally killed an innocent pickup truck. Sounds like an entirely civil matter to me."

Well, any way you look at it, cap a pickup truck and you need a cold beer. That's just what I had in mind after leaving Freddie Pointdexter at the gas pump. First, though, I decided to swing by the Heyman house and touch base with Sarah. But all I found there was a note that said she had gone shopping, and the kids were loose on the town. Go ahead inside, the note said, and make yourself at home. And please stay for dinner. About 7:00. That was what the note said.

I tried the door, and found it unlocked.

My first tentative steps across the hardwood foyer sounded hollow, almost as though the house were abandoned, not simply empty. I stopped short, and listened. The rooms were full of voices, of course, the kind that echo up and down the halls of your imagination. The kids late for school. Holidays. Laundry day and chores. Shouts of excitement and anger. Whispers of love.

Make yourself at home.

Make yourself at home. Did that mean toss our closets, paw through our drawers? Solve our life together?

I remembered the horde of family photographs in the sitting room. It struck me that I was best friends with a small town kid who became a doctor, but I was only acquainted with the drunken doctor who had tried to enlist me in his obsession.

And fuck you, too. See you around. The last words Gerry said to me that night outside the motel.

But what did I know about the man who had filled in the twenty years between those two versions of Gerry? *Where was he?*

I stood there in the foyer and stuck my hands in my pockets the way I would at a crime scene. I caught the faint odor of floral air freshener. I tried a narrow door to my left, and found a coat closet. Among the many coats inside were a London Fog trenchcoat, and a red and black plaid wool mackinaw, the kind old-time loggers once wore back in Montana. I stared at the mackinaw, trying to remember if I'd seen Gerry wearing it in any of the photographs.

And then I was reminded that there was still a third version of Gerry Heyman—the version captured in Freddie Pointdexter's crime scene photos. Why had I put off seeing those pictures? It was part of my job, part of what Sarah could expect for her money.

But I knew without seeing them what Pointdexter's pictures would show. A car, an empty road and a dead man. Limbs tight with rigor mortis, and molded exactly to the contours of the ditch. Tousled hair caked with dried blood. Flat eyes staring down into the heart of the earth. I'd seen it all before, seen it so often I could look at each picture and not bat an eye. But while I easily had the stomach for those pictures, I decided I didn't have the heart. The last thing I needed at the moment was to have my old friend transformed into just another stiff.

Well, one thing was sure: Gerry no longer lived in this big, clean house. Sarah did. My employer.

Or was she? Sure, she'd signed the check, yet I found myself barely able to be with her. So perhaps I was really working for a dead man. Working for Gerry. I guess that's always the way it is with homicide. Human being equals body equals evidence. Thing. Stuff. But there is someplace where the dead always go. Call it the outer office of your mind. And there they wait, your ultimate clients, while you do their work.

So rather than make myself at home in Sarah's house, I went back to the Hotel Mauvaisterre, where Mike set me up with a schooner that might have been custom made to fit my hand.

11

"P eople will talk about us," Sarah said. We were walking. It was after ten o'clock. She was dressed in a white cotton blouse and dark blue shorts, and had her hair done in a French braid. "They'll call me a merry widow. Or worse . . . probably worse."

We had finished dinner at Sarah's house, and installed the kids in front of the TV. Now we were out trying to walk off the lethargy brought on by eating enough fettucine to ballast a ship, and drinking enough Chianti to float it.

I circled an arm around Sarah's waist. "Screw a bunch of people and what they say," I said. My legs had a distant feel to them. I wondered if having too much food in your belly could cut off circulation to your lower extremities. Or worse, your brain. Our hips bumped several times before Sarah adjusted her gait to mine and we fell into an easy rhythm.

"You haven't changed a bit," Sarah said. She pulled away momentarily, just long enough and far enough to take my arm in hers.

"Yes I have."

I had told Sarah over dinner about my brush with death in the jaws of Pharaoh, and my slaughter of Matthew Turk's pickup truck. "A reversion to my desperado instincts," I said.

"What a luxury." She sounded like a woman who was wondering if she was getting her money's worth.

Sarah and I used to walk together for hours. Walks after concerts, walks after parties, with change in the air and the smell of marijuana smoke in our clothes. Walks after loving and before sleep. One step after another through the night. Tonight, we were looking over our shoulders at forty. The air smelled rich with wet soil and roses, and no matter how far we walked, we would never find our way back to 1966.

I said, "Did you ever wonder why I always stayed in touch with you and Gerry through letters, but never came back to visit?"

"No."

"Not even when my own home was nearby? Didn't it ever occur to you that I had to be in and out of this part of the country now and then, coming back to see my own people. How come I never got around to coming here? To Mauvaisterre?" The windows of the neat, prosperous houses we passed were either dark or flickering with the light of television sets. There was no traffic. We were out on the street after bedtime. We were committing sin. Trust me, I thought, I'm an expert on sin.

"No," she said again. "I don't really think about those things. I know that must sound crazy to you, but it's true. I just live my life straight ahead. All the time. Straight ahead."

"It doesn't sound crazy at all."

Sarah laughed. "Leo, you're the most cynical idealist I ever knew."

"I prefer to think of myself," I said, "as an idealistic cynic."

"Oh, of course." She laughed again. "How could I have made such a mistake?"

Nearly twenty-five years ago, I had climbed onto a bus headed for the Great Lakes Naval Station, while Sarah watched from the curb. I can still see her, all her long hair tucked up under a floppy leather hat, her slender arm falling slowly to her side after a last, desolate good-bye. Months later, after the breakup and the news about her and Gerry, I counted myself lucky she'd come to see me off at all. Even then, she knew more than I did what a long trip that would be, how long that good-bye would last.

"If we were in Montana—" I said, thinking of the place that was now completely my home.

"What?" she interrupted. "If we were in Montana, what? The birds would sing more sweetly? The moon hang closer to the earth?" She looked up at me and batted her eyes. "The course of true love be less bumpy?" I felt the pressure of her arm tighten on mine as she pulled closer. "I know better than that. And so do you."

We were nearing the four-way stop at the edge of what passed in Mauvaisterre for downtown. The street ahead brightened with the amber glow of mercury lamps. It struck me that I would never know who had murdered my friend Gerry Heyman, and that it didn't really matter. Some mysteries you're privileged to solve, others you're cursed to live with forever. Nothing profound in any of that.

Sarah turned away from the lights, steering us toward the boat ramp. The parking lot was empty, one of the two streetlights burned out. We bore left, along a gravel path behind the retaining wall. Soon, the ground began to rise, and the wall faded into a shallow hillside. We passed beneath a grove of trees, and came out in a park overlooking the river. I looked around. The park was like a small, grassy cup scooped out of dense woods there in the heart of town. The moon cast a dull glow on the muddy river.

"I knew what I wanted," she said, "from the time I waited my first table. Spending my whole life humping around under a load of burgers and fries wasn't in the picture."

I took her hand. "So I understand. Gerry told me you always intended to marry a doctor. I never knew that. Never even suspected it, even when we were living together."

"Doctors. Yes." She took a deep breath, and made a whistling noise as she let it out. "Doctors. They make a lot of money, and they spend a lot of time away from home."

"They also heal the sick, perform miracles. Stuff like that."

"Yes, that too."

"And all these years," I said, "I thought I'd been a victim of indiscreet politics. Of interfering with your plans to save the world through better chemistry, sex and picket lines."

When Sarah looked at me, her eyes were hooded with sadness. "Sometimes everybody needs to keep from feeling dead inside. I'm sorry."

"If we were in Montana," I said.

"You keep saying that, Leo." She was impatient. "If we were in Montana, what?"

"If we were in Montana, I'd do this." I grabbed her around the waist and kissed her, kissed her long and hard, then let her go.

"Dear God," she breathed, "I feel just like Maureen O'Hara."

"That's what I mean," I said. "I've been divorced in better style than you ever managed to be married. It's your loss."

"Maybe so." She sat down on the grass, and pulled me down beside her.

The river made tiny, lapping noises along the bank,

and all around us the night was damp and heavy. I heard the faint throb of engines, and pointed out the lights on a long line of barges approaching from upstream. As we watched, a great bulk of steel materialized out of the darkness. From the bridge, a long beam of light swept back and forth across the channel. The engines grew louder, seeming to vibrate up through the damp ground, then faded, leaving behind a moonlit froth churning up from the props.

And then it was quiet again.

When I looked at Sarah, she was crying.

"I'd have done anything to keep you," I said.

"You made the deadness go away," she said. She raised my hand to her breast, and kissed me.

Goddamn it, I thought, laying her back onto the grass and finding the buttons of her blouse. Goddamn it all.

"You always made the deadness go away, Leo," she whispered. Sweat glistened on her forehead. The inside of her thigh felt cool and soft, then warmed. "Always."

It was nearly midnight when I said goodnight to Sarah on her porch, feeling like a kid heading home from his first date. Sooner or later, I knew, guilt would hunt me down, leave me sliced up and bleeding. But for now, it was a lovely evening, warm and clear, with a thick mat of stars spread out above the silent trees. I had left my car at the hotel, and on the walk back I decided to make another swing down by the river. Rivers aren't an antidote to guilt, but sometimes they can soften the blow. When I got to the boat ramp, a pair of headlights swung in behind me. A moment later, the sheriff's cruiser went by and cut me off. Otis Wiesel got out.

"Hey, pardner," he said. His nasal whine sounded like that of a tomcat perched on a garbage can at midnight.

"Don't shoot!" I threw up my hands. It had been too long a day, and was now too nice a night to get rousted.

"Shoot?" Wiesel pushed his cap back on his head. "Naw, hell no, I ain't gonna shoot. That bidness last night, that was just work, that's all."

"And tonight?"

Wiesel tilted his head back and scratched his Adam's apple, then looked back at me and grinned. "This here's bidness, too. I got me some theories on that doctor's murder. Thought you might be interested."

"Maybe tomorrow."

"Whyn't you get in the car."

"I got someplace I have to go."

"I'll give you a ride."

"I'd rather walk."

"No you wouldn't." Otis flexed his scrawny shoulders and shook out his hands. "Wouldja?"

This was a man who could hurt himself just trying to look menacing. For his own protection, I gave up and got in the car.

"You must've worked on a lot of these things," Wiesel said as we got underway. "Murders, I mean."

"Enough to last me," I said. There were perhaps half a dozen radios stacked one atop another from the drivetrain hump to nearly level with the dash, enough radios to conduct a small war.

"That thing the other night," Otis said, "you shouldn't take that personal. Hell, you know how hard I gotta hunt to find somebody to bust in this here burg?" He tugged at the end of his mustache, then looked over at me and winked. "Bustin' people, you know, it gets in a lawman's blood. You get a little barn sour, you don't bust somebody once in a while."

I nodded wisely. "A man's gotta do what a man's gotta do." At this rate, we'd be peeing on light poles before the night was over.

As we cruised through the dark streets, Otis Wiesel began to ramble on about, as he had called them, his theories. First there was the escaped mental patient theory. Because who else but a crazy man would kill somebody like that? In the middle of nowhere and for no reason. Then there was the drug deal gone bad theory, in case there was a reason. Because, you see, everybody knew Doc Heyman had lots more money than he ever could have earned pushing pills. And what about the abortion theory, because everybody in town knew Doc Heyman flushed out a baby now and then. Let's say some gal's daddy got wind of her trouble, decided to settle the score. And hell, you couldn't even rule out A-rab terrorists, not these days, why just last week . . .

Okay, so somewhere along the line I had deeply offended God, and now I was settling the tab. I was about to demand that Otis take me back to the hotel, when one of the radios crackled.

Otis grabbed up the mike. "Yeah, 10-4, go ahead."

Otis listened to the call, a domestic beef, for about fifteen seconds. Then, before I could say anything, he threw down the mike, hit the overheads and siren, and jammed his foot all the way to the firewall. When the car rocketed ahead, I felt the muscles in my neck give way, and I hoped the damage wouldn't be permanent.

"You was a lawman, Banks," Otis shouted above the siren. "I bet you sure miss this kind of thing, huh?"

"Clyde and Dorie Phitts," Otis said, driving like a madman over country roads. "Clyde and Dorie don't get along."

We ended up at a little shack about five miles out of town along the river, a shack that made Tory Mc-Dade's place look like something you'd see in an *Architectural Digest* layout. After skidding to a stop in

162

the dirt yard, Otis shut off the car, and we could hear the snarl of a small engine.

"Chainsaw," Otis said, shaking his head.

Outside the car, Otis snugged both of his handguns into their holsters, then slipped the nightstick into the ring on his belt. As an afterthought, he kicked his right foot up onto the bumper and adjusted the fit of the Rambo knife.

Inside the shack, somebody revved the chainsaw.

"Fact is, Banks, Clyde and Dorie don't get along real bad," Otis said, breaking into a trot.

I figured that one of two things could happen to me. Either I'd get hacked up by a chainsaw, or I'd get shot half a dozen times by Otis Wiesel. So I hung back.

"They was supposed to see a counselor," Otis said over his shoulder. "I don't know what the hell happened."

As we neared the porch, there was a terrible crash, followed by a table, or what turned out to be half a table, which came flying out the door.

"Clyde!" Otis shouted. "Goddamnit Clyde, it's me, Otis."

The chainsaw raced again. A woman screamed.

"Clyde! You dumb asshole, what's goin' on in there!"

It occurred to me that if Otis Wiesel wasn't going to use any of his guns, the least he could do was give one to me.

Then the chainsaw stopped, and quiet swept over us.

"Otis?" It was a man's voice, hoarse and raw.

"Otis?" Now it was the woman. "Goddamnit, Otis, git him outta here."

We made it across the porch, past halves of chairs, boxes, dishes, even half a ratty floral sofa that looked as if it had been improved by the chainsaw. The screen door hung by only the bottom hinge. Inside, the cramped front room was wall-to-wall debris. Dorie stood in the doorway to the kitchen, holding a large pair of barbecue tongs in one hand, and a long-necked bottle of Budweiser in the other. And Clyde, of course, was holding on for dear life to a chainsaw.

"Jesus Christ on a crutch," Otis said, surveying the wreckage. Everything, once you got to looking at it, had been cut in half. "Clyde, I thought you two went to a counselor."

"We did," Clyde said, out of breath. He was dressed in grease-stained khaki pants, and a sleeveless undershirt. The tattooed wings of some kind of bird spread across his partially bared chest. His black hair was carefully arranged in the style favored by Elvis during the pre-Vegas period. "We did. Then I did it one even better than that. I went to a goddamn *lawyer.*" Clyde pulled a bundle of crudely folded papers from his hip pocket, and handed them over to Otis Wiesel. "And the *lawyer* went to a *judge,* and I got me a goddamn *order.*"

Otis unfolded the papers and studied them.

"Says right there," Clyde went on, "me and Dorie, we gotta divide all our property equal. That's all I'm doing, Otis, I just come over tonight to get my half." Clyde hefted the chainsaw and gave a yank on the starting cord, firing the machine to life.

"Clyyyyyyde!" Dorie shrieked above the engine.

"Clyde!" Otis shouted. "Goddamnit, Clyde, shut that goddamn thing off!"

Once again, Clyde Phitts shut down the chainsaw, and this time set it aside. "I'm almost done, Otis," he said. "Nothing left but the stove and the freezer. Refrigerator doesn't work anymore."

"Clyde, you stupid ox," Otis said.

"Otis, I'm just following the law. You read them papers."

"Maybe so," Otis said, "but you start in on that

freezer, all you're gonna do's tear up a good chain-saw."

"Who in the hell is he?" Dorie said. She was pointing a thick finger at me. "Who in the hell are you?"

When Otis took time out to make introductions, it was as though Clyde and Dorie took time out from their battle. Dorie smoothed back her mousy brown hair, then pulled her pink T-shirt down over her paunch. Clyde wiped his palms on his hips before offering me his hand.

"Hey," Clyde said.

Now that everybody had managed to take a step back from the brink, the situation calmed down. Otis told Clyde that the judge probably didn't mean for his order to be taken quite as literally as Clyde had taken it. And to Dorie, he said that, hell, Clyde was just trying to do what he thought he had to do, and now the damage was done, so why didn't she act like the good woman everybody knew she was and make the best out of a bad situation. Twenty minutes later, Clyde was headed back over to his brother's trailer, where he'd been staying lately, Dorie was calm and Otis and I were on the road back to town.

Although I thought Otis Wiesel had done a good job of defusing a lousy call, I couldn't help wondering why, if he needed to arrest somebody so bad, he hadn't punched a ticket for Clyde.

"Can't arrest him," Otis said, "he's my cousin. Come to think of it, Dorie's my cousin, too."

"I hope that doesn't mean she's his sister."

Otis thought about this long enough that I started to get queasy. "Probably not," he said.

Back in Mauvaisterre, most of the houses were completely dark now, the streets empty. Otis didn't have much to say as he herded the big white car through the quiet town. When I asked him to drop me off at the hotel, he ignored me.

"She sure is a beautiful woman," Otis said as he

approached the Heyman house. He turned off on the side street, cut his headlights, then turned again onto the street that ran behind the house. The only light burning was in a large window overlooking the backyard. "Goes out a lot, too," he said. "Surprised she's home."

"You seem to know a lot," I said.

"Yeah," Wiesel breathed. "Yeah." He reached into the back seat and dug into a black nylon bag, pulling out a large pair of binoculars. "I drive around these same little streets all night, why wouldn't I know things?" He focused on the lighted window. A figure passed in front of the window. "Mmmmmm, dear." Otis looked over at me, grinned and offered me the glasses.

I shook him off. "What do you know that you haven't told people? About this whole Heyman mess?" Cops always have a stash of information, bits and pieces they cling to tighter than money.

"Sure you don't wanna take a look?" Wiesel said, laughing now. He tucked the glasses in his crotch. A leer crossed his green-tinted face. "She gets around, I can tell you that much. Sometimes she even gets down to that little park on the river. Know what I mean?"

My arm shot across the car, and I grabbed Wiesel by his scrawny neck. He slapped my arm away.

"Easy, buddy boy!" Wiesel gasped. He swung his head from side to side, stretching his neck, then laughed again. "Ain't love grand."

I started to speak, but what was there to say? I got out of the car, and Otis drove off, leaving me there on the hot, spongy asphalt. When I glanced back up at the window, the curtains had been drawn but the light remained.

We're just alike. That's what Sarah had said afterward, in the tiny park alongside the river. "You and me, Leo. Too many things we had to figure out for ourselves. We'd have torn each other apart."

I could still see her standing there in the moonlight, looking down at me for a long moment, before stepping into her shorts. A bead of sweat had gathered between her breasts, and glistened like silver down her belly. "I made an accommodation with one man who understood. You divorced three women who, my guess is, couldn't. So what's the difference?" She slipped her long arms into the sleeves of her white blouse, buttoned it nearly to the top, then slowly tucked the tail into her shorts.

"My whole life since I met you," I said, "I keep trying to get back the way it was our first time. Like the whole world is holding its breath. You remember?"

"Yes."

"You ever come even close?"

"No."

"Not tonight? Not just now?"

She knelt down and kissed me. "No."

"You said I always made the deadness go away."

"You still do." Now she smiled. "But a person can't have everything, Leo. You can try like hell, but you can't get back what you're talking about. Not ever."

While I stood there in the street, the light in her window went out. I finally let myself relax, let the air explode from my lungs. That's where Sarah was wrong, where we weren't alike at all.

12

If I were back in Montana. Was it only last night that such a simple sentiment lured Sarah and me over the brink? The truth was that if I were back in Montana, I might at this very moment be sprawled out in a lawn chair on my broken-down back porch, chewing the fat with Pastor Roscoe Beckett, while the morning sunlight shot misty bolts through the cottonwood and willow trees, and lazy pigeons circled the Dolby Building across the Holt River. My mind would be clear of care. I would not be standing in a tepid shower, trying to sort out last night with Sarah. Strange as it may seem, I didn't feel that I had betrayed Gerry. But what about myself? What kind of luck is it that jars old love back to life? This whole case was stained forever with bad blood, half of it mine.

I tried to make the most of the water dribbling onto my shoulders. My father must have stayed in a hundred little joints just like the Hotel Mauvaisterre. After he gave up on farming—or did farming give up on him?—he traveled around the lower Midwest and

Midsouth for a chemical company, selling fertilizer, herbicides and pesticides. That was over thirty years ago, before developers started filling vacant lots with franchise motels. Once in a while, he would take me on a swing with him, perhaps through southern Missouri and northern Arkansas. I remembered sitting in rooms just like this one, which would be sweaty from a crowd of men playing cards and smoking cigars.

Dealing out hands of draw poker.

Glancing out of the corners of their eyes to see if the kid were listening.

There would be a bottle or two on the table, and the talk always ran to crops in the field and Jews on the Chicago Board of Trade.

And colored people who didn't even know the rudiments of proper behavior anymore. Infiltrated by the reds, you bet. J. Edgar Hoover said so himself.

And weather, both the kind of weather that came from the sky, and the kind that seemed to be building up a storm in people's hearts.

And of course they talked about church, too, because God still had a plan, even if folks had lately become blind to it.

My father was staying in a little hotel just like this in Chester, Illinois, on the summer night in 1965 when East St. Louis burned during a race riot. The next morning, on the highway not far out of town, he had a heart attack, ran his car off the road and that was the end of that.

Chester. That's the town where you'll find the Menard Correctional Facility. The joint. Where Mickey Cochran was doing time for murder the day my old man went over.

By God, I did not want to be in this little sweatbox of a town an instant longer, inside a hotel occupied by ghosts. This was the hotel where Otto Turk had brought his boy Matthew on the night of the murder. It was easy for me to imagine the boy trying to sleep through the noise of men coming and going all night, listening to them through the green, watery horror inside his own head.

The towel was threadbare and damp, unchanged from yesterday. It didn't matter. Despite the prized air conditioner, I broke out in a fresh sweat almost immediately.

Did I say ghosts? Wait a minute. Matthew Turk was certainly a long way from dead. Mickey Cochran was close to becoming a ghost, but close didn't count. And Otto Turk, people said, was still alive in St. Louis.

That left Grace Turk. But her voice was not among the sounds I kept hearing there in the old hotel. Whose face had she looked into that steamy summer afternoon? Was it true, what Cochran had said about her swimming? How could I ever know? What did Grace Turk have to say?

Cochran said that Otto Turk had beat him senseless for spying on his wife. I knew from much experience that men such as that also beat their wives for being spied upon.

Otto . . .

How old was Matthew Turk at the time of the murder? Fifteen? That night, he would have been in a man's world, a world of whispers in the hall, the bite of whiskey in the air. A man's world, wherein a boy would have no choice but to do the manly thing.

Otto Turk.

It was a relief when someone pounded on the door, jolting me out of my daydream. I pulled on a pair of shorts and opened the door just a crack to see who was there.

"Mornin', son," Freddie Pointdexter said, leaning past me into the room. Nick Serette was hot on his heels. "Whyn't you put some pants on, Leo," Pointdexter said.

As I reached for my jeans, I wasn't sure which made me feel more stupid, standing there in front of two men with my pants off, or being told by the hulking Pointdexter to put them on.

Serette slipped a hand inside his blue seersucker jacket and pulled out a long, thin cigar. "Mind if I smoke?" he said. As he spoke, he raked a kitchen match against the wall, leaving behind a smudge where the match had ignited with a long *whoosh*. "I didn't think so." He chuckled as he surveyed my accommodations. "I never been in these rooms before. What a dump. Banks, you ought to check out of here, then get yourself a blood test."

Pointdexter cleared his throat. "Nick here, being the State's Attorney and all, he's got a few details on his mind. Details about you."

Looking all the while at Serette, I said to Pointdexter, "He doesn't need you for that, Freddie. Most of the time, I'm pretty tame."

Serette said, "I'm going to ignore your bullshit, Banks." Which meant, of course, that he wouldn't—couldn't—ignore it at all.

It was tempting to tell Serette to go sit on a sharp stick. But he was, Pointdexter aside, the law in Big Sandy County. I'd already dragged him out of his car and humiliated him in public. What was the point in being a bully?

Serette rolled the cigar from the left side of his mouth to the right. "It's like I told you the other night, Banks. I've got a duty to look out for Sarah Heyman's best interests. And the best interests of other parties in this thing."

"Parties such as the Turk family?"

"They pay their taxes."

"I thought your duty was to find the truth."

"Give it a rest, okay?" he said. "I don't need a sermon from you on my duty."

"It's not my fault," I said. "Matthew Turk has managed to make himself look guilty as hell."

Serette gave his cigar a thoughtful, elaborate flourish. "I understand all that, Banks. Believe me—"

Pointdexter cut in. "We've known from the start about the letters and the phone calls. Sarah told us."

"Hell," Serette said, "Turk even admits to that stuff."

"Don't forget the two mouth-breathers at McDade's," I said.

"That, too," Serette said. He coughed, and scowled at the cigar. "You can make a case against Turk, hell's fire, more power to you."

"Assuming," I said, "he's the right guy."

"Hey, look," Serette said, "we're not a lynch mob."

I thought about old Mickey Cochran huddled around his cancer out at the nursing home. But I let it pass.

"All I really want to know," Serette went on, "is how much . . . what should I call it? Extraneous trouble? How much extraneous trouble you plan to stir up in the process."

"Beats me." I reached for the comb that was lying on the dresser, and began slicking back my hair. "How much extraneous trouble you got?" I stuck the comb in my hip pocket and dug through my suitcase for a clean shirt, then looked at Pointdexter. "What's he really after, Freddie? I can't believe he hauled you up here just to lean on me."

"Do you go out of your way to be a jerk?" Serette said.

I slipped into a pale blue chambray shirt. "Once in a while. But it seems like I never have to go very far." I smiled at Serette, and brushed a cigar ash from his sleeve. "Somebody always meets me halfway. Freddie?"

Serette flicked more ashes from his cigar to the floor. "I know you think Pointdexter and I are a couple of rubes. But we've spent a lot of time—a *lot* of time—on Heyman's murder. We still get calls in the middle of the night from little old ladies think there's a murderer crouching outside in the azaleas."

"And sooner or later," I said, "all those little old ladies will vote."

Serette nodded. "That's right."

When I glanced at Freddie Pointdexter, he looked embarrassed. I shrugged. What did I care who the people in Mauvaisterre voted for, as long as it wasn't Nixon?

"Believe me," Serette went on, "the evidence against Turk—if you can call it evidence—isn't nearly strong enough to beef him on this thing."

I smiled at Serette. "Okay."

Serette scowled. "What do you mean, okay?"

"Just, okay. That's all." I kicked my suitcase under the bed. "What do you think, Nick?" I straightened my collar. "Nice and conservative. Kind of salt of the earth. I think this shirt is perfect."

Serette shook his head, and his eyes looked slack. "You're a fucking maniac."

"Well," I said, "it's still a nice shirt. A Ralph Lauren knockoff, you know. I order them from this outlet place, a catalog they send me every—"

"I can't believe this," Serette said. "We come here like serious guys, trying to work this thing out . . ."

He turned away and stalked to the bathroom, where he threw his cigar into the toilet. Pointdexter looked after him, rolled his eyes, then put on his sunglasses. When Serette came back, he raised his finger toward me, and I just knew he was going to start wagging it. Luckily for us all, he was interrupted by another knock on the door. This was turning out to be quite the morning for visitors. Without consulting me, Freddie Pointdexter answered the knock, and found Sarah Heyman.

"Oh . . ." Sarah's face went blank with surprise. "I'm sorry, I didn't know . . ."

"It's all right," Serette said. I realized that Sarah was staring at him.

"No, please." She regained her composure. "I just stopped by to see Leo. See what his plans were for today." She was talking to Serette, too.

Pointdexter stood rocking back and forth on his heels. Serette seemed to have run out of anything to say. I smiled at Sarah, then stepped near her and gave her a short hug and a kiss on the cheek.

"You know me," I said, "busy, busy, busy."

"I know," Sarah said. She thanked me again, and said she would see me later at the house. I said that sounded like a wonderful idea to me. Then she excused herself to us all, and left.

Serette didn't waste any time deciding that he and Pointdexter would be on their way, too. Before leaving, though, he told me to be in his office at ten o'clock that morning. There was a man, he said, who wanted to see me. I pressed him for more, but he was off.

When the two men reached the head of the stairs, I called Pointdexter back. I could have looked him up later, but I wanted Serette to wonder what was going on.

"How long have those two been messing with each other?" I said softly, after making sure that Serette was out of earshot.

Pointdexter could barely contain his pleasure. "Oh, I don't know, I'd say off and on for about ten years. Ever since Serette moved into town."

"They must be getting good at it by now." If I listened very hard, it seemed that I could hear Sarah's light footstep all the way down the stairs, through the lobby, out the door. I swear I could.

"Must be," Pointdexter said, heading back down the dim hall. "Otherwise, you'd think they'd give it up altogether."

Downstairs, Big Mike was watching a beach movie from the sixties. Frankie was singing to Annette, who still didn't have any problem saying "no."

"This poor cluck," Big Mike said, pointing his thumb toward the TV. "Never gets any. You on your way to see Serette?"

"Maybe," I said. "Maybe not."

Big Mike laughed. "Walls like paper in this place. Anyway, I figured something was up, that Serette fella using Freddie Pointdexter for a bodyguard. That's what happens, you whip a guy's ass."

"I wouldn't say I whipped his ass."

"Sure you did, son. You go and drag a man out of his car, he lets you get away with it, that's an ass-whippin' in my book."

"I thought you didn't see anything."

"I didn't." Big Mike's face was tight with joy when he looked up at me. "I was watchin' this great show on the TV. Contest for women bodybuilders. I tell you, them gals could hurt you. I ever tell you I was a sports enthusiast? No, I never seen a thing."

Frankie got dumped in the ocean. Annette swooned. I boogied.

"God, I love cable," Big Mike said as I tugged open the door.

Lazy traffic circled the town square. Everybody, it seemed, stared at me as if I were some sort of invader, and everybody also smiled and waved. Hell, the whole town brought to mind a recurring dream I've had since making up my mind twenty years ago to stay in Montana forever. One day in the midst of my life, I become aware that I am back in my little hometown in southern Illinois. It is a beautiful morning in early summer. I don't know how or why I am there. I meet people on the street, whom I do not know, though everybody talks to me like an old friend. Nothing in their conversation tells me why I am there, what I'm supposed to do. But the people are all happy and confident, and the *rightness* of my being there is so obvious it need not even be discussed. Once, when I was still married to Deirdre, my third and final wife, I told her about this dream. She labeled it a nightmare.

As I cut across the town square, over lush grass under rustling oaks, through green, embraceable light past the bronze statue of Lincoln, I passed an old man and woman sitting on a park bench holding hands. The man wore clip-on sunglasses. His thinning hair was parted low on his head in milky blond streaks. Through a red and white striped straw, the woman sipped a cool drink from a large blue Dixie cup.

"You must be in town for the picnic," she said.

I slowed and smiled down at her. "I beg your pardon?"

"The picnic." She set the cup aside and dabbed at the corner of her mouth with the fingertips of her left hand.

"V.F.W.," the man said. "If he doesn't know, Betty, that's not why he's come to town."

"No," I said, "I'm sorry, that's not why I'm here."

"But you'll have to go," she said. "Friday. The day after tomorrow. There's a parade and everything."

I said I'd try to make it, then moved on. When I glanced back at the couple, I saw the man nod at something she whispered. And then he gave her a soft, grazing kiss on the temple.

It was just shy of ten o'clock when I started up the broad stone steps of the Mauvaisterre County Courthouse. The tall, solid wood door displayed intricately carved vines, and was as heavy on its hinges as time itself. Inside, I suppressed an urge to walk on tiptoe across the dark oak floor. The walls were lined with black and white photographs of men in the uniforms of assorted wars. I walked past the open doors of offices, inside which women with blue hair rolled into buns looked up from papers but said nothing and did not smile.

Nick Serette's office was on the second floor. His secretary was out, but I found Serette himself sitting behind a battered wooden desk in the inner office. He was turned toward the tall, open window, which was covered with Venetian blinds. The blinds were open. The window seemed to invite a breeze that was destined never to arrive. Serette was on the telephone.

"Come on in, Banks," Serette said, without turning away from the window. He hung up the phone, which sat on a credenza to his right. There was a faint squeak from his high-backed chair as he slowly rocked back and forth. His desk was covered with loose papers and manilla folders. Framed diplomas and certificates hung on the wall to my left, while the wall to my right was laden with shelves full of law books. As I wandered into the room, I ran a finger over one of the bookshelves, and found it dusty as a tomb.

The office had the feel of a heavy, cluttered box. I had already found my way to one of the two chairs in front of the desk, when Serette swiveled around and faced me completely. "Have a seat. Sorry about the heat, the damn air conditioner went tits up."

"Thanks," I said, wondering if Serette's newfound affability was on the level, or just a clever disguise.

The two chairs were upholstered in coarse, lavender fabric, and seemed incongruously modern, in contrast to the other office furnishings. Serette leaned back. When he clasped his hands behind his head, his chins developed several creases over the open collar of his white shirt.

"I watched you walk across the square," Serette said. "Saw you come up the steps, heard that big door open and close, heard you walk down the hall, climb the stairs." He leaned forward and balanced his elbows on his desk. "Before this goes any farther, I want to do something I intended to do earlier this morning at the hotel."

I debated any number of sarcastic replies, before deciding again that acting like a bully was not in the best interest of my long-term mental health. Serette took my silence as a cue to keep talking.

"I want to explain," he said. "About that night outside the hotel. You were right, I was following you. I was waiting outside the Heyman house, and I followed you when you left."

"So I was right. So what? We both knew it that night." I wondered if he wanted to explain why he was following me, or why he'd behaved like an asshole when I caught him at it.

"I don't know if anybody told you, but I'm from Chicago," Serette said. "In a little downstate town like this, that alone makes me a suspicious character."

I shrugged. "So you're the bogeyman from the big city." He was right, nobody from downstate had much use for highrollers from that cute, toddlin' town up north.

"Plus," he said, "I'm a bachelor." His face broke into a nervous twitch that could have been a smile. "Disreputable on two counts. Anyway, you put those two things together, sometimes I tend to push a little hard. Besides being a public servant, I like Sarah Heyman. She's one of those women . . . people . . . you know, the kind you want to do a good job for. I guess having her call you in made me a little defensive. I overreacted."

I started to say something, but Serette waved me off. "Let's not dwell on it, okay? The main reason I had you come over here, there's a gentleman wants to see you." Serette glanced at his watch. "Should be here any minute."

"A gentleman?" I wondered if Matthew Turk was going to call me to account for slaughtering his company pickup.

"An old fellow named Alfonse Leake."

I started to tell Serette that I was about to go looking for Leake myself, but decided that the less he knew about my business, the better. "And what's his claim to fame?" I asked.

Serette stood up and put his hands in his pants pockets. "Listen, Banks, I ask you to come over here, treat you like a human being, the least you could do is spare me the coy bullshit. Everybody in town knows Gerry Heyman was trying to climb up on the cross for this guy Cochran. And from everything I can see, you're climbing right up after him. A guy in your position, he's going to take a long look around, see who's holding a hammer and nails. And Alfonse Leake, he's the man who prosecuted Cochran." Serette smiled down at me. His right hand was busy jingling a pocketful of change. "But you knew that, didn't you?"

I smiled back. "You're taxing my modesty, Nick."

"Modesty? I thought that quality was reserved for young actresses and old athletes." Serette turned away and looked out his window, down at the street. "Well, here's Alfonse now."

"I was hoping," I said, "maybe I'd flushed Otto Turk."

Serette laughed. "You haven't really flushed anybody, Banks. You're just being humored, something people figure they have to do to get you to give up and leave town. Far as Otto Turk goes, I expect he doesn't give a shit about you one way or another."

As Serette spoke, I heard the heavy door downstairs open and close, followed by the echo of footsteps proceeding along the downstairs hall at a surprisingly crisp pace. Now the footsteps sounded on the stairs, and Serette straightened. When he moved away from the window toward the door, I stood and followed his lead. We met Alfonse Leake in the outer office. Serette was about to make introductions, when the old man extended his hand to me and said, "I'm

Alfonse Leake. Judge Leake. And you must be Leo Banks, that notorious detective from Nevada I've been hearing about."

Leake's handshake was brisk and strong. He was dressed in a cream-colored linen suit, with a pale yellow shirt and a navy blue bow tie. His brown brogans bore a perfect shine, and a gold chain hung from an ornate elk's tooth fob dangling from the button hole in his lapel. The chain disappeared into the breast pocket of his jacket.

I smiled and dropped his hand. "I think 'notorious' is too flattering a word."

"Ah, and charming, too." Patches of pink scalp showed through Leake's pure white hair, which he wore close-cropped and scruffy. Despite the tie, his shirt encircled his neck loosely, giving the impression that he had shrunk inside his clothes. All in all, Leake had the deceptively frail look of a wrought iron fence.

He went on: "I understand, Mr. Banks, you're interested in some of our ancient history."

"I'm not sure it's exactly ancient."

"Take my word for it." His smile was warm and practiced. "If the history you're after is as old as me, it's ancient."

Serette offered us the use of his office, but Leake declined, saying that he didn't want to disrupt any of the county's important business. Instead, he suggested that he and I visit for a while in the courtroom, which was at the opposite end of the hall, and presently not in use.

"Thank you, Nicholas," Leake said, dismissing Serette with a clasp of the younger man's elbow. "Shall we, Mr. Banks?"

The courtroom was fairly small, and in the end not a lot different from most of the other courtrooms where I've spent time. The ceiling was high, perhaps fifteen feet, the woodwork dark. The gallery consisted of about a dozen pews, and was separated from the main arena by a heavy, wooden railing, which made a ninety degree bend to form the front of the jury box. The oak jurors' chairs were fastened to the floor, and upholstered in cracked, black leather. The bench was predictably tall and remote, an aerie. Leake escorted me through a swinging gate in the railing, and nodded toward one of the two massive tables before the bench. The air inside the room was close, musty, and the light an odd mixture of yellow and gray.

Using the chain attached to his lapel, Leake fished a large, gold watch from his breast pocket. "You'll have to forgive me this one affectation. My grandfather carried this watch at Cold Harbor. In 1864. He was only a corporal." Leake studied the time, then snapped the watch closed and dropped it back into his pocket. "I have less than an hour." I noticed the gold Masonic ring, set with rubies, on the third finger of his left hand.

"Big Sandy County is part of a judicial circuit," Alfonse Leake said. That meant, he explained, that judges made scheduled rounds, and sat in a number of courtrooms in other towns. Also, a judge might be called to sit in another circuit in order to resolve a conflict of interest. Leake gave out a small sigh. "I sat on that bench—or others just like it," he said, "and sentenced a number of men to death. But the State of Illinois never managed to electrocute a single one of them."

13

The chairs crackled as Leake and I sat down. The old man took a moment to get himself settled, crossing his legs and straightening the crease in his pants. Then he cleared his throat. "I heard about your rhubarb with my friend Nicholas."

"We were a little intense," I said.

"Yes . . . yes. That's what Nicholas told me." Leake looked evenly at me. "He wanted you charged, you know."

"And?" I knew what was coming before he said it.

Leake chuckled. "And luckily for you, I managed to get him calmed down."

"The wise elder statesman intervenes," I said. "I'm impressed."

Now Leake laughed outright. "I'd rather hear you were grateful."

"Gratitude. Sure. The universal political currency."

"One of them, yes. Fortunately for you, Nicholas Serette knows how to honor it." Leake went on to explain that he'd met Serette several years before at a Bar Association meeting, when Serette was a struggling young Chicago lawyer who Leake managed to persuade to move to Mauvaisterre and run for State's Attorney.

"I'm surprised he could get elected," I said. "An outsider and all."

"No opposition," Leake snorted. "Job doesn't pay enough for any of the local boys to give up their practice for."

"And because Serette's from Chicago," I said, "there's no chance he'll ever develop a private practice."

"Exactly. He's a perfect fit."

Leake, I decided, was a master of perfect fits. For a moment, he closed his eyes, while he fingered the elk's tooth. When he opened his eyes, they were clear and focused. Focused on the bench.

"I became a judge in nineteen forty," Leake said. "Sat for thirty-two years." He coughed slightly and shifted his attention to me. "Well, enough about my concerns. I know you're here about Doctor Heyman's death. And, I hear you've talked to Matthew Turk and Mickey Cochran. Retracing the good doctor's fated steps."

I decided not to waste my time asking Leake about his sources. Instead, I chose to go at him straight up. "Why did Gerry Heyman believe Mickey Cochran was innocent?"

"Because he was young. Not young on the calendar, maybe, but young here . . ." Leake rested a bony hand on his chest. "In his heart."

"A fool?"

"Who knows? He was entitled to believe whatever he wanted. We're all entitled to that. It's how we use the entitlement that determines if we're fools."

"And you believed Cochran was a murderer."

"Absolutely. He admitted it to me. Why else, in God's name, would I have sent him off to prison?"

"That's right. You and Buckshot McCool, the sheriff. You guys took his confession. Late that first night at the jail."

Leake raised his thin brows and pursed his lips. "Then you're not talking to me out of complete ignorance."

"Not complete, no." I told him about my visit with Gerry Heyman earlier that summer in Rozette. "He wanted me to come back here and prove Cochran innocent."

"And you turned him down," Leake said, shaking his head. "So you didn't believe Gerry's contention from the very start."

I was willing to let Leake think whatever he wanted about my motives for putting Gerry off. The truth was, I really hadn't cared then if Mickey Cochran was innocent or not. And I wouldn't care now, if Heyman were still pushing pills and collecting fees.

I said, "Gerry based his belief more or less on what Cochran told him one day down at Menard. Did he ever ask you for your side of things?"

"Yes."

"And did you tell him?"

"No."

"Why?"

"It was none of his business."

"And have you talked to anybody since Heyman was killed?"

"Not in any great detail."

This time, I just looked at him, not bothering to ask why. Finally, Leake broke the silence: "Of course, I've heard it around town that Mrs. Heyman has advanced the theory that her husband was murdered because of his inquiries into that old case. I told Nicholas I didn't think that theory held water."

"Then why talk to me?" I said.

"Why you? Yes, well, let's see. You were a policeman. How many years?"

"Twenty."

"So you've no doubt had countless people tell you their stories. Why do you suppose they do that? Surely not always out of a quest for justice. Or, in the case of the guilty, to make the best deal they can."

"People talk because they talk," I said. I was getting impatient with Leake's lessons in human behavior. But I resisted an impulse to push him. The door wasn't that far away, and there was nothing wrong with the old man's legs. "They talk because they can't *not talk*. One minute, a little voice starts whispering deep down inside, the next thing they know, the words just explode right out of them."

Leake's face broke into a smile. "Ka-boom!"

"But Heyman asked—"

Now it was Leake's turn to be impatient. "That boy wanted an explanation. I don't owe an explanation to anybody, especially boys. Oh, I know he was a grown man. But when you get to be my age, anybody who still has all his own teeth will always seem a boy."

As Leake spoke, I thought about my encounter with Matthew Turk, and realized that I had been wrong back in June, when I told Gerry Heyman that people in a small town like Mauvaisterre would not talk to an outsider about the Cochran case. First Turk and now Leake, falling over themselves to tell me their side of things. They had no choice. How else could they get a stranger to go away? Their stories were obviously shaded by time, memory, and self-interest. But regardless of what a man's story might be, telling it can be a way to keep you at bay.

"So," I said, "one day a long time ago a woman was murdered."

Leake straightened his tie, then smoothed the tails of his jacket over his hips. "I was having a glass of iced tea and listening to the radio. My wife was off doing something, I don't remember what, and I was home alone. We didn't have any children . . . never did have any children." He hesitated for a moment, licked his lips. "Buckshot McCool came up on the porch all out of breath. 'Al,' he said, 'Al, there's been a murder. A murder. Out to the Turk place.' Who, I naturally wanted to know, and Buckshot said, 'Why, her, Missus Turk, who else.'"

"Why *who else?*"

"Oh, because she was from St. Louis, that's all. Old Buckshot grew up on the sand ridge. He never even trusted people from inside the city limits of Mauvaisterre. Not so much a provincial man as he was primitive. Grace Turk, on the other hand, was a rich, beautiful woman from St. Louis. That made her exotic, and exotic people are the kind who get themselves murdered. Especially when they attach themselves to a man like Otto Turk."

"Sounds to me like maybe you should have suspected Turk," I said.

"We might have." Leake's nod was solemn, somehow theatrical. "We might have. Except, of course, we had Cochran, didn't we?"

Buckshot McCool drove like a madman out to the Turk place, and Alfonse Leake, the young State's Attorney, followed along in his own car. "A new Packard," Leake said with assurance. "Best car I ever owned. Japs'll never make a car like that."

Out at Otto Turk's farm, a crowd of men were already milling around in the front yard, and everyone who came up to Leake and McCool had Mickey Cochran on his mind. It was Cochran. That's what little Mattie Turk said. Who else could it be? Cochran, whom the boy had seen running away when he wandered down to the pond and found his poor mother face down in the water. Mickey Cochran who'd gone and killed Mama, that was what young Matthew Turk said. Why else had the half-wit run? And where was Cochran now? Gone, that's where he was. Guilty and gone. Just ask the boy.

"All the other men in the neighborhood?" I said.

Leake fingered his lower lip. "It was the telephone. Back in those days, you wouldn't remember, but people out in the country had to make calls through an operator. That, and everybody was on a party line. Otto Turk called the sheriff right off. The way the telephones worked, he might as well have stuck his head out the kitchen window and shouted to the world."

Buckshot McCool took over as ramrod of the manhunt, while Leake telephoned for the doctor, Dr. Milbourne. But Dr. Milbourne was already on the way. "It was the telephone operator." Leake smiled. "Wanda Higgins. Wanda had already called him."

"And what about Grace Turk?" I asked.

"She was in her bed." The assurance dropped out of Leake's voice, and he sounded sad, mystified. I wondered if those emotions were authentic, or simply appropriate. "Laid out there with a blue chenille bedspread covering her. Before Buckshot and I got there, some of the men had carried her inside. So frail. She was a truly beautiful woman, you know. Not just rich, but lovely. Blond hair like cornsilk, high, strong cheekbones. Blue eyes. Well . . ."

"Gerry Heyman told me she was raped."

"That's right." Leake snapped out of his reverie. "At least, that's what Dr. Milbourne said."

"What do you mean?"

What he meant was that old Doc Milbourne's evidentiary standards in the nineteen thirties weren't exactly the same as a good forensic pathologist's today. Grace Turk was wearing a green cotton skirt and a yellow blouse. The blouse was torn, her bra pushed up. One eye—her left, Leake believed—was bruised and swollen, and there were bruises on her neck and shoulders.

"You still haven't described any evidence she was raped," I said.

Leake chuckled. "That's where we get into the delicacies of Dr. Milbourne's technique. You see, her underpants were torn. The crotch was partially ripped, and if I remember right, they were pulled down low on her hips. That, along with the other torn clothing, was enough for Milbourne. And if it was enough for him, it was enough for the rest of us. I mean, who among us was about to suggest that we examine the poor woman further? Right there in her own bed, with her husband and son just out there in the next room."

"What about the autopsy?"

"Don't you hear what I'm saying? What decent man that evening would compound an outrage, for no other reason than to tell us what we already knew?"

I wondered if Judge Leake's standards of evidence had improved by the time he started doling out visits to the electric chair.

It was at about the time that Milbourne finished his examination that Mickey Cochran had the bad luck to come wandering back to the place. Here, Leake's story fit with what I had heard the other day at the nursing home. The crowd fell upon Cochran like politicians pouncing on a dollar bill. Buckshot McCool and Leake impaneled a coroner's jury on the spot.

"We held the inquest that very night in the front room of Otto and Grace Turk's house," Leake said. "It took about an hour, and the whole house was jammed to the rafters with angry men. Halfway through, one of those crazy farmers threw a coil of rope with a noose tied on it into the center of the room. There was a great silence." Leake stopped talking, and canted his head forward and to one side, as though listening. "Buckshot McCool had a Smith & Wesson revolver tucked in his pants, and all I had was my vocabulary. These were all pretty good men, country men, and I knew Buckshot would be hard pressed to shoot any of them just to protect a murderer. And I knew all the words at my command at that moment were about as useful as spit."

So, to keep the silence from getting out of control, Alfonse Leake started talking fast to the jury. He summed up in a hurry, got his decision in a hurry, then had Buckshot McCool hustle Cochran safely off to jail.

Leake went on: "By midnight, Buckshot and I thought we had things under control. I was at home, just getting into bed, when Wanda Higgins—God love her, she's been dead thirty years—Wanda called me and said that folks were burning up the wires talking about poor Grace Turk and that murderer down to the jail. What were we going to do? That, Wanda said, was what people mostly had on their minds, and the answer—again according to Wanda—seemed to be that they should head to the jail and settle things. I was about dressed, when Buckshot called and said maybe I should get on back down to the jail."

What Leake found wasn't a classic mob scene. No crowd of men, no torches, no deadly confrontation at the jailhouse door. But there was traffic on the street. Too much traffic for one A.M. on a weeknight in Mauvaisterre, Illinois.

"Cars would drive by slow . . . three or four men inside," Leake said. "Or sometimes just a couple of fellows would walk by. Nobody ever stopped, but they all took too long and came back too many times. Once in a while you'd hear an unintelligible shout, sometimes the sound of a bottle breaking on the pavement.

"The temperature outside was about eighty-five degrees, my Lord, in the middle of the night, and the humidity so high it seemed like that air would condense around you at any second. And heat lightning. I remember watching the heat lightning flash on the horizon, and thinking how a rain would cool everything down, send people home. But hell, I knew it wasn't about to rain."

Leake talked things over with Buckshot, and between them they decided that the people outside—their friends, neighbors, family—would rile themselves into further tragedy unless the business with Cochran was settled once and for all that night.

"That boy looked like a wet dog," Leake said. "And his eyes, I can still remember just exactly the way his eyes looked, big around as old Buckshot's badge." Leake took time out for a good laugh. He opened his own eyes very wide, and shook his head quickly from side to side. "Bugga-bugga! Hah!" Then he laughed again. "Scared as hell. And he kept breaking wind, the way a scared man will do when you've got him cornered."

As Leake spoke, I tried to imagine him as a young man, younger than I, faced in all likelihood with his first murder. His first killer on the loose here in Eden. I tried to conjure up an image of Buckshot McCool, a good old boy, who did not trust people who lived in town. And Mickey Cochran, that dying cave of a man taking up space in the nursing home. When had all these old men slipped past passion? The passion for murder and vengeance.

"It took us a while," Leake said. "Buckshot took that boy under his arm and said something like, 'Son, everybody knows you done it. You know it, I know it, Al Leake here knows it. But the most important thing of all is them folks out there, they know it.' Because that was the real difficulty, wasn't it? As I told you, Buckshot knew, and I knew, that neither of us was about to shoot one of our neighbors just to protect the likes of Cochran, a strangler and a raper. There just was no question of us doing that, and everybody knew it.

"Think about it, Mr. Banks. Men you've known since the cradle turned into a lynch mob, and you're the one charged with keeping that from happening. In my mind, and I am as clear on this today as I was that night, the only tool I had to keep my friends and neighbors from ruining our life here forever, the only tool at all, was a confession from Cochran and an absolute guarantee of justice. Without that, all was lost."

So the serpent was offering an apple, and the town was about to take a collective bite. It was easy for me to be smug about any sort of deal with the Devil that McCool and Leake may have made. I, for all my years of policing, had never needed to point a shotgun at men supposedly my friends. Deals with the Devil had been done for a lot less reason than that. Ego, for example. How often were the rules thrown over simply because some copper couldn't stand the thought of losing to still another shithead? So you smile back at the Devil, and you say, Well, maybe just this once . . .

"What did he say?" I asked. "When he finally caved in?"

"What do you mean, 'What did he say?' " Leake huffed. "He said he did it. He said he came across her at the pond. And then he raped her there on the bank, and then he strangled her until she wasn't moving anymore and then he carried her out into the pond and held her under the water. Then he ran."

"He said all that? Said it just that way?"

Leake scratched behind his ear and stared at his shoes. "More or less."

"More or less?"

Leake's eyes met mine, and then quickly darted away. "He agreed with it all."

"And it wasn't many years after this that you took the bench."

"That's right."

"Where you sat for over thirty years."

"Yes."

"In that thirty years, if another prosecutor had brought Mickey Cochran's confession before you, would you have accepted it?"

Leake's answer was so quick that I knew this question had been with him for a long time. "Probably," he said. "And certainly I would have before, say, nineteen sixty. That's about the time the Supreme Court began tinkering seriously with suspects' rights in state courts. Or, as some people believe, handcuffing the local police."

"Some people believe," I said. "What do you believe?"

Leake's smile was tight, like the jaws of a trap. "I believe in the eternal struggle of good and evil, and in those virtues expressed by the Methodist Church and the Republican Party."

"Yesterday, Cochran told me he confessed for two reasons."

"Two reasons, I take it, other than guilt," Leake said.

"Yes and no. As far as guilt goes, he said he felt guilty. Guilty because Grace Turk was apparently in the habit of skinny dipping, and Cochran was in the habit of spying on her. Otto, I guess, caught him at it one day and gave him a good thumping. Did Cochran ever tell you about that? Or for that matter, did Otto?"

"Cochran did, yes."

"And Turk?"

"I wasn't about to ask a grieving man such a humiliating question about his murdered wife."

"Did you believe it? What Cochran said about Grace Turk?"

"That she went swimming in the raw?" Leake chuckled. He arched his brows and pursed his narrow lips, considering the question. "Those were different times, weren't they? Men and women—most of them, anyway—generally believed that knowing a person's name before you had intercourse was the decent thing to do." Leake folded his arms across his chest and looked at me evenly, his eyes bright.

I said, "Times do change."

"Yes," he said. "But nonetheless, we've been human beings all along."

"Then you believe it."

"Yes. I took it to be an element underlying his intent when he committed the crime."

"Cochran told me that he'd seen her swimming on the afternoon she was killed."

Leake's eyes widened slightly. "Is that so? I never knew that for sure. But, of course, that's exactly what I assumed had happened."

Had Leake pursued all this with Otto Turk in the summer of 1937, I wondered. What sort of response might Turk have made? Even more interesting, how would Turk have reacted had he seen his wife that day just as Cochran had? As Leake said, we've been human beings all along.

"According to Cochran now," I said, "he felt plenty guilty at the time just because of the fact he'd *wanted* Grace Turk so much all along. Said he got all twisted up inside, believed that wanting her like that, watching her while he hid in the weeds and got off, believed that was so bad, it must be why she was killed. So that meant he was responsible for her death. I'm curious, Judge. Do you remember exactly what it was he said that told you he was the right man?"

"I remember that quite well, yes. We had been talking for several hours, not getting anywhere, and we had fallen into a long silence. The air inside the jail cell was getting pretty nasty by then. My eyes . . . my eyes felt grainy from the smoke of those damned cigars Buckshot kept smoldering between his teeth.

"I was about to give up, but I simply couldn't get it out of my head, what had happened to that poor, pitiful woman out there. He had told us by then about the times he watched her swimming. I knew Grace Turk pretty well, of course, a small town like this. Certainly knew, as I told you, that she was a beautiful woman. Not only that, but she always struck me as a *good* woman, too. Bright, funny. Always gracious and kind.

"So as we sat there in that wretched cell, with the air like something rising off a cesspool, it was as though I could hear the water splash while she was swimming—

"I've never told this to anybody, Banks—

"I could see her blond hair in the sun, her white arms and breasts against the green water. I could feel —and I still can't shake this—feel how cool it would be if I were the water itself, flowing all against her."

Leake stopped for a moment and, with his thumb and forefinger, rubbed his eyes and pinched the bridge of his nose, as though his eyes were still burning from the smoke from Buckshot McCool's cigar.

"And so I started to talk. I said, 'Mickey, after the way she looked those other times, all spread out and cool there in the water, and you having to hide there in the weeds, all curled up and hunched down like some kind of animal, while you watched that beautiful woman out there . . .'

"It was at about this point that Buckshot started to get up and I thought he was going to hit *me*. He just couldn't believe I would talk that way about a dead woman. Hell, I couldn't believe it myself. But I motioned him to back off.

" 'Just trapped by the whole horrible mess,' I told him. 'Locked up there in those steaming weeds just as sure as you're locked up here in this jail tonight.'

"And as I continued to talk, Cochran began to nod his head. Very faintly at first, but stronger the more I spoke, nodding it *yes*. *Yes*. Finally, I said, 'Now son, I'm telling you the truth here, there's not a man in this town won't understand what you did. Not after they realize what you had to endure watching.'

"I let that sink in for a while, and then I said, 'The boy, Mickey, the boy saw you, there's just no getting around it.'

" 'What boy?' he said, and I said, 'Why, Matthew. Young Matthew, who else? He saw you running away after you did it. There's just nothing anybody can do about it, son.'

"That was when I stopped. Cochran shook his head once, No, and then he said, 'I done such a goddamn wrong.' " Leake was himself nodding "yes" as he finished his story. "That was when I knew we had him. That's what I told folks later on to send them home."

I thought about the dim old man, lying in what would be his deathbed at the nursing home, while he tried to explain to me his comprehension of guilt. "And you let it go with that? You didn't push him any further? Past any ambiguity?"

Leake took a deep breath and shook his head. "I know he's no mental giant. And it may sound to you now, half a century after the fact, as if it weren't clear what he was talking about. But believe me, it was that night."

"Then you've never had any doubt he was your killer."

"Absolutely none. Now, you said Cochran gave you two reasons why he talked. What was the second?"

"He was afraid of getting lynched."

The old judge didn't miss a beat. "That's true. I told him as much that night. So did Buckshot. And anyway, every time a car passed, you could hear the engine, see the lights play on the jailhouse walls. It wasn't any secret to Cochran that he was looking at the short end of a long day."

"And that's not coercion?"

"Of course it is. But what's life, if not a long series of coercive forces? Listen, Banks, if I were defending

195

Cochran back then, I'd say he was pressured into giving a confession to save his life at the moment. And if I were called to account—as I was—for getting such a confession, I'd say that I simply set down the facts for the man so he could make an informed decision."

"That's a good line," I said. "Maybe not an A line, but a definite B plus."

"Thank you. The point is, it worked. You think Cochran didn't eventually get a lawyer appointed on his behalf?"

"And who was that?" I interrupted.

"A young fellow named Eldon Sidwell. But I can save you some trouble. He was killed by the Germans somewhere in Europe. Late 1944, I believe it was. Anyway, I can assure you that Eldon Sidwell clubbed me over the head with all these issues in the pretrial. Hell, I've known for over fifty years Cochran claimed that confession was a lie."

"Claimed it," I said, "right up to the day of trial, when he changed his plea from not guilty to guilty."

"That's right. The sonofabitch pled out. And you know why? Because I told his lawyer that if Mickey Cochran was convicted by a jury, I'd ask for the death penalty and get it. On the other hand, if he pled guilty, I'd back off and just ask for prison. Now, as a prosecutor, I can tell that to a man's lawyer, and his lawyer can tell it to him, and that's not coercion. But if I tell it straight to the man in jail in the middle of the night—or if Buckshot McCool tells him, or even if you tell him, Banks—if that happens while a bunch of men roam the streets outside the jail looking to get blood on their hands, why, that's coercion, that's wrong. Now what's the difference? You tell me." Once again, Leake removed his watch and checked the time.

Inside, I winced at the sound of what I was about to say. "The difference is in what we pledge we will and will not do."

Leake stared down at the watch as he snapped it closed. The gold looked deep and burnished against the wrinkled, pink flesh of his palm. "When my grandfather had this watch at Cold Harbor, he almost lost it. He was clutching the watch in his left hand, while the surgeon amputated his left arm not far below the shoulder. Just before they carried him out, an orderly thought to retrieve the watch from the pile of bloody limbs and slip it into his pocket. You don't have to explain pledges to me."

"Maybe not," I said. "Maybe your grandfather should have."

But Leake had had his say, and now his patience was gone. Once more he returned the watch to his pocket, then slowly rubbed his palms back and forth against one another, as though restoring the circulation. "Where did you say you were a policeman? What utopia parted with its tax dollars to support you for twenty years? Look, we're talking about terrible secrets here. How else do you get people to talk unless you bring some kind of force to bear?"

I sat back in my chair, and rested my elbows on the arms of the chair, opening myself to Leake. Finally, I said, "Sometimes you only need to act stupid and listen. Poke a little here, a little there. But most of the time a guy will dig his own hole. All you've got to do is put the shovel someplace where he can find it."

Gradually, the sour look faded from Leake's face. "You arrogant sonofabitch."

"Arrogant? Me? Maybe so. But I don't think I ever threatened to turn a man over to a mob."

"I doubt we'd have gone that far."

"Oh, I see. You'd have let the mob come get him. You'll understand if there's a subtlety there I can't quite grasp."

"This is a small town, Banks. In societies like ours, we crave security and order. Peace. And it's just human nature to do whatever it takes to preserve that state. Disruptions are frowned upon, if you get my meaning."

"And Gerry Heyman's murder? That doesn't qualify as a disruption?"

"Of course it does. But it's also a disruption that's nearly run its course, expended all of its allotted energy. Tell me, Banks, other than the people directly involved in the case, who really cares now? When you sit over in the hotel cafe and bar, spending Sarah Heyman's good money, do people talk about any of this? Do they worry about it like they worry about the grain market or big government? Hell no, they don't. No sir, a community gets what it demands, and what a community demands most is the *feeling* of security and order. That comes with *time*. And the job of a true public servant is to provide *enough* time."

"The community," I said. "And who speaks for the community?"

Leake's face brightened, as though I had just led us to paydirt. "Why, in this instance, I do. I thought the fact that you're not in jail for assaulting poor Nicholas made that clear."

Leake's formality suddenly became sufficient to that required by a South American dictator. "Life is one long travail, isn't it, Mr. Banks?"

"Where," I said, "can I find Otto Turk?"

Leake sighed heavily, and got to his feet. "It seems," he said, "that I find myself completely out of time."

14

"You know, Leo, this town . . ." Freddie Pointdexter paused and took a sip of his drink. A cherry Coke. He was on duty. ". . . this town used to be someplace."

"Couldn't tell it now," Little Mike said. She dried an ashtray and set it on the bar near my left elbow. The air conditioning was giving me a chill.

There were about half a dozen other people in the place, men in their late fifties or early sixties, all huddled around a table at the far end of the bar. As with bars everywhere, the primary light came from an assortment of neon beer signs and a TV. There was a movie playing on the TV, a Clint Eastwood saga about a deputy sheriff from the Southwest who gets sent to New York City to collect some homicidal maniac. But it was turning out that there were a lot more homicidal maniacs in New York City than the one Eastwood was after.

"No, I'm serious now, goddamnit," Pointdexter said, moderately excited. "A man used to could buy a suit of clothes right over there across the square. Nice stuff. And Saturdays, you'd have to wait for a parking place uptown. But now . . ." He rested his huge hands palm up on the bar and shrugged. "Everything's gone to seed."

I told Pointdexter I knew what he meant. Mickey Cochran. Matthew Turk. McDade the wildman. Those three had taken up most of yesterday. And this morning there was Alfonse Leake. "Sometimes," I said, "it seems like all I've done here is talk to old men." I thought once again about Sarah. Talking to old men was at least less risky than talking to a certain woman my own age.

Little Mike started to laugh, but there was no fun in her face. "You ought to see Mauvaisterre from my side of the bar. You think about it, it's like the whole story of this town comes down to nothing more than the history of old men."

I elbowed Pointdexter in the ribs. "One of these days, Freddie, we'll be old, too. Hell, we'll even be dead."

He rattled the ice in his glass. "No, Banks, say it ain't so."

"Yes, Freddie, it's true." I finished off my beer. "Someday, a couple of fools might sit around getting shitfaced, talking about that big old sheriff and the has-been detective who tried to figure out who murdered that doctor." It struck me then that the Grace Turk murder over fifty years ago had created a present-day life for that little town, and the Heyman murder now gave it a future.

I decided not to drink any more beer. Not that night.

"What about Otto?" I said. "I've heard everybody's version of Grace Turk's murder but his."

"Good luck," Pointdexter said. "I haven't seen that old fart since, well, hell, probably not since before me'n Little Mike got divorced the first time. That's more years than I can count."

"Alfonse Leake didn't help on that account, either," I said. "Neither did Serette."

"Serette," Pointdexter said. "Yeah. Listen, I'm sorry about this morning. He just bumped into me in the parking lot behind the courthouse, asked me to come along. Really, Leo, I didn't know he was gonna go lawyer on us."

"That just happens, Freddie," I said. "They can't help it."

"I worry about the kids," Little Mike said, drawing us back into the here and now. "All that damned TV."

"Not just the kids," Pointdexter said. "People watch CNN, see about a mass murder down in Florida, Michigan, someplace, they act like it happened just up the road, like a mad dog killer's gonna bust in the door any minute. But hell, we're never gonna make CNN. Anybody could tell you that. We only got one stiff."

"I won't let the kids watch MTV," Little Mike said. "They're too young to wear garter belts."

"Yeah," Pointdexter said, "but you might try it sometime yourself."

Little Mike reached across the bar and punched him in the chest.

"I didn't know you had kids," I said.

"Two girls," Freddie said. "Age ten and three."

"Both of them honeymoon babies," Little Mike said. She smirked and pulled another ashtray from the deep sink behind the bar.

"Honeymoons are fun," I said. It was true. A little honeymoon never hurt anybody.

"Yeah, but there ought to be a way to have one without getting knocked up. I told Freddie, I said this divorce, it's gotta last, I don't need anymore kids."

The cluster of men at the table, Freddie told me, were all members of the local V.F.W., and they were thick into the planning of the coming town picnic. I heard snatches of conversation about potatoes, corn, chickens and ox tails. The numbers they tossed around were all big, hundreds of pounds and hundreds of gallons. They were talking about boiling up big kettles of burgoo. Burgoo, I remembered from my childhood, was a concoction that originated sometime in the nineteenth century down in Kentucky. I had eaten the stuff before, eaten it and lived. I bet Clint Eastwood never had to eat burgoo.

"How much soup they make?" I asked Little Mike.

She shrugged. "Coupla thousand gallons, I think. A lot."

"Must take a quite a few people." I said. "To cook up all that soup."

"About forty guys," Pointdexter said. "Maybe a hundred cases of beer. They stand around and stir soup and slug down Bud Lite all night. If we're lucky, nobody gets sick in one of the kettles."

That was an adequate definition of lucky if I'd ever heard one. "Spices," I said. Eastwood was kicking some guy's ass now. Maybe he had eaten burgoo.

"I guess," Little Mike said.

I looked at her across the bar. "You help out?"

"Me? Shoot no. No women allowed."

"Allowed?"

"Well, sort of. Women may want to be doctors and lawyers and politicians. Maybe even want to be soldiers and go off to war. But cook burgoo with those clowns? No sir, we're not *crazy.*"

Pointdexter slid his cherry Coke glass across the bar, and said it was time to hit the road. When I asked him if he could use a little company, Pointdexter didn't waste a minute before asking if there was something in particular on my mind.

"The Cherokee," I said. "Heyman's outfit. Sarah said you've still got it under lock and key."

When we pulled into the lot at Cletus Porter's gas station, there were three teenaged guys in T-shirts and jeans leaning against the gasoline pumps, shooting the breeze. Between the two overhead doors, a homemade sign advertised cigarettes and motor oil. It had rained again while we were inside the hotel, and the lights above the lot glistened in puddles of rainwater gathered on the pavement. Pointdexter pulled to a stop alongside the pumps, and when he shut off the car, I heard the sweet, throaty voice of Reba McIntyre playing over a radio inside the station. Reba was wondering what made love go wrong. Hell, if she couldn't figure it out, what chance did I have?

The three young guys, who had been laughing, abruptly stopped when Pointdexter and I got out.

"Evenin' gents," Pointdexter said, ambling toward the three boys. One of them lit a cigarette, then leaned into the other two and whispered something. All three snickered, then a second boy lit a cigarette.

"I see you got some groupies," I said to Pointdexter. Said it loud enough that the snickering stopped and a third cigarette was lit.

"That's Tommie, Lonnie and Ronnie," Pointdexter said quietly, with a wink. "They were all majoring in Gas Pump Jockey, till self-service took over. Now they're kinda like economic refugees. They got a buddy named Johnny actually has a job here. He must be inside doin' a grease job or something."

Freddie Pointdexter suggested to the three Musketeers that they might consider taking their smokes someplace far—very far—from the gasoline pumps, before one kind of explosion or another launched them into orbit.

"You got any gum on you?" I said to Pointdexter.

Pointdexter gave me a long look. "Juicyfruit?"

"Doublemint's better, but yeah, Juicyfruit'll do."

Pointdexter found a pack of Juicyfruit in his shirt pocket and handed me a stick. Headlights swept across the glass and cinderblock front of the station as a car pulled into the lot. A blue LTD dating from the mid-seventies. There were three teenaged girls in the car. Lonnie, Tommie and Ronnie piled into the back seat and the LTD was gone. I unwrapped the gum, then folded the foil into ever smaller squares.

Pointdexter looked at his watch. "Car's in a garage right around back. Let's go."

A single bulb burned above the door of the metal shed behind the gas station. Pointdexter removed a crowded ring of keys from the snap on his gunbelt, and easily found the key that fit the padlock on the overhead door. A moment later, he heaved the door open with a loud clatter, and found the light switch inside.

The Jeep Cherokee, dark blue with gold trim, was parked head first in the garage. A thin, uniform coat of dust took the edge off the paint job. The ragged remains of red plastic evidence seals were like wounds on both side doors, the hood, and the rear cargo door. The left rear tire was still flat, as Freddie Pointdexter had said he found it. For the second time that day, I was looking at the ride of a dead boy from Mauvaisterre, Illinois. I wondered if thirty years from now anybody would keep the Cherokee lovingly stored under wraps, the way Tory McDade kept his son's Corvette. Not much chance of that, I thought. Gerry's deep blue and gold outfit had *For Sale* written all over it.

"She's all processed," Pointdexter said. "You can go ahead and touch things, you want to. Hell, I could probably release the damned thing. Thought about doing that three or four times. Made me feel like I was giving up."

I made a circuit around the Cherokee.

"It's like I told you," Pointdexter went on, "we never got much of anything off the car . . . the truck

. . . hell, I don't know what you call these damned things. Anyhow, there were some prints, but all the ones of any value turned out to be Heyman's."

"What about the rear end?" I nodded toward the cargo door.

"Yeah, that was open. And like I told you, the handle was out on the ground, but not the jack itself or the spare tire. The jack and the handle are still in the vehicle here, but the handle, it's at the State Police lab."

"Any prints on those? Even prints of no value."

"None. Nothing at all."

"Smudges?"

"Not even that."

"What about the handle on the rear door?" I leaned close and studied the bright chrome fitting, which was streaked with black fingerprint powder.

Pointdexter shook his head. "Same story. I know the jack handle was wiped, because the dried blood was all smeared and streaked. But you just can't say about the other things. Hell, you know that."

"Inside?"

Pointdexter shrugged. "Nothing that tells you anything. The usual car junk. Registration, owner's manual. A bunch of generic paper napkins in the jockey box, like you stuff in there when you pick up fast food at a drive-in. Some loose change in the ashtray. Sunglasses. RayBans. The man had good taste in sunglasses," Pointdexter said.

"How about his medical bag?"

"Nope. That turned out to be at his office. I found it there the next day."

"Keys?"

"In the ignition, ignition off. Transmission in *Park*. The headlights were off, too, but the parking lights were on. And the battery was still charged enough to start the engine. Nine and a half gallons of gas. The lab fellas siphoned the tank and measured it."

I opened the driver's door and leaned in to look at the emergency brake, which was not set. When I looked up at Pointdexter, he shook his head. "Found it just like you see it there."

According to Sarah Heyman, Gerry had received a phone call late that last evening, then left the house not long afterward, without saying where he planned to go.

"That night," I said to Pointdexter, "where you figure Heyman was headed?"

"Anybody's guess," Pointdexter said.

"His wife said she thought he'd gone to check on a patient. Maybe to the hospital over in Jacksonville. But that doesn't add with his medical bag being at the office. At least not if he was making a house call, it doesn't."

"No, it sure don't. And I went through the charts of all his patients at the hospital. He never went there."

"So what do you think, Freddie? What do you think about Matthew Turk?"

Pointdexter chuckled softly, and his eyes brightened. "I knew you wouldn't be able to get your nose out of that old business."

"Let's say I owe the dead guy a favor." I leaned my hips against the Cherokee, crossed my ankles and waited. "Make his business my business. For old times."

"What old times?" Pointdexter sneered. "For stealing your girl? See Banks, I can get my nose in old business, too."

I thought about the Sarah I had come to know that summer, both in Montana and there in Mauvaisterre. I wondered if Otis Weisel had said anything to Pointdexter about my visit with Sarah last night to the park on the river.

"Okay," I said finally. "A man needs a reason, I guess that's as good as any." Piss on Otis Wiesel. He could tell anybody he wanted. Someday, I might explain it all to my buddy, Pastor Roscoe Beckett, explain it one evening while we listen to some Bobby Bland and drink some beer and watch some whitefish roll in the fading sun on the Holt River behind our decrepit mansion back in Rozette, Montana. But I wasn't about to explain it to Freddie Pointdexter in any tin garage behind a gas station.

"Well, Matthew Turk as the killer ain't a bad theory," Pointdexter said, "except Turk says it's bullshit. Hell, you talked to him yourself already. You ought to know that."

"You ask Mickey Cochran?" I said. "Maybe Cochran called Heyman at home the night he was killed."

Pointdexter snorted. "Oh yeah, Cochran. Yeah, I thought of that. Shit, Cochran's so old and cracked, been in the joint since before sliced bread. I bet he don't even know how to use a telephone."

It wasn't hard to accept that. When I talked to Cochran, he seemed like a guy whose abilities would be taxed just watching TV.

"Maybe Turk's lying," I said. "People do that now and then, you know." It bothered me, how much I found myself wanting to catch the big sheriff at something he hadn't thought of.

Pointdexter's laugh sounded as hard-bitten as I felt. "Yeah, they do, don't they? Imagine that. So try and prove Turk's lying."

"Let's say Turk didn't call, then," I said. "Let's say the call was nothing but a coincidence, and not long after that Heyman just decided to go for a drive. He drives out by the Turk cemetery because he's letting his mind wander, and he gravitates in that direction. He has a flat tire and Turk happens by and things get out of hand." Christ, who knew? We could talk that circle for days on end.

"That's real possible," Pointdexter said. "Heyman did that a lot, you know. *Therapeutic drives,* he called them. There's any number of people around town can tell you about that. And the way he was brooding those last few weeks about Cochran, it wouldn't surprise me at all, he decided to take a slow spin out through that country."

"But that takes you right back to Matthew Turk, doesn't it?" I said. "It may not make sense to you or me that Turk would be hot enough over Heyman's questions to kill him. But who else do you figure it might have been in that particular place in the middle of the night? Especially somebody even remotely inclined to be unhappy with Gerry Heyman. Nobody but Matthew Turk. Unless you think some zombie came crawling out of that old cemetery."

With that, Pointdexter threw up his hands and headed for the light switch. "But making sense still doesn't make a case, does it?"

I said, "What about the tire?"

"What tire?"

"What do you mean *what* tire? *That* tire, the tire on the Cherokee. The *flat* tire."

"Oh, you mean *this* tire." He stepped to the side of the Cherokee and gave the flat tire a solid kick with one of the largest black lizard skin cowboy boots I had ever seen.

"How come it's flat? You figure that one out?"

When Pointdexter shook his head, I told him it wouldn't take ten minutes to check out the tire. I told him we should get that Johnny kid in the station there to stop preening his tattoos or whatever it was he did with his spare time and give us a hand with the heavy work.

It turned out that Johnny didn't have any visible tattoos, and he was talking on the pay phone with his girl. Luckily, Pointdexter didn't have to break any bones to pry him loose. It wasn't long before we had the tire and rim off the Cherokee, inside the station, aired up, and in a tank of water. The funny thing was, there weren't any leaks. No stream of bubbles leading the way back to a puncture. Nothing at all.

"Well, I'll be dipped in shit," Pointdexter said.

When the kid Johnny started to laugh, Pointdexter looked for a flash like it might be him, the kid, who ended up taking a dip.

"How you figure this?" Pointdexter said.

"Somebody let the air out," the kid said. I couldn't tell if the kid was brave, or just too stupid to understand how close he was to getting hurt. I should have been ashamed of how much I was enjoying the moment. Nobody likes to miss evidence, even though everybody does. The best you can hope for is that what you missed didn't amount to much. There was no telling yet what our discovery about the tire meant. The only sure things were that Freddie Pointdexter was in no mood for small talk, and he was too big for anybody to risk tampering with his mood.

But this kid Johnny must have had a real death wish. "Yeah, see, first you take the cap off the valve stem, then you—"

The sweetness in Pointdexter's voice made my stomach flip. "You know, son, I bet someday you grow up and find a cure for cancer."

"Geez, you think so?"

"Oh, yeah, you bet. So think what a loss it'd be to all mankind if you was to suffer brain damage tonight."

15

The dash lights inside the cruiser cast a green glow on Freddie Pointdexter's face. I wasn't sure if his face wouldn't have looked green anyway, he was so contorted with anger over getting caught short on Heyman's flat tire.

"It's not like I'm a dumbass," Pointdexter said as he drove me back to the hotel. "I realize you don't know me well enough to have an opinion, but it's true, I swear to God it is. I know I'm a big guy, and sometimes I seem kind of, I don't know, *mellow*. But I'm not stupid."

I said, "No, Freddie, you're not stupid." As long as he continued not to blame the state police technicians for missing the tire, I was more than content to give him the benefit of the doubt. Pointdexter certainly hadn't struck me as brainless before, and there was no reason to let one little miscue change my mind.

"So what do you think it means?" I said, giving Freddie a chance to redeem himself. "Finding out somebody probably just let the air out of that tire?"

"Well, it broadens the field," Pointdexter said. He

glanced over at me. "But I'm not the one with what you might call a narrow field problem, am I?"

He was talking about my concentration on Matthew Turk. No, not a dumbass at all.

He went on: "Seems obvious the tire was meant as some kind of distraction to anybody trying to figure out what happened. Probably not a very good distraction. I mean, it doesn't really change much, does it?"

I was willing to soften my line on Matthew Turk. "I think it opens things up, too," I said. What I meant, I explained to Pointdexter, was that by removing the possibility that the killer had simply stumbled onto Heyman while he fixed a tire, it was now quite possible that he had met someone in that spot. Or, perhaps someone was following him, and Heyman chose that spot to pull over and see what was going on. The reverse of that could be true as well, with Heyman the one in pursuit. "Lots of chances in this lottery," I said to Pointdexter. This time, I made a point of looking directly at him. "And none of them rules out Turk."

Pointdexter nodded reluctantly. "Toss a coin."

"That's about the odds I'd give it," I said.

The tires squealed softly on the hot pavement as Pointdexter swung the big car to the curb outside the hotel.

"Most of the time," I said, feeling reflective, "doing a decent case doesn't amount to much more than a struggle with the obvious. But this one you've got, Freddie, it's kind of a sonofabitch."

"It's a *real* sonofabitch," Pointdexter said.

I started to reach for the door handle. Pointdexter kept talking.

"This whole thing's making me crazy. Because it all comes down to me. I've got those part-time deputies, and God help me one of them's got to be Otis Wiesel, and other than that, it's just me. I can call in help from the state police, like I told you I did, and they'll do anything I need, anything I ask. Hell, they'll take

211

over the damned case. All I've got to do is give the word. But no, not me. This one's mine."

"The thing people will always remember you for," I said, admiring Pointdexter's refusal—however foolish it might be—to dump the case on someone else.

"Bingo." He leaned out the window and looked up at the sky for a moment, then pulled himself back in and stared straight ahead. "This is a small town. People here don't know you, so you maybe don't see it, they maybe don't show it to you, but when I meet them on the street or in the grocery store or a cafe, I sure as hell see it. Day after tomorrow the whole county'll be out for that picnic, and I'll spend all my time telling folks I don't know anything. Don't know a damned thing."

I was no stranger to Pointdexter's bind. The last decent sleep he'd had, I was sure, was the night Gerry Heyman was killed, before that farmer came upon the body and called Freddie Pointdexter for help. I knew he was suffering self-doubt, excess humility and night sweats. Christ, I could tell him stories . . . but Freddie Pointdexter didn't need to hear my war stories, and God knows I didn't want to tell them. The only thing I could do at the moment to help Freddie Pointdexter was listen.

"And you know the worst part?" Pointdexter banged the steering wheel with the heel of his hand. "The worst part is I'll probably live the rest of my life here, rubbing shoulders every day with a goddamn lying, murdering, bloody *killer,* and him breathing a little easier, feeling a little more cocky every time he sees me, the idiot sheriff, and I don't see him at all."

"No," I said. "The worst part will be if the day ever comes when you grow a callus around all this. When you can play the whole thing back from start to finish inside your head, and it doesn't really matter."

I thanked Pointdexter for the lift, and left him to his own misery.

Inside, I found Big Mike and Little Mike in the darkened lobby, watching Wrestlemania on TV. Actually, Little Mike was dozing on the sofa, while Big Mike whooped and snorted at all the televised muscular mayhem. A fat man wearing a black leather hood was begging for mercy from a big guy with purple hair, a painted-on cat's face, and a lavender leotard.

"Kill the bastard!" Big Mike howled. He was in his customary chair, crouched forward with his elbows on his knees. The light from the TV cast a submarine blush about the well-worn lobby.

"Bunch of faggots." The voice was that of a boy, and it was coming from the dark corner at my left, where I saw Michael Heyman hunkered down with his knees under his chin and his back against the wall. "That's all those guys are, just a bunch of big, druggie faggots. It's all fake."

"He came crawling in out of the night," Little Mike said, sitting up wearily on the sofa. Her face was long and flat with sleep. "Said he was here to see you. I stuck around to make sure he and Pop didn't kill each other."

"Yeah," Big Mike snarled. "So get the little twerp out of here, Banks."

"See what I mean?" Little Mike sounded as if she'd just gone two out of three falls herself.

I looked at the boy, who was in the process of standing up slowly. "Your mama know you're here?"

"Get a clue," he said. He wore a black T-shirt again, over which he'd added a black leather vest encrusted with silver-colored studs. "Bunch of morons, you ask me," he said, nodding toward the TV. While his partially shaved head had before seemed merely weird, Michael had now moussed his remaining hair into thick spikes about three inches long. For the first time I noticed that a thin, braided tail hung down over his collar. The tip of the tail was bleached a nasty looking color somewhere between orange and blond.

Everybody in the room, I realized, except me, was operating off some variation of the name Michael. First we had Big Mike and Little Mike. Add to that Monster Mike. "How come you're such a rotten little shit," I said to the boy.

"You wouldn't talk to me like that if I was bigger."

"Probably not," I said. "I'd probably hit you with something heavy."

"I'd think about doing that anyway, I was you," Big Mike said. "I know I sure have."

"I've got a Louisville Slugger out under the bar," Little Mike added.

I thought about Little Mike's offer, but it seemed like a shame to ruin a perfectly good baseball bat.

"Let's go," I said to the boy. "Before you embarrass yourself anymore in front of these nice people."

I started for the stairway. When Michael didn't follow, I gathered up a handful of his studded vest without mangling my hand. I gave a short jerk, and Monster Mike managed to be persuaded.

Upstairs in my room, I could hear the rumbling bass line from the jukebox down in the bar. The air was lukewarm and smelled of pine disinfectant. Something deep inside the air conditioner ticked in almost exact counter-rhythm to the jukebox, and for an instant it seemed that the entire building was in harmony. Beside the bed, Michael lifted his foot, then bounced it up and down on the mattress, testing.

"This place," he said, "is worse than that dump you live in back there where we saw you this summer. That time you brought him back to the motel drunk."

"Him?"

"Yeah. Him. Gerry."

"How about *my dad?*"

When the boy shrugged, his vest jangled. "Suit yourself."

"What I'm going to do," I said, "I'm going to go in there and do my business." I nodded toward the bathroom door. "When I come out, if you're still here, I'll figure you've got something to say to me. I'll figure you're going to knock this shit off and get it said."

Michael opened his mouth, but before he could get anything out, I ducked into the bathroom and pulled the door behind me.

My business amounted to running cold water over my hands and splashing it on my face, over my head. I peeled the cellophane wrapper off a glass and as I drank, I felt beads of water run out of my hair, behind my ears and down my neck. I drank a second glass of water, then set the glass back on the narrow plywood shelf above the sink. When I shut the water off, I listened through the door. I didn't hear anything. One way or another, that had to be a good sign. I dried myself off, and went back to Monster Mike.

He was standing in the window, looking over the air conditioner out across the darkened square, through the trees and past the statue and on ahead to God knows what.

"I hate this town," he said.

"What's to hate?"

"It's stupid. All of it. Just a stupid noplace full of stupid people. Nuke it. That's what I'd do." He chewed on a thumbnail, then winced and studied the small drop of blood forming on the cuticle.

"Nothing you'd save?"

"Nothin'." He spit the word at the window.

"Then where would you go?" I asked. Montana, I thought, you could go to Montana. Demonstrate your charm for some red-blooded types and end up dumped along the interstate.

"Anyplace." Michael wiped his bleeding thumb on his T-shirt. "California."

"I used to live in a town like this," I said. I sat down in the matchwood chair and crossed my legs. "A couple of hundred miles south of here."

"Used to live there," Michael said. "Right."

"I went out with this girl, she was the Homecoming Queen. Her old man ran a hardware store. She was pretty enough to make you short of breath. That night at the Homecoming dance, I wore a brand new yellow mohair sweater that shed all over her dress. I think it was a navy blue velvet dress. She looked real cool with all that yellow goat hair stuck to her dress. It's like we were both sides of a strip of velcro. She still lives there. At least she used to. Married some guy sells insurance."

"You used to go with my mom." When he looked over his shoulder at me, I saw that his eyes were puffy. "She make you short of breath, too?"

"Sometimes. For a while, anyway. Then we both got over it." I hoped Michael believed that more than I did. I doubted that he would, though. Any kid who was smart enough to ask a question like that would know deceit when he heard it. I couldn't take back what had happened with Sarah. Not years ago, and not last night. "People get close to each other," I said, "you never can tell how it'll work out, what they'll mean to each other."

Michael sniffed derisively. "You talk to me like a kid."

"You are a kid."

He started to say something, then shifted his weight, and turned back to the window.

I said, "I never got a chance to tell you I was sorry about your dad."

"Sure, everybody's sorry about that."

"You sound like they shouldn't be." Maybe that was a hard shot, but the kid asked for it. "How come?"

"How come they shouldn't be sorry? Or how come I sound like that?"

"I thought we were through playing games."

"Game?" He glared at me. "What game?"

Michael Heyman was too smart for his own good. He hadn't yet experienced serious acne, and here he was doing his best Bogart from hell. At least he'd never have to worry about dying young. Christ, if he died tonight—not a remote possibility, the way he was carrying on—if he died in a minute and a half, he wouldn't die young.

"The night he was killed, did you see him before he left the house?"

"Nah. We ate supper late. He was raggin' on me about this." Michael pointed at his head.

"The hair? Or your brain?"

Michael looked at me again and rolled his eyes. "I dropped a hundred bucks for this do. At this place in the mall over in Springfield. You can't get a haircut like this just anyplace."

"I'll bet not," I said. That spiked hair made his whole head look like one of those ugly germs you see in microphotographs. Yep, Monster Mike was one chill dude—no mohair sweaters for him. God, how I was enjoying my adulthood. "And how do you come up with a hundred bucks for a haircut?"

"Dealin' crack, breakin' into cars, shit like that." The sarcasm in his voice told me he was lying.

"Must be tougher than hell being an outlaw and having your mother pop for your overpriced haircuts."

Without another word, the boy spun on his heel and started for the door. I got up from the chair in time to catch him by the collar of his vest and jerk him back. He winced and his vest sounded like a bucket of bolts when his shoulder slammed into the wall between the window and the bed.

"Asshole!" he hissed.

217

The hand that I laid along the side of his head sent him sprawling across the bed.

"I never read Dr. Spock," I said. "Any kid thinks he's big enough to talk the way he thinks a man talks, he's big enough to get his melon thumped."

I thought Michael was going to bite a hole through his lip, while he rubbed the side of his head above his left ear.

"You just did that because you could," he said. "Because you're bigger and you could get away with it and I couldn't hurt you back."

"Hey, I was right, you are the reincarnation of Einstein. Congratulations!" I gave him a few beats of weary applause. "Tell me when you're ready for your next lesson in how the world operates."

Michael scooted to the edge of the bed and put his feet on the floor. "He was tellin' me I looked like trash."

"Your father?"

He nodded. "He gave me this long rap about fathers and sons. Said they reflected on each other. People, you know, they'd take one look at me, and go, Hey, whoa, what's the matter with that guy's old man? How come he lets him be like that? And I go, like, don't tell me your life story, I'm just me, I got a right."

I looked up at the ceiling and took a deep breath. "Thank you, God," I said.

"What's that supposed to mean?"

"Nothing. Your mom says she thinks he left the house because he got called to see a patient. But she's not really sure. Did you hear the phone?"

Michael shook his head. "He kept after me, you know, and I finally got pissed and went upstairs and shut the door and got into some tunes."

"What time was that?"

"I don't know, who knows time, you know? Maybe eight-thirty. It was still daylight."

"You think he left because of the fight with you?"

Michael's silence told me that I'd found a nerve. A nerve, perhaps, that would end up keeping some therapist in meal money for several years to come.

"You afraid he got so pissed at you, he left the house, and if it wasn't for that, he'd still be here?"

He was staring down at the floor. "That's none of your business. Maybe. Big fuckin' deal. So what?"

"So why beat yourself up over something you can't ever know?"

When Michael looked up at me, his face was so drawn and intense, so like his father's, I felt as though I were staring back at a ghost. "Shit happens? That's what you're telling me?"

"Kind of. You can't hide behind that. But sometimes you can't avoid it, either. Guys have blowups with their old man everyday. People leave their homes all the time for all kinds of reasons, sometimes just to get away. Nothing to it. Yeah, sometimes shit does just happen. Anyhow, I think your mother would have said something to you that night, if it was because of you he left."

"She wasn't there."

"What do you mean?"

"I mean she wasn't home. At least not later on."

"How much later on?"

"I got hungry at about ten-thirty or eleven o'clock. So I go downstairs to the kitchen, and nobody's around. There's lights on and everything, but that's it."

"What about your sister."

"Yeah, oh yeah, I checked Lisa's room when I went back up to bed. She was zoned out. And I checked my folks', too, and they weren't there."

"Okay," I said. How, I thought, can I get to the bottom of this without tipping an unstable boy to the fact that his mother may have tagged herself with a very distressing evasion, if not an outright lie? As far as I knew, Sarah had led everyone to believe she'd

219

been home all night the night Gerry was killed. "Did anybody ever come up and check on you after you left the table?"

Michael laughed. "Get real, man."

"When did you see your mother next?"

"In the morning. When she woke me up, me and Lisa. Told us what happened."

"Did she say where she'd been that night? What time she left? When she got home?"

Michael shook his head. "There was too much going on. She was cryin' and everything. We never talked about that night."

"Later on? You talk then?"

"No."

"What about Sheriff Pointdexter?"

"He never talked to me and Lisa. Mom, she goes, no, they're too upset and she didn't think we ought to get dragged into things, we had enough troubles without that."

"How'd you feel about that?"

"It was okay with me. I mean, you know, I was afraid . . ."

"Afraid of what?" I was afraid myself of what he might say. For Michael, there was no good answer.

"You know . . . afraid . . . everybody would blame me . . ." His anger and fear now dissolved into slow tears. ". . . for bein' a freak."

I didn't know what to do. He was too old to hug, and too young to get drunk with.

"Part of being a freak," I said, "is you tend to make more out of it than it really is. Anyway, you don't seem like the same kid I saw a couple of months ago in Montana. What happened?"

Michael was staring at the floor again. When he shrugged once more, it was all he could do to lift the studded shoulders of the vest.

I said, "You get bitten during the full moon by mutant motorcycle zombies? What?"

For the first time since I'd known him, Michael Heyman almost laughed. "Would you . . . would you believe I was kidnapped by psychoyuppies? On that stupid trip?"

"I'll bet you never liked Disneyland, either."

"It was okay. Lotta chicks in tank tops."

So much for the adventurous allure of E Ticket rides. "How come you're here?" I said. "Why wander down here in the middle of the night?"

"I don't know."

"How come?"

"I just wanted to see, you know, what's going on." He glanced uneasily around the room. "Nobody tells me anything. I'm just a kid and they say don't worry."

"You want to know what I've found out."

"Yeah."

I considered the fact that the only significant thing I seemed to have learned about the murder of Michael's father might be what Michael himself had just told me about his mother. "Nothing," I said. "So far, I've been a bust."

We talked a while longer, long enough for Michael to regain his composure, but not long enough for him to go sour again. By the time we went back downstairs, it was after midnight, and the lobby was deserted. Outside, I saw Pointdexter's cruiser parked at the curb. Little Mike was leaning into the driver's window. Little Mike saw us first, and when Pointdexter looked our way I waved to him that everything was all right.

There was no traffic—not even a stray dog—on the streets as I drove. A few minutes later, I stopped outside the Heyman house. The porch was dark, and it looked as if only a single light burned somewhere deep inside the house. I asked Michael if anybody else was home. He told me that his sister had gone to bed before he left.

"And your mother?"

"Who knows." Michael popped open his door. "Sometimes she is, sometimes she's not."

"You going to run off?"

"No."

"You're sure?"

"Hey, man, give me a fuckin'—" He caught himself in the middle of a bored scowl, which matched his hairdo. Then his face softened, and it was once more Gerry's face. "I'm sure," he said.

I listened to the insects and the softly rattling leaves, to the hiss of a lonely car on a distant street, to all the night sounds, and I wondered if the night was listening back.

"Okay," I said finally. "That's fine." Maybe Michael had decided after all to work on being a man.

I watched him into the house, then pulled around the corner and stopped again. Then I walked back to the garage behind Sarah's house, looked through a dusty side window, and saw that the garage was empty.

16

Matthew Turk lived in an old, well cared for Italianate house perhaps a mile on down the road from the stone ruins of his parents' home. The house, set well off the road under towering oak trees, looked like a large, brick box. The bricks were painted dark gray, and the long, narrow windows were appointed with charcoal-colored shutters. There was a large red barn with white trim, which looked too neat to be heavily used, and a much larger metal shed, with sliding doors. There were several other outbuildings, as well as a large cluster of tall, cylindrical grain bins built of corrugated steel. A paved, circular driveway looped by the house off the main drive, but when I saw Turk's white Cadillac parked near the barn, I drove on past the house. As I parked beside the Cadillac, I saw that the barn was surrounded by a white board fence. Matthew Turk stepped out of the side door of the barn. Wiping his hands on a faded red shop towel, he walked slowly across the lot. I sat in my car and waited for him.

When Turk was within earshot, I said, "Sorry about that truck the other day." Actually, I wasn't sorry at all. "I figure it was just a couple of dumb yahoos took it on themselves to show the boss what good help they were."

"No." Turk laughed and stuffed the shop towel in the hip pocket of his green utility pants. "Truth is, I sent those boys out to hunt you up, convince you that place you come from in Oklahoma, wherever, is a much nicer place to live." He leaned his arms on the top board of the fence and glared at me.

"If that's the case," I said, "maybe I should have shot them instead."

"Well," Turk said, "I did hate to lose a good pickup."

"You mind if I get out?"

"Would it matter if I did?"

I opened the car door and stepped out.

Turk turned away and started back toward the barn. "If you're going to be a pain in the ass, at least let me get some work done."

I climbed the fence, caught up with Turk, and followed him across the muddy lot. Although there were no animals in sight, I noticed plenty of horse tracks, and twice had to step around piles of fresh, green horseshit.

"What's on your mind?" Turk said as we neared the door.

I told Turk that I wanted to talk to his father. That drew him up short.

"You're a bigger fool than I thought," he said.

"Maybe. Maybe not. Anyhow, I think I'd like to meet Otto. Figured you could put me in touch with him."

"You figured that, huh?"

"Doesn't really matter," I said, "does it? You make a couple of calls, or I go hunting. Either way, I get to him."

I followed Turk into the barn, where I was surprised to find a surrey, shiny and black, in a well-lighted workroom. The two seats were upholstered in new, tufted black leather, and a gold fringe hung from the flat roof. The four tall, wooden wheels had thin rubber tires, and a can of grease sat beside the left front wheel.

"For the parade tomorrow," Turk said. "I'll be up all night tonight riding herd on the soup making, so I've got to get this rig all cleaned up and in town this afternoon. I been packing the hubs." He nodded toward the grease can.

I heard a rustling noise from the far end of the barn, and saw the head, back and rump of a large white horse which was tied in a narrow stall.

"That's Buddy," Turk said. "Last horse on the place. I keep him around just to pull this rig in the parade."

"Sounds like quite a production," I said, "this picnic and parade."

"Biggest production in the whole damned town," Turk said. "We'll sit down there at the fairgrounds all night boiling up soup in great big kettles over open fires. Make a coupla thousand gallons of the stuff, sell it all out the next day."

"You're in charge of the burgoo?"

"Me? Nah, hell no. Recipe's a secret only this one guy knows. He makes the burgoo. It's my job to make sure nobody gets too drunk, gets in a fight, falls in the soup, nothing like that."

"Sounds like a fun job."

Turk shrugged. "I been doing it since I got back from the Pacific in forty-five."

"Marines?"

"Army. I got out a major."

It was tough to make sense out of Turk, out of the man who had tried to pick a fight the day before, then sent a couple of toughs to pick his fight for him, and

225

the man who always seemed willing to indulge my questions.

I ran my hand over the smooth, hard rubber tire on one of the wheels. "You really are the bull goose, aren't you, Turk?"

Turk squatted down beside the grease can and began using a putty knife to work grease into the left front hub. "Some folks seem to think so. Never hurts to have people want to make you happy."

"I take it Gerry Heyman wasn't one of those people."

"Not hardly." Turk looked up at me, his eyes narrow, and jabbed the greasy putty knife in my direction. "You think I got a case of red ass for the Heyman boy because he got it in his head I helped railroad that piece of shit Cochran. Well, you're absolutely one hundred percent right about that." Turk's thick, red fingers tightened around the putty knife. "But you gotta bear in mind that Gerry Heyman would've accused me of killing Martin Luther King and Jimmy Hoffa if he thought he could get anybody to listen."

"So I'm supposed to feel sorry for you?" I said. "Because Heyman thought there was an account to be settled, and you stomped on his fingers every time he tried to open the books?"

"Lemme tell you a story, Banks." Turk grunted as he got his legs situated under his hips and continued to work. "Six hundred and forty acres is a section of land. That's one square mile. Used to be, a hundred and sixty acres—a quarter section—was a decent-sized farm. That's because a hundred and sixty acres was what one farmer and his family could handle with a team of horses. Most of the roads were section roads, like that one right out there in front of the house, and every mile you came to a crossroads. I'm talking about up here on the flats now, the good farmland that used to be prairie before it was plowed up all those generations back. Time was, you'd find a family living every half or quarter mile or so along these roads, because of the way the farms fell into place in rough quarter sections. The houses were small, and there'd be a barn, a corncrib, chicken house, a bunch of hog sheds."

Turk balanced the putty knife on the grease can, then began fitting the cap back on the hub.

"Nowadays," he went on, "with all this big, expensive machinery we got, it takes seven, eight hundred acres for a fella to make a decent go of it. That's one farmer on the same amount of land that maybe used to carry half a dozen families."

"That's handy to know," I said. I strolled back toward the white horse. He was a tall, thick-bodied gelding. The air was hot and dusty. A set of black harness hung from pegs on the wall behind the stall. How many times had Turk just spoken the words *used to be?* "But I really didn't come out here for a lesson in agriculture. How do you figure that has anything to do with Gerry Heyman's death?"

Turk got to his feet and followed after me, again wiping his hands on the shop towel. "Maybe nothing to do with his death," Turk said. "But it sure God had plenty to do with his life. Within three miles of here, I can take you to probably ten places where there used to be a house, places somebody used to call home, and there's nothing there now but a cornfield. I know where those places are because I'm the one set a match to 'em. And like I told you the other day, one of those cornfields is where that boy and his family used to live. I think he always figured I stole a sizable chunk of his life. Torched it off, you know?"

No deposit, no return America. It jolted me to remember the way I used to feel when I was lying at night in my bunk at Great Lakes, dreaming about family, about all that I was leaving behind as I followed one day, as fast as I could, into the next. Gerry seemed to have needed monuments to his past, while I quite coldly reduced mine to a sentimental abstraction and moved on. Would it have helped him, I wondered, if that field were not a field at all, but prairie, growing not corn but lush grass, taller than a man's head on horseback? Would Gerry have recognized the difference? Or was he the kind of man who would see the prairie as simply a place to build a house, the river as a spot for testing your flycasting technique? That difference was something Montana had taught me. Not the Montana where I had investigated crimes, but the one where I had walked through cottonwood groves along rivers, and thought of nothing at all. I said, "You burned up his childhood."

"It's a sad business, I'll give you that," Turk said, jamming the towel into his hip pocket. "Sad as all hell. But what else can you do? Really? Shoot, you're talking about nearly subsistence agriculture here. A few crops and small-time livestock. Twenty beef cattle, maybe, a couple of milk cows, maybe three or four horses, fifty, sixty head of hogs. Nobody farms like that anymore."

Turk took a heavy brush from a narrow, worn shelf, and began currying the horse. "You know how much labor it takes to run that kind of nickel-and-dime operation? You can't even hardly get poor people to do that kind of work these days. I hear people talk all the time about how we ought to get back to traditional agriculture, make the family farm work again. Well, it's real easy, buddy. All you got to do is disconnect the electricity and start walking behind a team of horses. Believe me, son, you might as well spend your time looking for a chicken with lips as try and find people still want to work like that." The horse shied under Turk's touch as he worked the brush through its heavy, gray forelock.

And then I could see my father, his face free of wrinkles, his hair clipped short, and his eyes clear, looking over his shoulder at me and winking as he adjusted the first TV set in our little house. At that moment, it was as though the vacuum of twenty years of running away was sucking the heart right out of me. I imagined Gerry Heyman staring across an empty field, and being deafened by voices.

I almost asked Turk why the houses at least weren't saved. But why waste time listening to an answer I already knew? Buddy, he would say, those old houses, they're all small, the plumbing's like a sieve, the basements leak if they've got a basement, and the wiring's a death trap. At best, you go broke trying to keep them fixed up for a renter. Worst case, you get some miserable, raggedy-assed family burned up in the middle of the night, and a slick lawyer who keeps you tied up in court till hell freezes over. I knew that was the answer, because had I been Turk, it's what I would have said.

"None of this happened overnight, you understand," Turk said. He set the brush aside and began working his way around the horse, lifting each foot and pinning the hoof between his knees while he examined the steel shoes. "I guess you might say," he added, "it's taken farmers all of human history to succeed."

"Succeed at what?"

"At not having to work like a bunch of damned dogs anymore. I've got over a million dollars tied up in farm machinery. Four wheel drive tractors, plows, planters, combines. Every kind of machine you can imagine. What that means is I can accomplish today with money what my ancestors had to accomplish with sweat and broken bones. The up side is I can pay people better wages than ever before for doing farm work. The down side is I need fewer of them to do it."

I patted the white gelding on the rump. "Sounds like the American Dream come true."

"You got it, buddy. You hit the nail right on the head."

I was surprised to find myself enjoying Matthew Turk's company. But which was the real Turk, the ruddy-faced loudmouth, or the saddened restorer of the surrey with the fringe on top? I wondered how much it must cost one version of himself to keep the other going.

"I don't get it," I said. "Like you said, you're a man people in this county want to make happy. Why go out of your way to step on Gerry Heyman?"

Turk let the last hoof slide from between his knees, then straightened and caught his breath. "You mean those phone calls and that stupid goddamn letter. Well, lemme tell you right now, if I'd of known that poor bastard was going to get himself killed, killed right down the road from my house, I sure as hell would've done things different."

"It must have made you pretty uneasy," I said, "realizing you'd left behind a string of clues."

"No." He chuckled and wiped the sweat from his forehead with the back of his hand. "No, you'll have to set me up better than that, Banks."

"Did he accuse you of killing her? Killing your own mother?"

"Don't talk crazy."

"I'm not crazy. Believe me, sometimes I've wished I were crazy, but the world never let me off that easy."

Turk stepped behind the horse and began fingering the harness, now and then using the shop towel to buff a spot on the already polished leather. "Then let's just say maybe I've been more successful at being crazy than you. It's not much fun."

"Crazy enough to kill somebody?"

"Probably. Yes. But that doesn't mean I did. You think I'd be stupid enough to make such a big stink with Heyman, make myself the one logical suspect, if I planned to turn around and kill him?"

"Most people don't plan to kill anybody. They just do it. Simple as that."

For a long time, Turk stood with his back to me and continued feeling his way through the harness. When he finally spoke, he did so without turning around, and his hands were busier than ever with the harness.

"Listen," he said, "I've spent years just trying to forget what happened when I was a kid. And everyday I have to drive past that goddamn rockpile down the road. I've burned and bulldozed houses all over this county, but that one, that one I have to look at every day because an old man who lives in St. Louis says it's got to stay.

"And then along comes young Dr. Heyman, the boy wonder, and it's like he thinks it's interesting. Local color. *Interesting local color.*"

"When," I said, "did he first come to you with questions?"

"Last spring, when we all heard Cochran was getting out. And I talked to him, told him the story. Just like I told you yesterday. I mean, nobody had asked me for years, but I figured, what the hell, he's going to be Cochran's doctor, he might as well know what happened."

"And then he decided Cochran was innocent."

"That's right." Turk slapped the towel against the harness and faced me. "And that's when I told him to go to hell, that I thought all his nosing around was bullshit. Told him that plenty of times. Why the hell couldn't he just let the dead be dead?"

I shook my head and smiled. "But Cochran's not dead. Neither are you."

"And neither is my old man," Turk said. "Not by a long shot." Turk laughed, showing his teeth. "So here we are again, right back at square one."

"How do I find him? Your old man?"

"Forget it." His tone was that of a man delivering a

punchline. He hung the towel on one of the harness pegs, and walked out of the barn.

Outside, I followed Turk back across the lot toward my car. I considered asking him if it were true that he visited Mickey Cochran on the sly, asking forgiveness. Forgiveness for what? But those two questions might be the only heat I could bring to bear on Matthew Turk, and I didn't want to ask them until I knew I could do it with maximum effect.

"You can do whatever you want," he said, "talk to anybody you want. Just don't expect me to help you get it done."

I climbed the white board fence, then looked back across at Turk. "You know, Turk, it doesn't take a Clarence Darrow or an F. Lee Bailey to figure that maybe Leake and McCool put the fear of God in Cochran, and he told them just what they wanted to hear to save his neck."

Turk shook his head. "Leake and McCool wanted to hear the truth. Far as I'm concerned, that's what they got. I don't care if they had to beat the shit out of Cochran to get it."

I reached into my pocket for the car keys. But Matthew Turk wasn't quite through.

"You never asked me where I was the night Heyman was killed."

"Did Pointdexter ask you that?"

"Sure he did, him and Serette both."

"And what did you tell them?"

"I was home in bed asleep."

"Witnesses?"

Turk shook his head. "I live alone. Lived alone all my life."

17

The traffic grew more tangled as I neared downtown St. Louis on the way in from Forest Park.

Ahead to the left, the Gateway Arch, a bright, stainless steel swath across the gray, humid sky, towered several hundred feet above the city. St. Louis is an old, working class city that is not quite southern. The Arch is a gleaming monument to Lewis and Clark, who jumped off from St. Louis on their great expedition to the Pacific Northwest. It is also a monument to those pioneers who, for the next century, explored, settled, and pillaged the western continent.

Throughout the drive down from Mauvaisterre, I hadn't managed to shake my astonishment at the message that awaited me when I got back to the hotel from Matthew Turk's place that morning. Big Mike was wheezing when he handed me a pale green guest check from the restaurant next door. "Here she is," he said. There was a greasy thumbprint on the bottom corner of the check. "Roxanne answered the phone." Big Mike nodded toward the kitchen. "That's the gal cooks for Little Mike."

The note was simple: "Otto Turk. Busch Stadium, 7:00. Ticket at box office."

"It's the Mets," Big Mike said.

The Mets, sure, the Cardinals were playing the Mets, that's what it was all right. The Mets, the Cards, and Otto Turk.

Although it was about a two-hour drive to St. Louis, I left Mauvaisterre in the middle of the afternoon. Ever since arriving there a few days before, I had done nothing but talk to people, a circumstance that brought back vividly all my years as a policeman, those years when I did nothing but talk and talk and talk, day after day after day.

"We're nothing but a funnel for shit." That's what my old partner Red Hanrahan used to say about policing. He was right, of course, and his observation would be true of coppers from Las Vegas to Venus, Mars to Miami, and all points in between. For me, though, that was a perspective I had honed in faraway Montana, one that felt alien there in southern Illinois, the country of my childhood. This was a country of Sunday afternoons, with men wearing gaudy neckties and wilted white shirts, the sleeves rolled up to their elbows, revealing stark tan lines around their wrists, of kids racing across the lawn, of women busy with food. A country of generosity and prejudice, intolerance and love. As I said, a country of childhood. What kind of place is that to hunt down a murderer? Now that I thought about it, maybe the perfect place.

I crossed the Illinois River at Hardin, then drove south through Brussels, and crossed the Mississippi on the Golden Eagle Ferry. An otherwise modern craft, the Golden Eagle is propelled by a paddlewheel, an artifact that churned echoes of Twain from the murky water. The story of the Mississippi is a story of great jokes and cruelty, and I found myself wishing that the captain would swing the bow around and bear upstream for Hannibal, find us a new pass through deep water and all manner of trouble. The air thickened with the smell of mud and diesel fumes as the ferry neared the western bank. When the tires of the Chevy thumped off the ramp, I consoled myself with the thought that I was at least back on the proper side of the Mississippi, the Montana side.

Along with talking to Otto Turk, I also wanted to see where the old man lived. I had the impression he was rich as sin, and that all his wealth was the result of his marriage to Grace. I wanted to see for myself just how big a boost up in the world his dead wife had given him. Before leaving Mauvaisterre, I'd taken a chance and stopped by the County Courthouse. After applying some smooth talk to one of the blue-haired ladies, and spending about thirty minutes in a stack of musty ledgers, I found a St. Louis address, where Otto Turk received his tax bills. According to the St. Louis city map that came with my rental car, the address was near Forest Park.

Otto Turk's house, it turned out, was something of a palace. Constructed of gray dimension limestone, which was smudged with urban soot, it occupied grounds that took up most of the block. The grounds, a morass of untended shrubs, trees and vines, were surrounded by a low wall made of the same stone as the house, and the house itself was a squat, two-story bunker under a dull orange tile roof. As I drove slowly around the block, I saw the remains of a pool and pool house. The back of the main house opened into a conservatory. The glass panels were steamy, and it appeared as though the vegetation inside the house were as far out of control as on the grounds. Seeing a flash of color behind one of the conservatory windows, I slowed the car. The color turned out to be a large red and blue macaw. As I passed by the front again, I caught sight of the grill of a black Mercedes parked under a ragged gray awning on the north side of the house. A fat, orange cat darted through the undergrowth. All in all, a Mayan king in the market for a tomb might have decided Otto Turk's place was a little showy.

After seeing Turk's house, I still had a couple of hours to kill, so I found my way to nearby Forest Park, and took a walk through the zoo. Zebras switched their tails lazily in the heat. A peacock running loose on the grounds fanned his gaudy tailfeathers for countless photographers. An elephant rocked from side to side, lost, perhaps, in some vestigial savannah dream. I got my first whiff ever of hippo shit, and hoped to God it was my last. Later on, I saw elk and moose and wolves and bears, and had to remind myself that I had come here from a place where those animals live wild, where they bed down in the grass and trees at night through all kinds of weather, lowering their heads warily with their noses to the wind in the moonlight, in the rain or snow, while we in our houses turn on the lights and turn up the heat and believe that the laws of nature end at our doorstep.

And now I was making my way through the downtown traffic, trying to find a place to park near Busch Stadium. What the hell, I thought, if Otto Turk lives in a temple like that, he probably has great seats for the ballgame.

Busch Stadium is one of those circular modern stadiums that only a city booster could love. The field is covered with plastic grass, and comes equipped with an automated system that covers the infield when it rains, and once tried to devour a young phenom, Vince Coleman, at World Series time. Now, the Cards hadn't been to the Series for several years, and Vince Coleman was a Met. God, what next?

To get to the box office window from the parking garage, I walked past the National Bowling Hall of Fame. I could hardly wait for the day I was able to tell Pastor Roscoe Beckett I had seen the National Bowling Hall of Fame. He'd probably wonder why I went ahead and wasted time with baseball. To my left stood a tall bronze statue of Stan Musial. Now, there was a ballplayer. Suit Stan the Man up today, and he'd make Ricky Henderson's contract look like pocket change.

The crowd was picking up, and the vendors were out in force on the sidewalk around the ballpark. I lavished twenty bucks on a cap. Not one of those universal models with the adjustable plastic strap on the back, but a genuine red wool, size seven-and-three-eighths St. Louis Cardinals baseball cap. Then I loaded up with a couple of Polish sausages, a tray of nachos, a cup of beer, and some Milk Duds. I had come all the way from Montana, by God, and I was going to have a good time, even if I was working. And even if the necessary diet ate a hole in my gut. You know, there's no beer like the beer you get on a warm summer night at the ballgame.

Well, I wasn't wrong about Otto Turk's seats. They were in the first row of a field box just off third base. My seat was the third in from the aisle, and the rest of the row to my right, as well as the row behind me, remained empty while the nearby area began to fill. Plastic or not, the playing surface was bright green and perfect under the high banks of lights. Swallows darted through the lights, zeroing in on insects, while the players went about their business on the field, throwing, hitting, spitting. Everybody knows it's a rule that you can't play ball unless you spit a lot.

For the next half an hour or so, I didn't give a thought to anything but batting practice. In the outfield, kids hung over the railing, talking to the ballplayers, throwing down baseballs and gloves and programs to be autographed. I marveled at the relaxed grace of the infielders, at the outfielders shagging fly balls behind their backs at the center field wall, at the warm-up throws that reduced the baseball to a blur. The one thing TV doesn't communicate about baseball is how good you have to be just to be a bad player in the big time.

As the starting lineups were being announced, I heard a small commotion behind me. When I looked back, I saw a skinny old man making his way down the aisle with the aid of both an aluminum walker and a tall, muscular black man with his hair cut in a stove-pipe. As the pair neared, I could see that the black man carried a baseball glove tucked under his left arm. He wore a red Cardinals T-shirt, black warm-up pants, and red hightop basketball shoes.

"Banks?" The old man glared down at me with narrow, black eyes. He had on a white *guayabera* shirt with long sleeves and elegant embroidery, and shiny, gray, sharkskin slacks.

"That's me," I said. "You must be the ghost of Ferdinand Marcos."

The old man was out of breath. "Shut up," he said. With his right thumb, he made a stabbing motion over his right shoulder, like an umpire who had just rung me up. "Stand up and get out of the goddamn way."

I stood, and stepped over into the vacant row behind me. The walker clattered against the empty seats as Otto Turk made his way along the front row, then settled into the seat to the right of the one he'd just run me out of. The black man took charge of the walker, laying it on the cement between the first and second rows. When he finally took his own seat, immediately to Turk's right, he fitted the glove onto his left hand, smacked the pocket into shape with his fist, then leaned forward and sat with his elbows on his knees. The leadoff man for the Mets, Vince Coleman himself, was just stepping into the box.

I climbed back over the seat and sat down. "Shagging souvenirs?" I said, nodding toward Turk's companion.

"Huh? Nah . . ." He was still catching his breath. "Nah . . . Thing is, see . . . you get a right-handed hitter in there against a right-handed power pitcher . . . throwing inside . . . so the hitter's gotta fight 'em off to save his ass . . . them foul balls come this way like bullets . . . like goddamn bullets. I'm too old, I come too far just to get killed by a pitch fouled off by some overpaid Negro. So I got me a overpaid African American . . . that'd be Mr. DeWitt here . . . to field 'em. Ain't that right, Mr. DeWitt?"

"That's right, Mr. Turk."

Turk grinned at me. "Mr. DeWitt cooks for me, too, fries me up a skillet of potatoes and onions every night. And a slice of ham. Or a catfish rolled in cornmeal. Ain't that right, Mr. DeWitt?" Turk found a red and white pack of Marlboros in the breast pocket of his shirt.

"Sure is." Mr. DeWitt found a Zippo lighter.

I noticed that all of the nearby seats were occupied except for the block around us—fifteen seats, I counted, not including the three in which we sat—in the first two rows. I asked Turk if he happened to know the story of all these empty seats.

"I own 'em," he said. "Own the tickets, anyway."

"You got a lot of friends?"

"Nah. I just don't like to be crowded. So I buy 'em all up. Season tickets. I like it Mr. DeWitt's got a little room, case he has to make a play."

"You come to all the games?"

"About three-fourths."

"I guess you could donate a lot of tickets. Like to an orphanage or something."

Turk drew on his cigarette and thought. "What the hell for?"

I had trouble finding any shadow of Matthew Turk in his father's face. Otto's cheeks were caved in, and he had a habit of working his dentures back and forth on his gums. His hawk nose was nearly purple in the corners where the nostrils met his cheeks, and his freckled scalp showed through scraggly white hair. As

I studied Otto, though, I began to see that he was a decomposing version of his son.

I held out the tray of nachos to the old man, but he waved me off. "Damned stuff gets stuck under my teeth."

"I grew up a Cards fan," I said. "But I've never seen the Mets except on TV. I got a pal in New York who's a big Mets fan."

"Mets're all a bunch of whiney punk bastards," Turk said, "worse'n the fuckin' Cubs."

Otto Turk was a fan's fan.

With a two ball, two strike count from Ken Hill, Coleman grounded out to Ozzie Smith at short. Mr. DeWitt seemed to play his position with about the same intensity as Ozzie, gathering himself slightly as the pitches were delivered, then relaxing while Hill went through his idiosyncracies on the mound. When Tommy Herr, another ex-Cardinal, stepped in and fanned on five pitches, it looked like Hill was in good form that night. Dave Magadan was up third. He popped up high over the infield. Turk turned to me before the ball reached the ground, and said above the crowd noise, "I never thought I'd live to meet a true life de-tective."

I watched Pedro Guerrero glide under the pop-up and measure the catch. "What'd your son have to say about me?"

"Said some fella from Colorado was snooping around."

"So you decided to be generous with your time."

"And my tickets." Turk tried to blow a smoke ring, but the smoke dissolved into an indistinct cloud. "I watch a lot of baseball. Somebody comes along, entertains me between innings, I figure, what the hell. Ain't that right, Mr. DeWitt?" He nudged Mr. De-Witt with his elbow.

"That's right, Mr. Turk."

Then, Turk said to me, "My boy Mattie says people

think he killed that doctor fella. Heywood . . . Heymaker . . . Hey-some thing."

"Heyman."

"Yeah, sure." Turk chuckled. "I knew that all the time. I heard all about that stuff. Heard about Cochran getting out . . . the Heyman boy . . . all of it." Turk studied his cigarette, then blew softly on the burning tip. "Killed out there by that old ruin where the tragedy happened. That's all it is, you know, all just a bunch of goddamn bullshit."

"I'd say it's more than that. You think people just pulled your son's name out of a hat? What you call bullshit, some people might think is evidence."

"What do I care what people think?"

The stadium organist plinked out a tune, while the huge video screen above right center played a live shot of the Mets pitcher, Ron Darling, throwing his warm-ups.

"Well, if Matthew's a murderer," I said, "I guess you might care about that."

Turk dropped the cigarette and turned back to the game.

While the Mets finished taking the field in the bottom of the first, I heard a soft *tic-tac* heading toward us down the steps. A moment later, a tall young woman stepped in and sat down on my left. She had a pale complexion, as though her skin never saw the sun, and a wild mane of auburn hair with henna highlights. She was dressed in emerald green spandex tights and a pale yellow, sleeveless leotard. The *tic-tac* sound came from her black high-heeled shoes. She was carrying two large cups of beer. She reached under my nose and handed one cup to Turk. She looked like a mis-colored Laker girl.

Out of the corner of his mouth, Turk said, "You get the car parked?"

"Sure," she breathed. After giving Turk the beer, she held her hand in place, the first two fingers extended, until Turk fumbled in his shirt pocket and outfitted her with a cigarette. That long, white arm made me feel like a big old catfish watching a piece of bait glide by. My eyes followed her hand as she slowly retrieved it past my face. She wore a ring set with one large sapphire and a supporting cast of diamonds. The blue sapphire clashed with her green pants, but sapphires, especially sapphires accompanied by diamonds, can clash with anything they want. Then my eyes bumped into hers. Her eyes were hazel.

"Nice to meet you, honey," I said.

"I'm Ronette," she said. Her lips looked red as blood.

Turk said, "I know what you're thinking, Banks. But I'm rich, so she don't mind."

I looked up again at the video screen above the outfield, half expecting to see a replay of Ronette's entrance.

"You must be the cowboy detective," she said through a cloud of smoke. She gave me a once-over that made me feel like a steak, then shook her head.

"Me? No, I'm more of a social scientist. I came down to study your squeeze here." I nodded toward Turk, who was busy giving instructions to Mr. DeWitt.

"That old reptile?" A smile played on her lips, as she idly thumbed the sapphire ring.

I smiled back. "I guess that makes you a biologist."

"That would be the *art* of biology . . . *honey.*"

Before I could say anything more, I heard the crack of a bat and an immediate burst of cheers. When I looked out onto the field, a new kid for the Cards named Gilkey was stretching through his last strides toward first, just behind a throw from Howard Johnson deep in the hole behind third. The cheers quickly faded.

For the next twenty minutes or so, the game took its course, and Turk didn't have much to say, except to express the opinion that the Mets ought to be playing ball in places with wooden bleachers and picket fences. Turk volunteered nothing more about the purpose of our meeting, so I decided for the time being to wait him out. I thought about making small talk with Ronette, but every time I started to say something, my mouth went dry. In the fourth, the Mets took a two-to-nothing lead on a homer by McReynolds with Hubie Brooks on second after a double. With the Cards down, Turk's interest in the game seemed to wane.

"I drove by your house this afternoon," I said to Turk.

Turk let out a dry laugh that jarred his teeth loose. "Quite a showplace, ain't it?" He didn't seem interested in how I had learned where he lived.

"Looked like you could use a flock of sheep," I said, "to clean up the yard."

Turk laughed again. "Mr. DeWitt here don't tend livestock. He's a sports enthusiast. Ronette, she can't afford to mess up her nails. And I'm retired from agriculture myself."

"How long you been retired?"

"Since the boy got home from the war. My wife's mother died in forty-three—her old man was dead before we got married. Died of a heart attack when he heard his little Grace was gonna marry me." Turk stared at me for a moment, looking, I guess, for some sign of whether or not I believed him. "Anyhow," he went on, "after the boy got back a hero and all, I decided maybe I'd just move to town."

"How'd you meet her, anyhow? Your wife? Grace."

"Oh, when I was a young man, I used to get duded up and take the train down here to St. Louis. You know, nightclubbin' and such. This was during Prohibition, and I knew a couple of joints they'd let me in. Me and Grace just ended up at the same watering hole one night. You know how it is. Nothing special. Not at the start, anyhow."

"Why you?" I said. "How come a rich society girl from St. Louis latches onto a dirt farmer from out in the country?"

"Kind of like Cinderella in reverse, isn't it?" Turk said. "And me wearing the glass boot. Well, it's not like anybody liked it. Not any of her people, I mean."

Just then, a hot foul screamed our way. His glove instantly ready, Mr. DeWitt jumped forward, but at the last millisecond, he twitched aside and pulled the glove back. Ronette ducked my way, and I doubled down over her just as the ball whistled not more than a foot past Otto Turk's awestruck face before crashing into one of the empty seats behind us.

"Jumpin' Jesus Christ!" Turk howled. The purple veins around his nose were drained. "What in the goddamn hell was that! Mr. DeWitt—"

"I got a good eye," Mr. DeWitt said. His voice was a cool, level drawl. "That's what you pay me for. That's why you say you don't want a *white* man."

"I might remind you," Turk said testily, "I'd be just as dead from a heart attack as a baseball between the headlights." Then he turned to me and said, "You gotta watch these colored all the time."

When I saw the light snuff out behind Mr. DeWitt's eyes, I decided that Otto Turk's racial views were a self-fulfilling prophecy.

"But then," Turk said, laughing nervously and clapping Mr. DeWitt on the thigh with a bony hand, "Mr. DeWitt here is an African American. A *major league* African American."

It occurred to me that perhaps Mr. DeWitt would escort Mr. Turk home by way of one of the bridges over the deep, muddy river. And it also occurred to me that Ronette was taking a long time getting her head out of my lap.

"So her people didn't like you," I said to Turk, trying to get the conversation back on track.

"Not exactly," he said. "I had calluses and blackheads. But I was wild." Turk looked at me and laughed deep in his chest. "And Gracie wasn't exactly tame."

I wondered aloud what had gone sour in Turk's relationship with his son.

"Oh, it was the murder, that's all," Turk said.

"Right," I said, "the murder. I talked to some people about that. Back in Mauvaisterre. It all makes for quite a story."

"Quite a story," Turk echoed. "Yep, quite a story." He appeared to study the game on the field.

I settled back and crossed my legs. "When I talked to Alfonse Leake, he said your boy, Matthew, was the first one pointed a finger at Cochran. Said he saw him running away."

"That's right."

"I talked to Matthew, too. Twice. But he didn't mention that."

"Mention what?"

"You know, didn't say he'd seen Cochran running away from the pond. He told me a lot of things, more than I expected. But he didn't say anything about that."

"Must've slipped his mind." Turk gazed up at the scoreboard.

"Maybe."

"That happens, you know. Things happen when you're a kid, you forget 'em. Even black 'em out, they're bad enough."

"You're right," I said. "And sometimes old men leave home and move to St. Louis."

In the long moment that followed, I could feel Otto Turk gathering inside himself. Finally, he leaned closer, and began to speak in a soft, almost conspiratorial voice. "See, there was a problem at the start with Cochran, one that nobody but me and the boy knew about."

The next several minutes were like one of those

dreams you have. You know, the kind where a boy with wings might fall from the sky into the ocean, while a shipful of people goes sailing idly by. The game progressed without our attention. I heard the ebb and surge of the crowd, but it seemed somehow elemental, like the pulse of the world. I felt the arch of Ronette's foot sliding rhythmically up and down along the back of my calf, but I didn't care. Well, I almost didn't care.

Otto Turk went on to tell me that it was Matthew who had found his mother, which I already knew. When Otto showed up not long afterward, the boy was nearly wild.

"I told him," Turk said, "told him there wasn't any question it was Cochran done it. Killed her. I told him about catching that half-wit watching his mother swim one time before, how I'd give him a good whippin'. So the boy didn't have any trouble believing it was Cochran, either."

But that wasn't good enough for Otto Turk. He went on to tell his son that it didn't matter what the two of them knew, nobody actually *saw* what had happened. How could the two Turk men take a chance that Cochran would get away with it? So somebody had to be a witness. What other choice did they have?

"I told him I'd do it myself," Turk said. By now, his voice was hardly more than a coarse whisper. "But there were people, people I'd been with, who'd know I couldn't of seen anything. So I told him it was up to him to be the witness. For his mama."

"And you knew," I said, "they'd be more likely to believe the boy than they would you."

"I ain't sayin' I knew that, and I ain't sayin' I didn't. Anyhow, he stood up and did what he had to."

"And who were the people? The ones who would say you weren't there?"

Otto Turk chuckled, and his voice got even lower. "You know, that's just what the boy said." Turk glanced over his shoulder at Mr. DeWitt, who was eyeballing a woman in the next box.

"I talked to Cochran, too," I said. "He claims he didn't do it."

"Maybe I should've killed *him*," Turk said.

"Who were those people, Otto? The ones you were with?"

"I kinda forget."

I put my hand on his shoulder. "That's a lie." I squeezed slightly, smiled at him, and squeezed just a touch harder. "You caught her swimming all right, caught her that day, just like you'd caught her before. Showing herself. Leake said her clothes were torn. He figured that happened when Cochran tried to take them off. But you and I know it happened when you put them back on."

Turk's breath smelled like cigarettes. "I told her the first time, I said, You carry on like that again, do that to me again—"

"That's the first time you caught her," I said. "In the pond?"

"Nobody rubs my face in it like that. Didn't matter how rich she was. Anyway, I thought she'd got all that out of her system. We were all settled down, you know, after Matthew. Then I catch her carrying on that way where the moron could see her."

"What changed?"

"Changed? Hell, how do I know what changed."

"Maybe she was just going for a swim."

Turk shook his head sharply. "Didn't matter. Nobody shames me like that. Not after she pledges to you, gives you a baby. Maybe before, but not after that."

"So you beat Cochran."

"Had to. How else you supposed to teach somebody like that?"

"And what about Grace? You said she was wild."

247 🚗

"Not anymore," Turk said, his voice falling off to a whisper. "Not anymore."

Briefly, Turk seemed lost in thought. Mr. DeWitt and Ronette stood and screamed with the surging crowd.

Finally, Turk said, "So what? Huh? Just what the hell is it you think you're gonna do? There must be thirty-five, forty thousand people here, not a one of 'em heard anything. Not even that chippie Ronette, or this coon over here thinks he's Reggie Jackson."

Turk was right. So what? I was sick to death of old men and old murder. What could I do? Call the police? Tell them to arrest Otto Turk for a crime that Mickey Cochran had long since settled?

"It's a done deal, Banks," Turk said. "Done since the night old Buckshot McCool and that nitwit Alfonse Leake decided they had to make it all work. Had to scare up some justice so all those god-fearing souls wouldn't lynch a half-wit, ruin their precious little town. Hell's bells. I'll let you guess what that town ever meant to me."

"You're a regular genius," I said.

Turk popped out his upper plate and swished it around in what was left of his beer, then thumbed his teeth back into place. "Just lucky," he said. "That's all it was. I was a genius like you say, I'd of taken her on a vacation. A long vacation." He turned his attention back to the game for a moment, before he looked back at me and started to cackle. "That's it! A nice long vacation out West. Where there's lots of wide open spaces. You know all about life in the West, don't you, Banks?"

Otto Turk's laughter was drowned out by a mixture of cheers and boos for Ken Hill, who had just put Vince Coleman in the dirt with a pitch that brought the Mets to the railing of the dugout.

18

As I drove back into Mauvaisterre around midnight, I could see the red glow in the sky above town. That would be the cookfires for tomorrow's picnic. Well, I for one was not in a picnicking mood. For two hours on the road, I had been trying to get the echo of Otto Turk's reasoning out of my ear. Trouble was, the old man was probably right. Grace Turk's murder had been a done deal since Buster McCool and Alfonse Leake chose to save, at any cost, the town from itself. And now I was heading back into Mauvaisterre, where the night sky looked like a cauldron.

So I had indulged myself, followed Gerry Heyman down the gullet of that old case and nothing there had taken me any closer to finding his killer. My friend, Gerry Heyman, the amateur detective. What was he doing that night at the Turk cemetery? Brooding? Brooding on Mickey Cochran's bad luck, all the while stumbling over some bad luck of his very own? Or brooding on the cosmos? That would be more like

Gerry. Well, Dr. Heyman, meet the cosmos. Have a nice stay.

Why did he leave the house at all that night? Sure, it might have been his habit, as Pointdexter had said. But that seemed too pat, especially when you put it together with the phone call he took just before going out.

I drove steadily and the red sky seemed to urge me on. I thought about the men huddled around the kettles, talking through the night in low, slurred voices interrupted by laughter. I thought about a boy named Gerry Heyman, a kid roaming those perfect, tree-lined streets, finding his way to a town picnic, where there would be, besides that world famous burgoo, cold chicken, hamburgers, hot fried carp, pies, carnival rides and fancy ladies in bright cotton dresses. Bands playing. Probably even a beauty contest. And it would all be beautiful, yes sir, beautiful, dazzling, your eyes practically tearing at the sight of children running across the broad shimmering fields, perhaps setting loose wonderful bunches of helium balloons and the balloons would glide off into the blue sky, red and green and yellow dots sailing away. Gerry Heyman, a farm kid, whose boyhood home had been torched, plowed under, and turned into a cornfield. Gerry, my buddy, who knew what he wanted, Sarah and a decent life in his hometown, and got them both.

Those same streets were Sarah's streets, too. The lovely Sarah, sleeping alone in her big yellow house under that smoldering sky. Showering in the morning. (I remembered the line of her shoulder and back from our year together in Champaign.) Sitting down to breakfast. (Did she still like to curl up with a glass of orange juice in a patch of early sunlight?) I remembered the smell of her, like crushed roses. (Would she still daub perfume between her breasts at bedtime?) I thought about Sarah a lot. I thought about her leaving home the night her husband was killed. Thought about her miserable, renegade son, who had given me that information by accident.

And then I thought: Drop it. All of it. The dead and their killers, the living and their lovers. Just let it all go. How much more did I really want to know?

The streets were deserted, but there were maybe a dozen cars parked around the Hotel Mauvaisterre. Inside, the bar was loud and smoky, the jukebox an unintelligible din above voices. Little Mike was behind the bar, swamped, and Tory McDade was at the end of it, smashed, which added a nice symmetry to the small crowd of drinkers, men and women in their twenties. The uniform of the day seemed to be some variation of blue jeans and T-shirt, with gimme caps for the guys and pushed-up sunglasses for the gals. Which way to the tractor pull?

"Banks!" Tory McDade waved an arm wildly in my direction.

Little Mike put her hands on her hips and gave McDade the evil eye. I wandered in his direction, not anxious to drink a lot, but needing to drink a little. Drink a lot in my mood, and I could become a dangerous man. I looked at Little Mike and pointed to the tap, then sat down on the stool next to McDade.

I said, "Cooking burgoo tonight, eh?"

"The miserable pricks," McDade said.

Little Mike slid a schooner in front of me. "They eighty-sixed him. From the picnic grounds."

"Said-I-was-drunk," McDade slurred.

"Imagine that," Little Mike said.

I took a long pull on the schooner, then paused to catch my breath. "I can't imagine that at all." I finished off the beer, and slid the empty glass back to Little Mike, who knew what to do with it.

"Anything I can't stand," McDade said, "it's being called a drunk by a buncha drunks."

The second beer was just as good as the first. By the

time the third arrived, I was feeling a little more sedate.

"What was the score?" Little Mike asked.

I remembered that the summons from Otto Turk had come to me through Little Mike's kitchen, just like an order of fries. I told her I left before the game was over. "This whole damned trip," I said, "it's starting to feel like a bust."

Little Mike laughed. "That's because you didn't come back here to solve any murder. You came back to get your mitts on an old girlfriend."

Could that be true? Up until those moments with Sarah along the river, I would have argued to the end that Little Mike was wrong. "No," I said with great formality, "that is a completely separate issue."

Now Little Mike laughed harder. "And that's a crock, Leo. Trust me, I've been an old girlfriend, I recognize the signs."

"What signs?" I said.

"Here's to love!" Tory McDade said, hoisting his glass before draining it. "Love and kisses!" He rattled the ice in Little Mike's direction.

McDade, thank God, was more interested in murder than in failed romance, so I explained why I had made the trip to St. Louis to meet Otto Turk. But I stopped short of telling him about Turk's veiled admission.

"Turk!" Tory McDade spit the word down at his glass. "This whole town's had people named Turk stuck up its ass ever since that night."

"What night?"

"Be serious, Banks. Night of the murder." McDade twirled his cigarettes around and around on the bar, then stopped them abruptly and pulled a smoke from the pack and lit it. "I was there, you know."

"What do you mean?" I said.

"*There.* At the jail." He worked on his fresh drink. "That night they talked to Cochran."

I glanced at Little Mike, who shrugged and shook her head.

"Poor bastard," McDade mumbled.

"Who?" I said.

"Who? Cochran, that's who. Who'd you think? The miserable retard."

McDade explained that he was fourteen that year, and he had a job swamping out the jail. The job didn't pay beans, but there were rarely any prisoners, so the work consisted mostly of sweeping up cigar ashes after Buckshot McCool. For Tory, the job's most valuable asset on the night of the murder turned out to be his key to the front door, which he used to sneak inside and listen to McCool and Leake take Mickey Cochran apart.

"He sobbed," McDade said, "Jesus God, you never heard anybody sob like that boy. After about an hour, they got him to say he used to slip around and spy on her . . . then he started sobbin' even more."

"You said you had to sneak in," I said.

"Right." McDade nodded quickly, trying to make his eyes focus. "That's right. For a long time, I hid out in a coat closet. But I couldn't hear, so I went creepin' out, found me a corner by the door leading into the cells. Wasn't but three cells in that old jail . . . it's gone now . . . big old stone building over behind the Methodist church." He shook his head and drank. "Ugly place. Burned down back in the fifties."

Once he left the closet, McDade could hear the traffic and the voices out in the street. As Alfonse Leake had told me yesterday, so Tory McDade told me there in the Hotel Mauvaisterre bar: that July night in 1937 Cochran was in deep trouble.

"They'd of took him," McDade said. "That's what Buckshot and Leake kept tellin' him, and by God I believed it. I still believe it. Because everybody knew it was him, see? It was all over town that Matthew Turk had seen Cochran running away from the pond just before he found her. Everybody knew it, I knew it even before I snuck in the jail and heard Buckshot and Leake saying it over and over to Cochran."

"And Gerry Heyman?" I said. "You didn't tell him any of this, did you?"

"I told you the other day," McDade said. "He pissed me off." McDade suddenly let out a growl and stubbed out his cigarette. "I'm gettin' outta here."

I tried to tell McDade that I wasn't done talking, but he wasn't having any of it.

"The night's young," he said, "and adventure calls." McDade stepped behind the bar and pulled down an open fifth of Jack Daniel's. "It may take a Russian," McDade explained patiently, "to make decent vodka. But trust me, son, those crackers down in Tennessee, they know about whiskey. Little Mike, put this on Banks's tab."

"I don't have a tab," I said.

"Yeah you do," McDade said. "I been drinking on it since this morning."

Little Mike shrugged. "He said you were blood brothers, Leo."

"Kimosabe!" McDade bellowed.

The fifth was half empty. "It's half empty," I said to McDade.

"That's where you're wrong, bucko. Half full. Always half full." McDade wrapped his arm around my neck and pulled me close. People in hot weather should change their clothes more often than McDade did. "Let's go, Masked Man, let's go annihilate some goddamned evil!" He mashed his ever-present fedora onto his head.

"Well then, give me a drink," I said. All of those vivacious young people at the table were laughing, and I'm afraid they were laughing at us.

"A drink? Why the hell not. Here, have one of mine." He handed me the bottle of Jack just before he fell through the red Naugahyde door, pulling me after him out into the unsuspecting town.

"Everybody knows," McDade said, "a real man can chew tobacco and drink sour mash whiskey at the same time." We were on North Water Street, heading for Memorial Park. He fitted a fistful of Red Man into his mouth and offered me the packet, which I waved off. But I didn't wave off the Jack Daniel's when he offered that.

"This here's Theona Gresham's house," McDade said, pointing to a huge gray brick house with more windows showing than McDade and I had fingers and toes between us. Since turning down North Water, McDade had been conducting a travelogue of Mauvaisterre's smart set, the people with old names, old houses, old manners, and most of all, old money. The Gresham house sat back from the street, and was surrounded by well-tended gardens. All of the many windows were dark.

"Theona Gresham," McDade muttered. "She tried to help me once . . . rehabilitation . . . what an insult! Christ preserve us from the folly of old women. See the smoke?" McDade pointed ahead at the orange haze rising from the end of the street, maybe six blocks away. He picked up the pace.

How would all those good people behave if they knew what was passing by outside their bedroom windows?

"What else about the jail?" I said. My eyes were starting to feel numb from the whiskey.

"The jail? Oh yeah, the jail. That. Nothing much. They keep hammering on Cochran, see. Leake, he's all the time telling him it's pointless to lie, 'cause the boy saw him, and who's not gonna believe the boy? You know? Hell's fire, a kid sees his mama dead, sees her killer . . . all that kinda shit.

"Then every once in a while, Buckshot jumps in

255

with his size fourteen Ds, and he says the real problem is what are they gonna do that night. Says people are pissed off enough about the murder and all, but what's got 'em so fired up at the moment is the fact old Cochran there won't stand up and take it like a man. Lyin' about it, see. I mean, it's bad enough you kill some poor woman, but then you tell a whole town to just, you know, just go fuck itself, well, people don't like it.

"People think they oughta just come on down here and hang you, Buckshot says, and then he says, *By God, I think I might as well let 'em."*

Now Alfonse Leake's story made even more sense. I said, "So Alfonse Leake tells Cochran if he'll just admit he did it, they can persuade everybody to go home. Then they can deal with the consequences of the confession later on, after everything's cooled down."

"You're smarter than you look," McDade said. "You sure you don't want a chew?" He spit onto the sidewalk, leaving a wet smear about the size of a dinner plate, then took a long hit from the bottle. "Arrgghhh!" He gulped his lungs full of air. "Wait till we get to the park, Banks. You'll have a great time. I haven't missed one of these picnics since I got out of the army after the war." As we walked, I heard a few coins jingling in his pocket. "Except for that year I spent in the hospital," he said.

"Hospital?"

McDade drank again. "It was nothing. Forget I said anything."

It seemed to me that we had been walking for a very long time. I was dead tired, and angry as hell that I hadn't slipped McDade back at the hotel and gone to bed. We had passed Sarah Heyman's house several blocks back, and I'd barely noticed it until we were almost by. Her house wasn't among Tory McDade's points of interest. What the hell did Little Mike know about me and old girlfriends? I remembered eating burgoo one time when I was a kid. Was there a pay phone up ahead in Memorial Park, where I could run and call home . . . I still remembered the numbers of parents, grandparents . . . but who would answer, after all these years and the line gone cold? How long until I can put a rock down on this country?

"I was gonna bring Pharaoh," McDade said. We were within sight of Memorial Park now. "Put him on display for the kiddies. But he's been under the weather. Got something on his stomach. Maybe from the paint on that pickup truck the other day. Whatever it is, it ain't real pretty." McDade wrinkled his nose.

I wondered what it would be like to spend time around a fifteen-hundred-pound dyspeptic boar with the shits, and decided that such an experience would really be just excess baggage on the freeway of life. I held out my hand for the bottle, and McDade slapped it into my palm like a surgical instrument. When I was done, the bottle was empty. With a hook shot, I deposited it in a hedge of yew bushes that lined the sidewalk leading to someone's door. A dog barked inside the house.

"Shhhh!" McDade hissed. He was hissing at me.

The large, scorched kettles, several dozen of them, were set up in three rows and a string of lights had been hung from the four power poles that bracketed the area. There was a big, open barn about fifty yards from the kettles, and as we got nearer, I could hear both the voices of the men, who were maneuvering paddles inside the kettles, and the sounds of uneasy movement from inside the barn, the low rustle of horses kept awake, I decided, by the noise of the soupmakers, and by the vague panic of smoke.

Tory McDade straightened the collar of his green suit jacket, cocked the fedora at a rakish angle over his right ear, and cleared his throat. "Yes, and a lovely evening," he shouted. "We shall by God stir soup until the ice around Theona Gresham's heart melts. Turk! Mr. Matthew Turk! A paddle, if you please."

With that, I looked more closely at the men, and sure enough there he was, Mr. Matthew Turk, standing near a large, silver-colored stock tank.

"Go away!" Turk cupped his hands to his mouth and called across the dark, open field. "Go home, McDade. We got plenty. And take that over-the-hill cop with you!"

Now that we were closer, I could see that the stock tank was filled with peeled raw vegetables. All of the soup crew were watching us.

"Now listen, Turk," McDade said, "my friend Banks here, he's looking for a cultural experience. And I have a certain civic duty."

Turk's face looked as if he were choking back a sudden attack of heartburn. "No, you listen, McDade. I finally got everybody calmed down. I don't want you getting 'em all hopped up. Not again this year. I told you that earlier." He pinched the bridge of his nose with a grease-brightened thumb and finger. "You're a menace. A goddamned menace."

"Don't repeat yourself, Mattie," Tory McDade said. "Just take it slow and calm." He picked through the potatoes and carrots and onions and corn and peas and lima beans in the stock tank. "Good vegetables this year, Mattie. I hope you got meat as good as these vegetables. Anybody bring pigeons this year?"

"Just your basic ox tails and beef shanks," Turk said, his tone curiously defensive. "Just your basic ox tails and beef shanks. And chickens."

McDade made a clucking noise. "It was a mistake to substitute chickens for pigeons. I tried to tell 'em that years ago. And squirrels." He gave me a mournful look. "They gave up putting squirrels in back before Korea."

I followed McDade around the tank and out among

the kettles and the men. A small ladle hung from one of the posts that held up the string of lights. McDade took it down and began making the rounds of the kettles, dipping a sample from each. The kettles—I counted forty—were fitted into metal bases that were vented by a length of stovepipe, so that the considerable smoke was released into the air above everybody's head. I was intrigued by the robust bouquet of woodsmoke, sharpened by an impudent hint of grease. The color of the liquid inside the kettles was predominantly gray, with shimmering orange highlights. Now and then, a long, bony ox tail wagged up out of the boiling delight, reminding me that there is always a touch of heaven in simple country pleasures.

Tory McDade moved easily from kettle to kettle, exchanging greetings and insults and much backslapping. Matthew Turk shadowed McDade, and I shadowed Turk. I spotted the two boys from the pickup the other day at McDade's place. Neither of them seemed to want anything to do with me.

"Good soup," McDade said to the men. "You're doing a fine job. Excellent soup this year. Mattie," he said to Turk, "you are a true master of the soupmaker's craft. I salute you." McDade threw back his shoulders, tried to suck in some of his belly, then touched a finger to the brim of his hat. "Now"—he leaned against a stack of cordwood and let his belly out with a loud *whooosh*—"now we got a lot of work to do."

"Last year," Turk said to me, "we caught him pouring half a case of beer into his kettle. Took four men to hold him down while we called Otis Wiesel. Nobody cared much about the soup, but it was getting late, and they couldn't abide wasting the beer."

McDade shrugged. "It was nothing. The cast was off in a coupla months. But this year, Mattie, this year I'm at the peak of my form."

"That's what I'm afraid of." Turk lit a cigarette and threw the match disgustedly on the ground.

"Fine way to treat a war hero," McDade said. "A man who waded ashore at Guadalcanal. No shit, Mattie, I'd get a better welcome than this in Japan."

Turk exhaled a cloud of smoke and turned away.

McDade shot an arm out, grabbed Turk by the sleeve and spun him around. "Don't you turn away from me!" We were standing next to a kettle being stirred by a big, curly-haired guy in a Chicago Bears T-shirt. The guy was a little big to play linebacker, but not quite big enough for offensive tackle.

"Fifty years!" Turk ripped his arm away. "Almost fifty years ago. That time's all gone now, gone. Can't you just let what's gone go?"

I stepped between the two old men, hoping to keep McDade, you might say, out of the soup. "Tory—"

But McDade shoved me aside. I didn't much mind, but the guy he shoved me into, the behemoth in the Bears T-shirt, he minded plenty.

"If I forget—" McDade said.

"Knock it off, McDade," the Bears guy said. He looked as if he were listening for the snap count.

"Don't worry about it," I said to everybody, "he's as drunk as I am."

"Drunk?" Turk said. "If all he was was drunk, I wouldn't mind. Jesus Christ, everybody here but me's drunk. Why do you think these guys come down here and stand around all night? But him, he's crazy! Two years ago he passed out and fell in a kettle and if we hadn't fished him out when we did, half the town would've been made into cannibals!"

"Fuck you, Turk," McDade said.

"Cannibals!"

"McDade, take a hike," the Bears guy said.

"You keep out of this, you big dumb sonofabitch." McDade addressed the Bears guy with great assurance, if very little wisdom.

"What?" The guy rested his paddle on the rim of the kettle.

"I said—"

Again, I tried to steer McDade away. "Take it easy." Once more, McDade shoved me aside. This time, I reached out instinctively to catch myself, and ended up with my arm elbow deep in simmering burgoo.

Out of the corner of my eye, I saw Matthew Turk fade, grinning, into the gathering circle of men.

"You hear that?" the Bears guy said. "He tried to call me a sonofabitch. Nobody does that." Being called big and dumb didn't seem to bother him.

When the Bears guy drew back a huge, bronze fist, I thought about trying to stop him. Sooner or later, though, McDade was going to need a fist like that. More merciful, I decided, that it come from somebody who could put him down with one shot. For all the shortcomings of his life, I hoped that Tory McDade at least had good insurance.

I'm not sure if it was my scalded arm or the hay scratching through my clothes that awakened me. For a while, I lay on the stack of bales with my eyes closed, and listened to the horses shift from hoof to hoof and sigh. I could smell them, a smell like sweaty animal dust. I was sober enough by now to feel like hell.

Once McDade hit the ground, a couple of the soup crew had helped me drag him into the horse barn, where we left him passed out on the ground. Then I decided that the best course for me would be simply to go to sleep. Now, I prayed against all reason that when I opened my eyes this miserable midwestern murder gig would be over.

Then I heard a series of loud, rapacious snores.

So McDade at least was not dead.

I opened my eyes. It was still dark. I sat up. I

retched once, and promised myself not to do it again. "McDade?"

He was sprawled under a rail lined with saddles and tack, where we had left him.

"McDade!"

It was quite clear. If he didn't shut up those snores, I was going to have to kill him.

McDade moaned and dabbed his fingers at his jaw. Even in the dark, I could see it was swollen and ugly. He tried to sit up, but got tangled in a pair of stirrups. Finally he freed himself, and crawled out from under the saddles, where he sat back and rubbed his fists into his eyes.

"I guess I'm not making sense," McDade said.

"How could you? You haven't said anything yet."

"Oh . . . yeah. I thought I was just talking to you," he said.

I told him he hadn't said anything at all, unless you counted the snoring, which hadn't sounded exactly human. And then I told him it seemed as if he had pretty strong feelings about Matthew Turk, about as strong as those he'd expressed before about Gerry Heyman. I was curious to know if what he thought about Turk had anything to do with some murder or another.

For a while, McDade didn't say anything. Then he felt around inside the breast pocket of his jacket, retrieving finally an object, which he tossed to me. It was a medal, a dark cross hanging from a wrinkled red, white and blue ribbon.

"DSC," he said. "That's for Distinguished—"

"Distinguished Service Cross," I said. "Yeah, I know. Guadalcanal?"

"Sure. Why not."

"What happened?"

McDade began smoothing down his stubby gray hair with his hands. "Nothing much. Bunch of us got blown up." His laugh was unexpected, a dry bark.

"There was this guy named Collins. Big gangly kid from Philadelphia. Drove us all nuts, all the time talking big stories about the women back in Philly, and shooting snooker all day. Nothin' but mouth, that's all he was. We was so fed up with him on the ship, we'd of killed him ourselves, but the Japanese saved us the trouble."

It was very quiet there in the barn, and the men outside were quiet, too.

"We go ashore, that goddamn worthless Collins, he gets one in the chest that turns him around so he's walking back out into the water, back out toward the ship. Then he starts screaming, screamin' so loud we can hear him over all the goddamn shooting. *Paulette, you bitch, how come you,* he screams, then a big wave knocks him on his ass and he never gets up.

"Rest of us, we end up in a hole there on the beach and every now and then somebody tries to make a move and gets hit. Long time, I kept looking back out there at Collins, there at the edge of the water, and every time a breaker rolls in, it's like he's waving at us. Waving good-bye . . . good-bye . . . still see it. The miserable shit. Who you suppose Paulette was?"

I shook my head.

"Well, she's better off, that jerkoff a pile of bones back there on Guadalcanal."

"You get wounded?" I asked, remembering his comment about the hospital.

"No."

"How'd you get this?" I held up the medal.

"That's nobody's fuckin' business. I done some stuff." McDade turned away quickly and began feeling around on the ground. "You seen my hat?"

"Not since that guy knocked you out from under it."

"I got a hat around here someplace. Fine old felt hat. Kind of hat Jimmy Stewart wore in a movie once. You haven't seen it?"

"I told you I haven't."

McDade crawled back under the saddles, feeling through the loose straw and hay. He kept crawling until he was among the horses, where he stood up. For the first time, I looked closely at the horses. There must have been thirty head tied to both sides of a rail that ran the length of the barn. The night had cooled, and their breath gathered around their muzzles in erratic bursts of warm steam. At the far end of the barn, I saw Matthew Turk's surrey, and his white gelding tied nearby. I started working my way through the horses, talking softly and patting them on their rumps and backs to keep them calm.

"What about Turk?" I said. "His old man told me he was a war hero, too."

"Oh, he was," McDade said. "He was. Takes a brave and skillful warrior to fight his way up to the rank of major. Especially you never leave Honolulu." The horses on McDade's side of the rail were starting to sound edgy as he moved among them with growing abruptness. "Nothing wrong with that," he said, "unless you let people go on thinking you're the greatest swingin' dick since MacArthur."

"And nobody caught on?"

"Sure they did. See, there were enough of us who really went through something, it didn't take but a year or two before people understood what he was . . . or what he wasn't, really. But he kept the bullshit alive, and after a while folks just said, well, this here's Matthew Turk, the fellow who won the war."

I was about to pump McDade further about Turk, when I heard him gasp.

"Shhhhit!"

"The hat?" I said.

"Standin' on it," McDade moaned. He was leaning against the rump of a pinto horse. "Get offa there, you sonofabitch." He started ramming his shoulder into the horse's butt. I told him to stop before he got kicked into next week, then I ducked under the rail and joined him.

The brim of the hat was spread out in all directions under the pinto's left rear hoof.

"He's just a horse," I said, "he doesn't know any better."

"Well get him off it," McDade moaned. He leaned again into the horse's haunch. "Come on, you big piece of dog food, move it." He strained harder against the animal. The horse looked back at McDade, as though measuring him.

I pushed McDade back, then bent down and lifted the hoof and plucked away the hat. The pinto let out a long sigh that made his lips blubber. I handed the flattened hat to McDade.

McDade turned the hat over and over in his hands, shaking his head. Then he went to work punching out the crown and carefully reshaping the brim. When he finished, he put the hat on his head with great dignity, then walked to a bale of hay and sat down.

"This calls for some thought," Tory McDade said, resting his elbows on his knees. "This calls for restitution."

I didn't like the sound of that. McDade seemed to have a way of devising plenty of wreckage without the aid of a plan.

"It's just a hat," I said. "A hat's not that important."

"Exactly," McDade snapped. "That's exactly the point." He jumped up and began pacing. "Don't you see?" His eyes bulged out like shot glasses. He spoke quickly and shook his index finger at me. McDade might be a certified war hero, but I didn't really consider him to be someone I was willing to go to jail with.

"That's why it's so bad, Leo, because it's *not* important. It's just petty trifling, that's what it is. Petty trifling and I won't stand for it. There was no need for those men to throw my hat to the horses."

McDade suddenly kicked a five gallon bucket across the barn.

The horses bolted, straining against their halters.

I wished to God I was drunk again.

McDade walked back down the line of horses until he came to the pinto. A moment later, he had untied the horse, brought him back down to the hay bales and was busy saddling him.

"I think I'll call him Jingles," McDade said, drawing the cinch tight. "You can take that one there," he said, pointing out a Palomino tied next to the bales. "Call him Champion."

Me? All right, so I was still drunk.

"The Japanese tried to kill me," Tory McDade said, "and damn near did. But I'll tell you one thing, Leo, the Japanese understood a man's honor."

"Champion, eh?" I said. I don't know how this happened, but when I looked down at my hands, they were busy untying the leather lead strap on the Palomino's halter.

"They used to call a bunch of horses like this a *remuda,*" McDade said. By now, he'd finished saddling Jingles and he was moving down the rail, slipping the halter from the head of each horse. "But hell, you know all about this, you're from North Dakota. That's real cowboy country." The horses began to mill uneasily inside the barn.

"In the old days," I said, "the Indians believed putting the run on a man's horses was a point of honor."

"I understand completely," McDade said. He threw the reins over Jingles's head, then grunted loudly as he tried to reach the stirrup with his foot. "Leo, your assistance, if you please."

"Wait a minute," I said, then took a moment to pin the Distinguished Service Cross on his lapel.

I felt dizzy as I leaned down and put my shoulder

under Tory McDade's backside and heaved him up into the saddle.

"You ready, Masked Man?" Tory McDade said, squaring his hat of incomparable value.

"What the hell," I said, swinging aboard Champion, "let's go count some coup."

We moved out under the cold morning stars, the *remuda* leading the way at a trot, until they broke into a canter as Tory McDade and Jingles cleared the barn behind them, McDade now holding the reins in his right hand and the saddle horn in his left, urging Jingles faster and faster until he pulled abreast of the *remuda* and on ahead, turning the stampeding herd hard to the right, then falling back again as the horses bore down on the kettles, the crazed animals on the run through the night, rich turf flying above their heaving backs, closer and closer to the men until the lead horse faltered, sensing the fires, and Tory McDade yelled, "Yaaaaahhhooooooo!" and, as one, the *remuda* thundered straight for Matthew Turk, who looked up from the tank of vegetables and screamed, "He's gone berserk he's gone berserk!" and the men scattered and the horses went crashing through the cluster of kettles, overturning one, kicking up dirt and debris into others, before they raced headlong out across Memorial Park toward all the fancy old homes on North Water Street. Through it all, Champion turned out to be worthy of his name. He never lost his head, and I was able to hold back and enjoy the entire show.

Tory McDade rode among the wreckage. Jingles stopped, then raised himself on his hind legs. McDade grabbed frantically for the horn with both hands, and when Jingles's front hooves hit the ground, he was off like a bolt of lightning.

I pulled up beside Matthew Turk, who was wiping hot soup from his shirt with a burlap bag. The other

267

men, unaccountably, were cheering and clapping and calling for more beer.

Matthew Turk reached up and tried to pull me of the horse, but I shoved him away with my boot. I was so goddamn mad that out of all the pandemonium there at the park that night, the luckiest thing that happened was that Turk didn't get me down off that horse.

"It was you fingered Cochran," I said. "You never told me that." After leaving Otto Turk at the ballpark, I'd been going over and over my conversations with all those old men. Cochran. Leake. McDade. Otto Turk. Everybody had something to say about the effect of Matthew Turk's statement in settling his mother's murder. Everybody, that is, but Matthew Turk himself.

For once, Turk seemed caught short. "I never thought to. It just didn't seem to matter anymore."

"You're a liar," I said.

I could tell by the sickened look on Turk's face that he knew exactly what I was talking about. "Then he told you," Turk said.

"Your old man," I said. "That's right. Told me he got you to lie. I just didn't realize until tonight how much the lie counted for." I was referring to what McDade had said about the effect of the lie on Cochran's statement. But I wasn't in any mood to explain that to Turk.

I looked down at the big shot, who had come home from Honolulu a war hero. I wasn't angry because he'd been the kind of boy who would lie for his mother and father, or even because he'd become the kind of man who didn't know how to set it right. I was angry because he was the kind of man who would let the lies stack up, and then expect everybody to understand and go along. Not just go along, but forgive and forget. Because once Tory McDade had told me about Turk and the war, then I knew that Mickey

Cochran wasn't just crazy down there in the nursing home.

"How many times you been to see Cochran?" I said. "How many times did you sneak down there and stand outside that window like it was some kind of confessional?" I was angry at last because Turk's lies had been easy, so easy that anybody might have told them. Anybody. Even me. "How many? Jesus Christ, giving him candy."

When Turk didn't answer, I suddenly felt exhausted. I reined Champion's head around and trotted off into the darkness and the calm, away from all the shouting and lunacy around the kettles. But Turk ran after me.

"Banks! Banks, you don't understand."

It was as though Turk were hauling my anger after me, so that I wouldn't leave it behind. I pulled the horse up short, and waited for him.

"After your old man told you," I said, "that he couldn't lie about Cochran because he'd been with people, how long was it before you knew there weren't any people?"

"There wasn't anything I could do," he said.

"You could have told the truth," I said.

He shook his head. "There wasn't anything I could do."

"I don't mean when you were a kid. A kid gets stuck, that happens. But later, once you understood it. You could've saved that poor damned Cochran maybe thirty years in the joint."

Turk was still shaking his head. "There wasn't anything I could do," he said a third time.

Worst of all, I'd met Otto Turk. Maybe Matthew was right.

"You should have stayed in California," Turk said. "Stayed out there in California where you belong."

That did it. I started to laugh, laugh harder than I had since I'd quit the cops and stopped trading pervert stories with the guys at the station. Matthew Turk did the only thing I guess he could. He reverted to the loudmouthed guy in a white Cadillac that I'd so grown to enjoy.

"What's so funny, Banks?"

"I'm from Montana, you moron," I said. I kicked Champion in the slats, and as Jingles had done before him, he reared gallantly on his hind legs. When Champion came down, I gave him his head and he lunged off into the night, turning my testicles into puree.

There were horses grazing on lawns all along North Water Street. When I passed Theona Gresham's house, I spotted Tory McDade passed out in a lush clump of peonies. Jingles stood beside him, his head bent low as he nuzzled McDade's face.

On down the street, I tied Champion to the porch rail at Sarah Heyman's house, where people could find him, then I went back to the patio and collapsed onto a long, padded lounge chair. Maybe I could get a little sleep before Otis Wiesel, or, if I was lucky, Freddie Pointdexter, showed up to arrest me.

19

I heard the long whoop of a siren through my sleep, and soon after that something smashed into the soles of my boots and I could hear a guy talking about horse thieves and hanging. And I thought: So this is morning.

God. Goddamn, what a head.

When I eased my eyes open, the light slashed into my brain like a razor blade.

"Kill me," I said. Nothing in the world out there was worth looking at.

"I would, son, I truly would." The voice belonged to Freddie Pointdexter. "But bullets cost fifty cents a pop, and I'm on a budget."

This time I forced my eyes open, and sat up. "I think there's a dollar in my pocket. "That's two bullets. More than enough. I promise not to move."

Pointdexter was holding a large, black flashlight, an excellent tool for smacking drunks on the bottoms of their feet, which is one way to wake them up. Sarah Heyman was at his side. She handed me a tall glass of orange juice. The juice cut through the gravel in the back of my throat, and when I rubbed the cold glass against my forehead, I got a chill. Sarah was wearing a long, clingy kimono made of dark red silk with gold trim. I got another chill.

"There was a horse tied to my porch," Sarah said.

"What the hell did you expect?" I said. She didn't have to tell me I wasn't making sense.

"I come to take you for a ride," Pointdexter said.

"I'll bet."

"It's not what you think."

"Trust me," I said, "nothing could be what I'm thinking right now."

Pointdexter slid the flashlight into the leather trimmed sap pocket sewn into the left leg of his pants. "The boys down at the park, they say you had words with Matthew Turk last night."

Sarah Heyman took a slight step back. She raised her brows slightly and glanced uneasily at Pointdexter, a look that seemed to mean "be careful."

"Last night?" I said. "The park?"

"Don't give me a ration of shit, Leo. Okay? I got Matthew Turk dead in an automobile crash."

I remembered the look of fading bombast that I had seen on Turk's face just a few hours before. "You think I had something to do with that?"

"Not directly."

"What's that supposed to mean?"

"Goddamn," Pointdexter said. "I hate talkin' to a guy that can't get his own trouble out of his head."

I got to my feet and handed the empty glass back to Sarah. "Then you better find another line of work." Ignoring Sarah, I unfastened my jeans and tucked in my shirt.

"Leo," Sarah said, "I don't think Freddie's after you for anything."

"Oh, I'm sure he's not," I said, but not exactly believing it. "I was pretty drunk, though. You know how it is, Freddie, sometimes a guy gets so shithoused, he can't remember anything. Can't even say he knew what he was doing enough to *intend* doing it. You know what I mean?"

Pointdexter smirked. "That happens. Can't charge a guy with crimes if you can't show he intended to do something. I hear that's especially true with crimes involving horses."

"Crimes?" I said. "Horses?"

"Well, not exactly crimes," Pointdexter said. "Way I hear it, some old boys were thoughtful enough last night to exercise all those horses out there at the 4-H barn. Those fellas on the soup crew were entertained as hell. Somebody even said all the dirt those horses kicked up in the kettles kind of improved the flavor of the soup."

Sarah pulled the kimono closer around her shoulders. "Sounds like we're talking about heroes instead of criminals, Sheriff," she said.

"A welcome addition to the local mythology," I said.

"Absolutely," Pointdexter said. "Why hell, we'll probably make it a tradition. The Banks/McDade Memorial Stampede. Now how about that ride?"

I excused myself to use Sarah Heyman's bathroom, where I took a much needed piss, then gave my head a good soak, and finished off with a sizable dose of mouthwash. When I came out, Sarah stopped me in the kitchen. Pointdexter was still waiting out on the patio.

"Leo?" She stepped up close to me, and her hair brushed my cheek. "Leo, tell me you didn't do something."

"Do something?" I knew, of course, what she meant. "Well, sweetheart, I got drunk and put the run on some horses. But that's about it. Unless that horse I left tied up out front ate your shrubs."

"That's not what I'm talking about, and you know it." The day was barely underway, and already she

273

had her makeup on. Smudges of green eyeshadow gave her a sloe-eyed look.

"I forgot how much I loved you," I said. I folded my arms around her.

"Me too." Sarah leaned into me, and I could feel her breath on my throat.

"I'm sorry I asked you for all that money," I said. "Before I came back."

"It's okay," she said. "I should have tried harder. All those years ago. You know, to accept what was happening—"

I lifted her face and gave her a short kiss.

"—when we broke up," she said.

"I know." I kissed her longer this time, the kind of kiss you wait twenty years for. "But you didn't. And I always counted that a kind of favor."

It took a moment for what I had just said to settle into her eyes. Then her shoulders tightened and she pulled away.

"You don't care about helping me at all. It's all just easy money to you."

"Listen to me, Sarah. Nothing in the world feels like putting a murderer in jail. Nothing. Marriage, the birth of children, the impeachment of bad presidents. Nothing. You just look into the eyes of a guy you've got the goods on, and you think; you're a murderer, slick, and I've got your ass. Getting a murderer feels so good, only a fool would go about it without some kind of restraint."

"I thought—" she started.

"What you thought," I said, "is that for fifteen grand, maybe I just took care of Matthew Turk."

"I never said that."

"No, you just handed over the check. Believe me, sweetheart, nobody ponys up that kind of money for any kind of easy reason."

"If you thought I was hiring you to kill some-body . . ."

We were cut short when Pointdexter tapped on the sliding glass door and motioned me outside.

"Don't worry," I said to Sarah as I left, "I'm sure he'll come to me."

I followed Freddie Pointdexter down the path toward the gap in the rhododendrons. When I looked back at Sarah, she was standing at the edge of the patio. Her chin was held high, and the sharp, clean lines of her face looked as beautiful and perfect as marble.

The morning was cool, but I was too busy sweating out last night to notice much or care. As we headed out into the country, toward Matthew Turk's house, I slouched down in the seat and cranked open the window. The inside of Pointdexter's cruiser smelled like stale cigarettes and puke and air freshener, smelled like all police cars everywhere. I suppose it had smelled like that the other times I'd ridden in it. Before, though, I'd never been sick enough to notice. Driving too fast, with one hand on the wheel and the other draped over the back of the seat, Pointdexter explained.

"According to the boys at the park," Pointdexter said, "once you and McDade left on the last roundup, somebody went to the pay phone and called Otis Wiesel. Little while later, old Otis comes swoopin' in like he's making a crash landing on the deck of an aircraft carrier. Given a choice, Otis only talks to important people, so right away he talked to Matthew Turk."

Talked to Turk. Amazing. Amazing that I wasn't in jail. I glanced over at Pointdexter. "And?"

"And Turk tells him to forget it. Then Turk sent a bunch of those boys—half of them probably work for him anyway—sent them out to round up the horses. They get back, Turk's gone."

Later on, just after daybreak, Otis Wiesel was out

cruising, trying to finish out his shift without falling asleep. He moseyed out toward the Turk farm, and that was when he found that white Cadillac, crashed head-on right into the front door of that big old stone house. Turk himself ended up as a hood ornament, after his skull and chest got rototilled on his way past the steering wheel and through the windshield.

By now, Pointdexter and I were coming up on the house. A second patrol car, a wrecker and several cars and pickups were parked along the road, and a small crowd, men and women, but mostly men, stood smoking cigarettes and talking. Otis Wiesel stood before the group like a choir director.

"Accident?" I said.

"You tell me," Pointdexter said, braking abruptly on the gravel road. "You can still see where he left the road, cut a path through the weeds. Maybe it's just me, but I don't think there's any skids. And there's sure as hell no reason for him to be doing anything but driving straight ahead."

Pointdexter was right. He pulled to a stop, and we got out. There were two clean sets of tire tracks crossing the right shoulder, then plowing through the shallow ditch, the heavy weeds, toward the house. The swath was straight and true, heading directly for the wide gate through the stone fence. The gate had been ripped free of the fence, the rotten porch was in splinters, and the Cadillac sat imbedded like an ungainly white torpedo in the front door. As Pointdexter neared the house, ignoring calls from Otis Wiesel, I saw the shattered windshield and the long, wide smear of blood along the hood of the car.

"I figure," Pointdexter said, "he was going about a hundred miles an hour."

I said, "Hey, Mom, I'm home."

Pointdexter gave me a funny look. "What's that supposed to mean?"

Before I could explain, we were distracted by Otis

 276

Wiesel, who was headed in our direction, trailing a stream of gawkers behind him. Freddie shouted at him to keep those people the hell out, and to stay the hell out with them. Then he looked back at me.

I told Pointdexter what I had pieced together from the Turks, father and son, from Alfonse Leake, from Tory McDade and Mickey Cochran. And I told him that just a few drunken hours earlier, for better or worse, I had sprung the trapdoor under the Turk family's scaffold of lies.

Pointdexter took a step back and gave me an exaggerated look from head to toe and back again, obviously impressed to be in the presence of such a wise man. Then we sat down on the rickety porch beside the demolished Cadillac, and Pointdexter offered me a stick of Doublemint.

Out on the road, Otis Wiesel was conducting an animated blow-by-blow account of how the wreck had surely happened. His scrawny arms flapped in the air as he gestured toward the road, then the stone wall, and finally the house. The cluster of farmers and their wives nodded a steady chorus of agreement. I could hear Wiesel's voice, a high-pitched howl like the whine of a power saw. Mercifully, his words were lost in the humid distance, in the growing hum of insects, and in the rustle of a July breeze blowing hotter by the minute.

"Someday," Freddie Pointdexter said philosophically, as he gazed at Otis, "I'm gonna fire that man. Gonna do it just for recreation."

"It won't help," I said.

"Maybe I could move to Montana," Pointdexter said.

I nodded. "Worked for me."

Once Pointdexter was satisfied that there was nothing else to be gained from the Turk ruin, he left Otis Wiesel in charge of getting the Cadillac hooked out of the house. Then Pointdexter and I piled into his cruiser for the short drive back into Mauvaisterre. Neither of us said much. I wondered if Pointdexter were trying to make up his mind whether or not the blowup with Turk also meant that it really was Turk who had bashed in Gerry Heyman's skull. I know that's what I was thinking. Maybe the fact that Pointdexter wasn't doing any talking meant that he hadn't made up his mind, either.

By the time we got to town, the parade was already underway. The streets were mostly deserted—more deserted than usual—until we neared North Water. There, the crowd was substantial, and the music of marching bands was everywhere. As we neared Sarah Heyman's house, where Pointdexter planned to drop me off, I saw Nick Serette's Mercedes parked a block away. At first, I thought Serette might just be in the neighborhood to watch the parade. Well, that turned out to be true, I guess. Except that he was doing his watching with Sarah from a glider on her front porch.

"Looks like company," Pointdexter said, staring up at Nick Serette and Sarah Heyman. Pointdexter decided that sooner or later he'd have to give Serette a report on what had happened with Turk, and it might as well be sooner. He left the cruiser double parked, and the two of us climbed the steps up onto the porch. Sarah stood and came to meet us, but Serette kept his seat.

"So it's over," she said, with nervous relief. "Isn't that right, Leo? And I was right about Matthew Turk. It is over, isn't it? Leo?"

I couldn't manage to take my eyes off Nick Serette, whose attention seemed to be absorbed by the parade.

"I called Nick," Sarah said, pacing slightly, then composing herself. "I thought if he was here, you and Freddie could tell us both what happened. I mean,

Nick has to know, he's the state's attorney. And I . . . Well, I obviously *need* to know."

Pointdexter and Serette still hadn't said anything, as though they were in some unspoken compact to let Sarah and me play things out. But there was nothing, really, to play.

Sarah realized that I was still watching Serette. "I know," she said, "there's more between us, Nick and me, than that. I know. I know it was wrong. We just—" She glanced at Serette, then back at me. "I know . . . I'm sorry—" Then she stepped quickly to the glider, where she sat down close to Serette and took his hand. Serette finally got the idea that something was going on besides that goddamned parade. His smile at Sarah was something less than lame.

"I'll let Freddie tell you," I said. "See what he thinks. See what the two of you think."

While Pointdexter made his report, I leaned against one of the heavy, white columns and watched the parade. There were a couple of bands, maybe seventy kids all told, all dressed in heavy uniforms, one red, the other purple, that both looked like what I imagined a Prussian postmaster might have worn in the days of the Kaiser. There was a squad of Boy Scouts, too, and Campfire Girls, and floats from local businesses. On one of the floats, a miniature cornfield built on the bed of a wagon that was pulled by a large, green John Deere tractor, I spotted Lisa Heyman. She was dressed like an Indian princess in a brown cotton shift with fringe, a wig with long, black braids, and a single, tall, black, crow's feather sticking up from the back of her headband.

My head was in the middle of an interminable detonation, and my stomach was full of snakes. I could hear Pointdexter's voice behind me, interrupted now and then by Sarah or Nick Serette.

A column of classic cars passed, fifty-five Chevys,

Model Ts, an old Imperial with enough chrome to give a Hollywood mogul the orgasm of a lifetime.

Pointdexter still wasn't finished. I couldn't stop sweating.

Then came the horses. The horses always come last in a parade because they shit on the street, and nobody wants to have to walk through it. None of the horses looked the worse for wear after their adventure of the night before. There were a lot of large American flags flying among the mounted contingent. I found Jingles, who was ridden by a young woman wearing red cowboy boots and powder blue jeans tight enough to cause gangrene.

And there was Champion, prancing along under who else but the man whose fist had set Tory McDade on the road to equestrian retribution. Instead of a Bears T-shirt, though, the guy was decked out in a snug silver brocade shirt, with a bolo tie and a straw cowboy hat. His saddle blanket was midnight blue and orange, team colors of the Chicago Bears. When he came abreast of the house, Champion caught sight of me and balked, then began to dance and buck, straining at the bit to break from the parade and come up on the lawn. The Bears guy realized immediately what was happening.

I thought: If he gets down off that horse, I'm going to need an orthopedic surgeon.

But the man's grin was as wide as the sky above a new homestead. Sharply, he reined in Champion, and when the horse stood back on his hind legs and hesitated before cantering away, the Bears guy pulled off his hat and waved a salute.

I heard Sarah: "Then it really is over."

The crowd began to mill around after the horses passed. But there was something else, the rumble of a set of good, throaty glass-packs muffling a big engine.

And there he came, Tory McDade in the red sixty-two 'Vette, idling along after the horses, weaving back and forth around piles of dung, waving at the crowd. And in the seat beside him, why there was Michael Heyman, his hair done in those lethal spikes, and the sun glinting off the studs on his black leather vest.

"Mom . . . yo, Mom!" He was laughing and he waved at Sarah. Not seeing him, she had stood and walked into the house.

"Look at that little fucking jerk," Serette said. He cupped his hands around his mouth. "You're a jerk, Mikie!"

The laughter faded from Michael's face and he gave Serette the finger. Then Michael said something to Tory McDade, who found it within himself to give Serette the finger, too.

"Well, anyway," Serette said, composed now, "I guess it's like Sarah said. Done. The way I see it, when Gerry started picking at Matthew Turk's old wound, Turk just lost it. Boiled over one night and killed the poor bastard. Happens all the time. Then Banks here solves the old murder, calls bullshit on Turk, and he can't live with himself any longer. Freddie?"

Pointdexter sucked on a tooth. "Sounds a little lean on evidence."

"So what else is new?" Serette said. "There hasn't been any evidence from the gitgo. Even if it is all theory, I think Turk's suicide gives it a lot of credence. And that's the best we may ever have."

Pointdexter shrugged. "Plays as well as anything, I guess."

"Sure it does," Serette said. "Listen, Banks, we had our problems, you and me, but I want you to know this might never have been wrapped up if you hadn't solved that old case."

I told Serette I hadn't solved anything. I'd just crawled down into a hole and made the people I found there uncomfortable enough to crawl out. I didn't feel particularly good that my *solution* had launched Matthew Turk head first into a glass-and steel oblivion.

"Now," Serette said, "what about old Otto? Wha do we do with him?"

"Nothing," Pointdexter said. "You know it, I know it."

"That doesn't mean I like it," Serette growled. "I gotta tell you, Freddie, it really galls me, letting a killer walk. Even on a deal like this."

"Can't help it," Pointdexter said. "Leo here, he's got a lot more experience in these things than me, and I bet he knows it, too."

Yes, I did know it. And so had Otto Turk when he'd come clean last night in the sixth inning. So big deal, I thought. Freddie Pointdexter could keep getting re-elected forever, and Nick Serette could go on pretending he was one crimebusting sonofabitch.

Without saying anything more to Serette and Pointdexter, I stepped down off the porch and started through the crowd, heading uptown. I was thinking about Sarah Heyman's check, which was still folded neatly in my wallet. It was time to go to the bank. Before I changed my mind. And before Sarah thought to call and stop payment.

20

Fifteen thousand bucks makes a nice lump in the pocket of your jeans. I managed all the appropriate smiles and thank-yous necessary to get in and out of the bank, then cut across the square, under Lincoln's gaze. Most of the stores were closed, and there was hardly any traffic. Everybody, it seemed, had followed the parade out to Memorial Park. Well, I wasn't everybody, and I was going to bed.

At the hotel, I found the front door askew on its hinges. There were splinters on the sidewalk, as well as on the threadbare carpet just inside the door. Big Mike was sitting in his chair, watching more kickboxing on TV. In his hands, he held a big spoon and a big white bowl. He glanced over his shoulder and saw that it was me. Big Leo.

"Hell of a game, huh?" He slurped a spoonful of something gray and stringy from the bowl. "Card's pullin' it out in the ninth like that. Wished I could of been there with you."

"Terrific game," I said.

"Yeah, I always listen on the radio. Jack Buck and

Mike Shannon. Shannon used to play for the Card
you know."

"I know."

"Thought they'd both lost their voice last nigh
they was shouting so much when Guerrero hit tha
one out." He slurped again from the bowl, and con
tinued looking at the TV.

"What happened to the door?"

"Horse," he said. "Got up this A.M. and there was a
goddamn mare. Standin' right here in the lobby."

I surveyed the damaged door, and cringed. "Could
have been worse," I said.

Big Mike coughed and dropped the spoon into the
empty bowl. "You ever have to mop up two gallons of
horse piss?" He wiped his mouth on the sleeve of his
white shirt.

I wondered how it was that the lobby did not smell
any worse after being showered with horse piss, and
decided that this, too, was among the things I did not
want to know.

"What's in the bowl?" I said.

"Burgoo." Big Mike hunched over and refilled his
bowl from a large plastic bucket. "I can't take the
crowds anymore, so somebody always brings me a
couple of gallons." He sat back and blew across the
steaming bowl. "Best ever this year."

"So I hear." I started for the stairs.

"You ever watch this stuff," Big Mike said after me.
"This kickboxing stuff?"

"No."

"Damnedest way to beat somebody up I ever saw. I
can't get enough of it. Throwing their legs up like
that. You'd think they'd all get ruptured."

By the time I got out of the shower and headed for
the bed, I was practically on my hands and knees. The
crippled air conditioner kept the room passably cool,
and the window shade kept it passably dark. I thought
about all those people at the picnic, who would visit

and eat throughout the sweltering day, and later that night dance to the best bad band anybody ever heard.

I rolled over and punched the pillow and thought of Matthew Turk, aiming his car straight into the heart of the awful house.

So there's a solution, Banks. A solution you can live with.

And I could have, too. I swear to God I really could have. I knew what I could prove and what I couldn't prove, and I'd learned a long, long time ago how to live with the difference.

It was nearly evening when I answered the pounding on my door, and found Little Mike. There was no mistaking the look on her face for anything but trouble.

"Leo," she said, "that Michael Heyman boy, he just called. Said he needs you over at the house. Needs you there quick."

I tried to imagine what Michael Heyman could possibly need from me. Nothing came to mind, but at the same time it seemed impossible that he could need me for anything good. "How'd he sound?"

"Hard to say," she said. "But he didn't sound like the little twerp that came to see you the other night."

"Maybe you'd better get Freddie, too," I said.

Little Mike said she would try, but that could be tough because of the picnic. Pointdexter and any other deputies on duty spent a lot of time out at the picnic, away from their radios. Little Mike would see if she could hunt him up.

"Don't call that goddamn Otis," I said.

Little Mike understood my aversion to Otis Wiesel. "Relax," she said. "Super Cop doesn't come on shift till later tonight. Anyhow, he's not all that bad. He's just got a big mouth and a small brain to run it."

When I parked outside the Heyman house, I saw that Nick Serette's old Mercedes was still parked where I had seen it that morning. I hadn't even made it up onto the porch when the front door crashed open and Michael Heyman stalked outside, with Sarah close behind him.

"Michael!"

"Forget it, Mom, he's an asshole." Michael threw himself down the steps, and I caught his arm on the way by.

"I'm sorry, Leo," Sarah said. "He shouldn't have—"

"Why don't you go back in the house," I told Sarah.

"How come?" Michael said. "How come you don't wanna talk to *her?*"

"Shut up," I said. Then I turned back to Sarah. "Go on. Go back inside."

After a brief stare-off, she left. I turned loose of Michael's arm. "Let's have it."

"Why don't you ask her? Or *him.*"

"Because you're the one called me. I talk to you first. Now what's the deal?"

The deal, it turned out, was no more, no less than Nick Serette. I remembered the way Sarah had taken Serette's hand that morning, the way she had looked at him, the way I had not allowed myself to feel.

And now it had all broken loose for Michael.

"How long?" I said.

The boy shrugged and the pout stayed on his face.

"Don't be a jerk. How long?"

"I dunno. He was here when I got home. Couple of hours ago."

"That's not what I mean." I knew from Pointdexter how long the affair had been going on, but I wanted to know how long Michael had been living with it.

Michael lowered his head and closed his eyes. "A year. About a year."

"Did your dad know about it?"

The boy nodded.

"How do you know that? Did they fight?"

"No. Not really. Sort of, I guess. I don't know. I heard them in their room one night. That's how come I knew. But they weren't really fighting. He wasn't like that. My dad wasn't."

He wasn't like that. No, not Gerry. He would be calm and reasonable. And wounded. He would drive you crazy.

I told Michael to sit down on the steps and to wait there. And then I took a deep breath and went into the house, the big, warm old house filled with elegance and taste. The home that Gerry and Sarah had built.

They were in the sitting room and the room was filled with evening sun. Serette was on one of the love seats, pitched forward with his elbows on his knees, his head hung low. Sarah sat on the arm beside him, with her hand on his shoulder. I went to the marble-topped table in the bay window, then looked back at them.

"You're a real peach," I said.

When Serette lifted his head, I could see that he was drunk. His eyes were bloodshot, and wouldn't focus. His hair was pasted to his forehead in sweaty strands. He looked ten years older than he had that morning.

"What's your fuckin' problem?" Serette said.

"I wasn't talking to you," I said. "I was talking to her."

"Excuse me?" Sarah said.

From the table, I picked up a delicate brass box with a glass top, and examined it. Then I put it down, and smiled across the room at Sarah. "I said you're a real peach. Just a term of endearment."

Sarah stood up and momentarily covered her face with her hands. A heavy gold link bracelet on her left wrist caught the light. "I didn't want it to come out like this," she said. "With Nick, I mean. But he was here, and I was . . . we were so relieved that everything was finally over. So . . . relieved."

"And then Michael came home," I said.

"I wanted to tell him first," Sarah said. "Him and Lisa both. Tell them the right way."

"And just what way is that?" I said. *The right way.*"

Serette lurched to his feet. "The kid just went batshit, Banks. I mean, what the Christ was I supposed to say?"

"That you been bonin' my mother." It was Michael. He was standing in the door.

"I told you to wait outside." I started for the boy, but Serette was ahead of me.

"Bonin' my mother!"

"You little bastard." Serette moved quickly around the end of the love seat, and by the time he neared the boy, he had a good head of steam. I was still a couple of steps behind, when Serette caught Michael over the eye with his fist. "Little prick!"

The blow made a loud *thump,* and threw Michael against the door, but he kept his feet under him. Serette was ready to hit the boy again, when I buried an elbow in his kidney. That wasn't enough to put him down, but it did turn him around, and when that happened, I mashed his nose in a shower of blood. Sarah finally managed to start screaming by the time Serette hit the floor.

I looked at Michael. "You deserved that."

"But I—"

I took him by the arm and shoved him through the door. "I told you to wait outside. Now shut up and do what I told you."

He started down the hall, and I closed the sitting room door. Sarah moved toward us, and I wondered if she was coming to Michael or Serette. Serette moaned and tried to sit up. I kicked him in the ribs, and he stayed down.

"Leo, my God, Leo." Sarah stopped, and took a step back.

"This isn't what you wanted," I said, "is it?"

"What?"

"All that money," I said. "The fifteen thousand. That's what it was for, wasn't it? To find out about him. To make sure he was okay." I nudged Serette's leg with my toe. He moaned and tried to sit up, but fell back onto his side and coughed specks of blood onto the ivory carpet. "Well, sweetheart, I'm afraid I came without a guarantee."

Serette's voice was raw. "You're out of your mind."

I said, "Shut up."

"All right," Sarah said. She walked back across the room to the marble table and the bay window. I could sense more and more composure radiating from her with each step. "So I was worried. Scared."

"Where did you go that night?" I said.

"What? What are you talking about?"

"The night of the murder. Michael told me."

"Michael . . ." she breathed.

"Your son," I said. "You let everybody believe you were home all that night. The night Gerry was killed. Pointdexter never second-guessed you because he was too busy being polite to the grieving widow. And I was still being a chump from twenty years ago. So Michael told me. Told me you left the house not long after Gerry."

"Sarah?" Nick had managed to get to his feet. He wiped his palms against the front of his shirt and licked his lips. "This is stupid." The look of uneasiness on his face had to mean that he didn't know until that moment that she'd been out that night, too. And since he didn't know where she had gone, what she had done and seen, then he couldn't risk a lie.

"I figure you just planned on another quickie," I said to Sarah, making it sound as matter-of-fact as a grocery list. "Gerry gets a call, he goes out. No explanation. So you decide to run over to see babydoll here. Only babydoll isn't home. That wouldn't matter much, if he didn't just happen to be gone somewhere at the same time your husband was getting his brains beat in."

"And just how is it you figure," Serette said, "it wasn't Turk? What's to say it wasn't him, just like we settled on this morning? You can't bullshit me, Banks, there's no evidence."

He was right, of course. I was working without a net. There was no evidence one way or another. There was only the fact that Sarah was afraid to ask questions. "Did you ever ask him where he was that night, Sarah?"

"Who says I was anyplace?" Serette said.

If I couldn't get him to *act* like a killer, there was a slim chance anybody could ever prove it. I said, "We checked the tire the other night, you know. Freddie and I did. Turns out it holds air. So I figure somebody calls the house, asks Gerry to a meeting out at the cemetery. Then beats him to death, sets up the flat tire scam, figuring that'll be enough to make people think it was just coincidence he was out there. A coincidence, and Turk finds him."

"Turk," Serette said. "That's what I'm telling you, it's the perfect setup." He began to cross the room tentatively toward Sarah.

"If it's a chance meeting," I said, "then maybe it's Turk. But you're right, Serette, this was cold, a great setup. The kind of setup an amateur detective couldn't resist. The secret meeting at the scene of the crime in the dead of night. Jesus Christ, it's a wonder somebody didn't murder the poor dumb shit before now."

"Don't say that," Sarah said. "Not about Gerry."

"But that's what you paid me for, isn't it? To call everybody by the right name. So what am I supposed to call you? What's the right name for a woman who

:an't even ask her chippie if he murdered her husband?"

"That's out of line, Banks." Serette turned on me,
but thought better of it. Maybe the taste of his own
blood was still in his mouth.

"Go on, Sarah," I said. "Ask him where he was. It's
your money, here's the big payoff."

Serette moved closer to her. He raised a hand tentatively, then dropped it. "Don't you see, honey, it's
over. All of it . . . all behind us."

"He's pretty good, Sarah," I said. "I could almost
believe him myself. Why don't you ask him where he
was?"

"Gerry didn't seem to care," she said. "Not anymore."

"Michael said you and Gerry talked about it . . .
about him." I nodded toward Serette.

"Michael?" she said.

"Yeah, Michael. You know, your son? He told me
outside he heard you and his dad talking about Serette a year or so ago."

"He wasn't jealous," she said. "Not this time."

"This time?" I said. I glanced at Serette, who
seemed caught by surprise, too.

She shrugged. "You know how it is, Leo. People do
what they do, they are who they are. Of all people,
you should know that. I try to be better than I am, but
sometimes it doesn't work out the way you'd like." As
she looked at me, the long years ahead seemed to
settle into her face. "I try to be a good person, I
always try, but I'm just me. I'm just Sarah. That was
the thing Gerry always understood."

"It's okay," Serette said, now closing the distance
between him and Sarah, taking his chance. "I understand, too."

Sarah's voice turned dreamy. "I always wanted that
sick feeling, the kind you get when you're just falling
in love. I don't know why, but Gerry understood that.

291

He could do without that part of me in return for the rest."

I said, "Ask Serette where he was."

Now Serette looked at me. "Goddamnit, you stay out of this!"

"Where were you, Nick?" she asked. Her voice was quiet, resigned.

Serette jammed his fists in his pockets and nodded sharply. "Okay. Fine. Have it your way. I was home. Home all night. How about that?"

She shook her head. "But it's not true."

"And who says it's not?" he said. "A woman out whoring around on her husband, while he's getting murdered? Who'll believe you? You want to have it this way, Sarah, fuck you then. I was home. And who's to say you didn't kill him yourself?"

She screamed and rushed him, her fists flailing. But Serette managed to hold her at arms' length, while I caught her around the waist and pulled her back.

"But he wasn't even jealous," Sarah said. "Gerry wasn't. Just disappointed and sad. Jesus Christ, he wore that sadness around like armor."

"You still don't get it, do you?" I said. "No jealous husband means no jealous lover. You really believe that. Goddamn, Sarah, you're a more dangerous woman than I thought."

Serette was about to speak, when he was distracted by something outside the bay window. Freddie Pointdexter was pulling up to the curb.

"You sonofabitch," he said to me. "Come here and run this bullshit on me." His eyes were moving quickly now, skipping from me to Pointdexter to the door.

I looked at the door myself, and held tightly to Sarah. *Run,* I thought, *run away so the world will know it's all true.*

"Think you're some kind of fucking genius." There was a long V of sweat from the collar of his shirt, pointing down his chest. "Lemme tell you, Banks, I can beat this shit in court in a heartbeat."

"But it's true!" Sarah cried.

"Poor baby," he said, smiling at her and shaking his head. "So what? Only thing counts is what you can prove. Ask your hired hand here."

I kept silent and caught Serette's eye. I held his gaze for a moment, and then I very deliberately looked again at the door. I could hear Freddie Pointdexter on the porch.

But Serette didn't budge. "You can't prove any of this," he said, now starting to sound like a lawyer instead of a murderer.

And so I started to laugh. "I don't have to prove it anymore. That's Pointdexter's job. Me, I just have to go on back home. That would be Montana."

21

I t didn't take long for me to explain to Freddie Pointdexter why I believed that Serette had killed Gerry Heyman. The whole thing was absurdly simple, once we all stopped treating Serette's love affair with Sarah Heyman as an open secret. Pointdexter told me later that he had suspected Serette all along, but every time he tried to shoulder the case in that direction, he was blocked by the bogus leads against Matthew Turk. I told Pointdexter that I was surprised he'd let a guy like Serette keep him at arm's length that way.

"Wasn't Serette," Pointdexter said. We were riding around in his car, coming back down to earth. "It was her."

"Sarah?"

"I couldn't ever pry her away from things long enough to get past Turk." Pointdexter gave me an apologetic look. "She's your old girlfriend. Hell, I didn't know what to say."

Had it not been for Michael's chance comment to me, we might all still be sitting around scratching ourselves. "Believe me, Freddie, I'm the last person in the world that needs an explanation of that woman."

Pointdexter was smart enough not to try. He was also smart enough to know, as I did, that the case against Serette was far from a lock. Life, God knows, isn't like TV. The criminal never gets scared and runs, gives you a chance to blow his brains out so you don't have to take a loser case to trial. But, as I had told Serette, that wasn't my concern. Sarah Heyman had hired me to give her an answer. If she didn't like the answer she got, that was her problem. And getting Serette in front of a judge was up to Pointdexter. No, the avenging angel business was not my line of work.

The next morning, I went out to the nursing home and paid a visit to Cochran. I don't know what I expected. Certainly not trumpets and banners, not to greet the news that, yes, it was true that fifty years ago his life had been stolen. No, he lay there in the bed, his breath labored, and he listened. And when I was done, he closed his eyes and turned away.

"Now who gonna bring me candy?" Cochran said.

As I looked down at him, nothing but a sack of bones and guts, I figured the time he had left could just about be measured with a stop watch.

That afternoon, I drove out to the cemetery. Not the little graveyard on the Turk place, but the main Mauvaisterre cemetery, which was outside of town, where the land first began to rise above the floodplain. There, I stood on the grassy slope beside Gerry Heyman's grave in the heat of the day, and I said good-bye. Said thanks. Said I was sorry. There was nobody there to listen, of course. A hot breeze ruffled the grass from time to time, and all about me the chiseled stones were implacable.

Looking around, I realized that the cemetery was on an alluvial fan, a wedge of sediments spreading from a gap in the bluffs. Through the centuries, run-off from the hills had coursed through this spot, and as the rate of fall decreased and the water slowed, its cargo of sand and clay had settled out, leaving behind high ground. I remembered what Tory McDade had told me about the many Native American sites in the area, the artifacts from thousands of years ago recovered from deep in these Illinois valley sediments. At my back, deep woods rose up from the base of the bluffs, masking the limestone outcrops. Before me the valley spread flat and green, shimmering under the July sun, until it faded into the haze along the river. And here the dead come to rest, I thought. But what other dead, unknown and unmourned, lay in the dark horizons below these graves? At least those particular Indian dead were safe from shovels and brushes and cameras, for it's a sure bet we will never dig through our own graves to get to them. That's the main difference, I figure, between being six feet or six thousand years deep.

I closed my eyes and tried to remember how it had felt to be young, to be on the way home to pack, to say good-bye, and head north on the bus and meet Gerry and Sarah, my friend and my first lover, who would help me change the world. As I looked out over the valley, the river's home, I thought about Gerry that night in Rozette, the look on his face as he watched the fisherman and the storm scattering rain across the Holt River. His face was that of a man with an eye for windmills. Wind and water. Rain. Stand in one place long enough, and you'll be dissolved away. It's not all bad.

When I went back into town, I drove the rental car too fast. I stopped by Sarah's house to tell her I was leaving the next day. She wanted me to stay over for dinner with her and the kids. I thought it was a bad idea. She seemed relieved.

"My savior," she said.

"What?"

She took my arm and walked me to the door. "I think you saved me."

"From what?"

"I don't know. From myself, maybe. Do you think I betrayed you?"

"Which time?"

"Ouch!"

We were at the door now. I looked back into the house, cool and clean. Perfect. "No," I said. "No betrayal." Perhaps she had betrayed others—her husband and children, for instance—but not me. Not anymore. For my part, I figured Sarah was just living her own life. Doing, as the cons say, her own walk.

"You were half right," she said. "I had to know the truth about Nick. And I was afraid to find out on my own. But I also needed somebody to make me face the truth. Whatever it was."

"And I was the only one."

She smiled. It was the smile I remembered seeing through candlelight. The smile that can still get me up in the middle of the night, leave me staring back numbly at the late show until dawn. "The only one," she said, "who hated me enough to do it."

"I'd have done it for free," I said, "but with the money, I figured you'd know I really meant it."

By the time Serette's case was resolved, guilty or not guilty, Sarah would have to face a lot more. And face it this time in public. I wondered who she really was. I had never known, never would. No more than had Serette, or even Gerry. I felt sorry for her children. Her grandchildren, too, for that matter. I said good-bye and left, hoping that Montana was far enough away from Mauvaisterre and Sarah to get me through another twenty years.

Back at the hotel, I had a last hamburger with Freddie Pointdexter. By the time he left, and I adjourned to the bar, I had said enough good-byes to last a lifetime.

Savior, I thought, what a crock of shit. What a angle. I wasn't anybody's savior. As I had told Nic Serette, I was just a guy who crawled down into hole and flushed people out. What they did in the dayligh was their business. At least that's what I liked to tel myself. Had Matthew Turk considered me any kind o savior?

That's what I was thinking about later that night in the hotel bar, when Tory McDade came strolling in and pulled up a stool beside me.

"What's happenin', Jackson?" He slapped the bar. Little Mike produced a bottle of Stoly from the ice chest, and a shot glass.

I looked at McDade and I remembered the parade. "So how is it you know Michael Heyman?"

"I didn't tell you that . . ." McDade tossed off a shooter. ". . . did I?" He poured another drink. "One time when Gerry was out trying to buy that Corvette, he brought the boy with him. The kid liked the car, hell, what kid wouldn't? Turns out he likes country life, too. So he comes out on his bicycle every couple of weeks or so. Takes a look at the car. Scratches old Pharaoh behind the ears. Does a little fishing off the dock. I just saw him wandering around the other day when they was putting the parade together. Figured he'd like to go for a ride."

"He'll have a tough time," I said. "The girl, too. But I got a bad feeling things'll be worse for Michael."

"Well, that's what fishin's for, ain't it?" McDade pounded down another drink.

"Good luck," I said.

"Thanks." McDade slid the bottle back down the bar toward Little Mike, who seemed shocked that it wasn't empty. "Just keep that on account," he said to her. "On account of I got business to attend to." He slapped me on the back and slid off the stool. "See you 'round, Jackson."

"About that car," I said.

McDade stopped abruptly, and his eyes narrowed. "What about it?"

I thought about the lump of cash upstairs in my bag. "Ten grand. I don't know what it's worth on the market, but it's worth ten grand to me."

McDade looked bewildered, as though he had never thought about the red Corvette while sober. "I don't know. I got a lot invested in that car, Banks."

"Maybe too much," I said. "Ten grand. That'll buy a lot of fishing."

McDade chewed on a lip. "Ten grand, *and* my bar tab in this joint."

I glanced at Little Mike, who had been following the conversation. "Round it off low," she said, "I'll take two thousand."

Now I looked at McDade, stunned. "How come you're not dead?"

"Just bad luck," he said.

"And then, there's what he drank on your tab," Little Mike said. "That's another three hundred."

"Three hundred?" He had only started my tab a few days ago.

McDade shrugged. "It's been a busy week."

I was getting hosed, but this was as good a way as any to leave some bad money behind. I had a feeling, too, that somehow the Heyman kids would be the better for it. We shook on the deal, and I told McDade I'd be out tomorrow to pick up the car.

The next morning, I settled both bar tabs with Little Mike. Then I figured up about how much the rental car would cost, added a hundred dollars to it, and persuaded Little Mike to return the car for me, keeping whatever money was left over. Just before noon, she drove me out to McDade's place and dropped me off.

All the while keeping a careful eye and ear out for

Pharaoh, I checked the house and buildings, but Tory McDade. When I climbed the levee, though, saw him out on the end of the dock, sitting in a law chair. He looked back and stood up when he hear me on the planks. He had his driver with him, the on he used on Pharaoh, and he leaned on it like a can

I gave McDade his money, which he didn't bothe to count, and he pulled the title and the keys to th Corvette from his hip pocket.

"Things change, huh?" he said.

"That's what they say."

"Everything but this big ugly river here." We bot looked out over the water moving by the dock in long, muddy slab. "What the hell," he said, "you se one river, you've seen 'em all."

For an instant, I could feel water rolling over my shoulders, and I knew that he was exactly right.

I heard a car engine and doors, and looked at Mc Dade.

"Don't worry about it," he said. "Anybody wants me bad enough, they'll find me. You did."

A moment later, a tall auburn-haired woman appeared on the crest of the levee. She pointed at us, then had words with somebody on the other side. It took a moment before I realized that it was Ronette. Otto Turk's Ronette. She tiptoed on spike heels down the levee to the dock, and was halfway out to us by the time Turk, with the help of Mr. DeWitt, reached the crest.

Ronette said that they were in town because of Matthew Turk's death. That explained why she was wearing a snug gray dress, which had more imagination to it than fabric. Otto wanted to talk to me. She didn't know why, but it was important enough that he'd come all the way out to this . . . this place. Ronette looked around, and turned up her nose.

"He wants to talk to me," I said, "I'm here."

"He said he'd meet you on the levee."

I shook my head. "Sorry. I'm busy."

Ronette said that none of this mattered to her one way or another. She looked back at Turk, and waved her arm for him to come out on the dock.

I heard a shout from the old man. It sounded vaguely like *Goddamn you, Banks,* and then Mr. De-Witt began helping him down to the dock. Both wore plain black suits, white shirts and ties.

I introduced Ronette to Tory McDade. "How come," I said to her, "you work for him? Or whatever it is you do?"

Ronette laughed. "What I do is I drive the car. And I do it for money, like most people do most jobs. That other stuff, like he was letting on at the ballpark, that's just his line. He likes people to think he's still got it. Think he's hot stuff."

"I apologize," I said.

"Don't worry about it," she said. Her smile was genuine. Her eyes flashed, and I thought of all that auburn hair blowing in the wind as the red Corvette sped down the highway.

I said, "You ever been to Montana?"

At least she didn't hit me. Tory McDade had a coughing fit, and I thought he was going to pass out.

"I always liked to travel," she said. "But there's my job to think about."

The tips of Turk's walker thudded on the dock. Mr. DeWitt was right behind him, easing him along. Now Turk shouted again. This time, the words were clear: "Banks, you sonofabitch."

Ronette looked at me and raised her eyebrows and smiled again, one of those *you know how it is* smiles. McDade let out a quiet gasp, and searched desperately through his pockets for a cigarette.

"Sure it's a bad job," Ronette said, "but it's better than no job. Maybe a long weekend in the Ozarks?"

McDade moaned.

"You'd like Montana," I said.

Turk was about halfway down the dock now. "I just wanted to see you, Banks," he wheezed. "Look you in the goddamn face and ask you if you're satisfied. Satisfied my boy's dead."

I started to say something back, but before I got the words out, there was a long sucking noise from inside a clump of dense brush at the base of the levee, as Pharaoh drew himself out of the cool mire, and waddled onto the dock.

McDade stepped in front of me and Ronette, holding his driver at the ready.

"Jesus Christ on a crutch," Ronette said. "What in the hell is *that?*"

"Shhhhh!" McDade warned.

I wished that I had a cannon. Or at least a sand wedge.

Deliberately, with an awful rhythm, the boar gnashed his tusks until his mouth began to foam. None of the humans on the dock moved a muscle.

And then Pharaoh charged, charged as fast as a fifteen hundred pound hog can possibly charge.

Turk shouted: "Mr. DeWitt, stop that goddamn boar!"

But as Pharaoh neared them, Mr. DeWitt stepped deftly aside, and let him past.

The boar caught Otto Turk squarely between the legs, gashing both calves open with his tusks, then tossed the old man and his walker off the dock, and continued to bear down on us.

Tory McDade stood his ground, and at the last possible instant, whipped the driver down onto the point of Pharaoh's snout. The boar came to a dead stop and shook his head.

"That was three hundred yards if it was an inch," Mr. DeWitt said.

Tory McDade let out a long breath, and buffed the head of the driver on his pants leg.

Then we all looked over the side of the dock to see hat had become of Otto Turk.

The old man was buried head first up to his waist in allow water and mud. His legs were kicking faintly, aking tiny splashes in the brown water. By the time r. DeWitt and I jumped in after him, the kicking ad stopped. When I pried his mouth open, he oughed a spray of mud that sent his false teeth sailng past Mr. DeWitt's head.

We got Turk back up onto the dock, carried him to he yard beside the house, and set him down on a atch of grass. The job had left everyone about as nuddy as Pharaoh, so McDade began rinsing us all, ven the homicidal boar, with a garden hose.

It was several minutes before Otto Turk could peak. "You thought I was dead . . . didn't . . . ou?" he panted. He was looking at me.

"There was always that chance," I said.

"I'm too mean to die," Turk said. His mouth looked awkward without teeth in it. "Mr. DeWitt?"

"Yes, Mr. Turk." Mr. DeWitt had peeled out of his black suit coat.

"Mr. DeWitt, you're fired."

Mr. DeWitt shrugged. "Suits me. You wanted a matador, you should've hired a Mexican."

"And you." Otto Turk turned to Ronette.

"I'm going to the Ozarks," she said.

Otto Turk looked like the remains of a giant slug after someone had poured salt on it and sucked out all the life.

Ronette pulled her wet hair back tight against her head.

"The Ozarks, eh?" I said. At least we would be on the way to Montana.

"Maybe we could stop by my place in St. Louis," she said. "To get my makeup."

Tory McDade reached in his pants pocket and pulled out the wad of money I had given him. He

peeled off three soaked hundred dollar bills. "So it
the Ozarks, is it? You'll need this for a chiropracto
Banks. Consider it a loan."

Retirement, I thought. A guy might as well mak
the most out of it. I could hear Pastor Roscoe Becke
now. *Be careful, Jim, be real careful.*